MW01139083

Murder on the Lunatic Fringe

By
Debra Gaskill

DISCARD
LOUISVILLE PUBLIC LIBRARY

© 2014 Debra Gaskill
All rights reserved.
ISBN: 13:9781495998850

No part of this publication may be reproduced, stored in a
retrieval system or transmitted, in any form or by any
means, electronic, mechanical, photocopying, recording, or
otherwise, without the express written consent of the author.

Cover design © 2014 Scott Shelton

Published by D'Llama Books, Enon, Ohio

This is a work of fiction. The situations and scenes described,
other than those of historical events, are all imaginary. With
the exceptions of well-known historical figures and events,
none of the events or the characters portrayed is based on
real people, but was created from the author's imagination
or is used fictitiously. Any resemblance to actual events or
persons living or dead is purely coincidental.

DISCARD

Prologue

Is this how it will end?

The steel exam table felt cold against my naked back and legs. My neck was cradled on the hard metal headrest, immobilizing my skull. The back of my head felt soft, mushy and wet. Something pushed against my left eye and cheek. The room smelled like medicine... and death. At least a sheet covered me.

I was going to have children, then grandchildren. There were supposed to be big meals on Sunday with all of my family surrounding me and I'd end my days by dying in my sleep. I was supposed to spend my later years like Mother had, leaning out the window of our apartment, watching the young children play in street, walking to markets to get the ingredients for dinner. Our fire escape would be decorated with potted flowers and I would knit in front of the television at night, making mittens or hats or baby booties.

It wasn't going to end like this. Not this way. *Was it?*

A man spoke, a voice I'd heard before. "Doctor, whenever you're ready to begin documenting the case..."

Someone else sighed, then began to speak in a singsong Indian accent: "It is one forty-five a.m. on Thursday. We have a Caucasian female, approximately 32 years old. She is approximately five foot eight inches tall and approximately one hundred thirty five pounds. She has bullet wounds to her left eye and cheekbone, with exit wounds at the back of the skull..."

Is this what it's like to be dead?

Chapter 1 Graham

A week earlier

The biggest disasters are always preceded by days like this, days when the news is so slow it crawls. I've only been in this business a little while — five years — but that's the pattern I've seen, at least here in Jubilant Falls.

"Hey, some Russian woman won something at the state fair." Elizabeth Day, the features and education writer was opening the morning's mail. "She lives here, it says. Well, out in the county, I mean, according to her address."

I looked up from my computer where I was working my way through the appeals court website. When news was slow, like now, sometimes I could generate follow up stories on previous court cases I covered. Generally the Common Pleas Court decision was upheld in appeal, but at least it provided local copy and kept us from running wire stories on the front page.

Addison extended her palm over the top of the copy desk computer. "What Russian woman? Let me have a look at that."

Elizabeth smoothed her purple chin-length hair and handed Addison the press release, along with a photo. "Ekaterina Bolodenka. She lives out on Youngstown Road. She just bought that one farm where the barn burned a couple years ago."

"Ah, yes. The old Jensen farm." Addison scanned the one-page release. "She's apparently re-christened the place Lunatic Fringe Farm. She's a fiber artist, whatever the hell that is, and she's won best of show for a woven wall hanging. This release is a month old! I wish they'd gotten us this stuff when the fair was still going on. The photo would have been better than what they sent. It's just a picture of the wall hanging—she's not even in it!"

It was mid-afternoon, long past the morning deadline. The police scanner crackled only with the occasional traffic stop, nothing in terms of real news.

City and county reporter Marcus Henning was at city hall searching for tomorrow's story. As Labor Day approached, it was probably the annual round up on how bad the receipts for the city pool were over the summer and, once again, whether city council would take up the debate about closing it. I'd seen that story every summer for the five years I'd been here.

Jubilant Falls wasn't a bad little town, I guess. I mean *I* liked it. It was a little more than an hour northeast of Cincinnati and the same hour's drive southwest from Columbus, and not unlike a lot of fading small towns across the country whose best times were in the past.

The big limestone courthouse, where I spent the better part of my day, dominated the center of town. The town's only other big building was Aurora Development, an incongruous tall glass building, that stared back from its place across the street from the 1840's-era courthouse, demanding it keep up with the times and smug that it couldn't. To the east of the courthouse, across a narrow one-way street, were the jail, the sheriff's offices and the county offices. The city offices were in an Art Deco building a block north of the courthouse.

Further north was the empty storefront of what used to be a department store called Hawk's, and four blocks from the intersection of Detroit and Main were a string of storefronts that housed second hand shops, the occasional lawyer's, accounting or insurance offices, and a restaurant called Aunt Bea's. In the brick building it occupied since its founding a century ago, sat the *Journal-Gazette*, a block south of the court house, facing west.

Golgotha College, a small fundamentalist institution, sat at the prosperous east edge of Jubilant Falls. The ever-smiling, well-dressed Baptist students who attended were at odds with the other south side faces I saw daily, pockmarked and toothless from meth or heroin addiction, their refuge from poverty and unemployment.

When the weather and the leaves began to turn, it wasn't unusual to see a combine or tractor come through town en route to harvest the corn, beans or wheat from the fields that filled surrounding Plummer County.

On summer weekends, farmer's markets filled the block-wide municipal parking lots that connected Jubilant Falls' downtown and, in the fall, festival booths. I didn't have plans to stay here for the rest of my life, but the *Journal-Gazette* was my first job out of college and I liked what I was doing.

Like most small towns, the Great Recession hit Jubilant Falls hard, taking with it a lot of jobs, including a big chunk of the *J-G* staff.

We worked hard, we worked as a team, but when the news was slow, like it had been for a while now, none of us could stand it so we spent the better part of the day scraping the bottom of whatever journalistic barrels we could find.

I was getting ready to head back to court, to see if the jury had reached a verdict on an assault case. The defendant would probably get a suspended sentence and probation for assaulting his roommate in a drunken brawl over the cable bill. He had no prior record, but broke his roomie's cheekbones, nose and jaw.

I spent the morning with our photographer Pat Robinette, looking into who toilet-papered Mayor Dwayne Yoder's house overnight one day after he declared his decision to run for an unprecedented fourth term.

It was that time of year for us, just past the county fair and a few days before school started again, when the action was so slow I'd cover a Dumpster fire if I had to. That was why, at eight this morning, Pat and I were standing in the mayor's front yard, surrounded by toilet paper streamers hanging from the branches of a big maple, listening to Yoder swear. With a number of detractors in the city, Yoder could be abrasive. I could see somebody getting pissed off if he decided to run again.

But turning it into an entire story? There was a new word for it: *hyper-local.*

We ran it on page one.

The sports writers hadn't come in yet and wouldn't for another hour. At the end of the summer, their pages would consist of photos from the high school football two-a-days and previews for the upcoming season.

What I needed — what we all needed — was a good story, one we could sink our teeth into.

Like most afternoons, Addison and our city editor Dennis Herrick usually put together the advance pages for the next day's edition. It was Thursday, so they were at work on Friday's edition. That meant putting together a food page, a religion page, the comics and searching the Associated Press wire for a story to put on top the half-page of real estate ads that the *Journal-Gazette* ran.

Addison handed the release back to Elizabeth. "Give Bolodenka a call. It would make a great story. Make sure we get pictures, too. At least better than this one."

Elizabeth nodded and winked at me as she walked past my desk on her way to her own in the corner.

I hung my head over my keyboard, trying to look busy and hoping no one noticed. My private life was just that—private—and I wanted to keep it that way.

Quiet returned to the newsroom as Addison turned back to her computer screen and I turned back to the Court of Appeals website.

I closed my eyes and just listened as Elizabeth spoke on the phone, making an appointment with the Russian woman for the next afternoon, then chatting with our photographer Pat about his schedule and asking if he could come along with her on the interview.

"If you could come with me, Pat, you know you'd take a better picture than I ever would. Aww, c'mon," she wheedled. "It won't take more than a couple minutes. *Pleeeeaaase?* OK, thanks."

She sounded like heaven, but then, her voice did that to me.

Her computer dinged as the information passed electronically through the editorial system to the news budget, the running list of stories that were slated for the week.

There was another computer ding as Addison finished a page and sent it to Dennis to be copyedited and checked for errors. She stood and stretched.

"You know something," she said. "It's been a long time since we've had a big story happen around here."

Dennis poked his thick glasses up his nose. "Now you've gone and done it. We're now cursed with whatever unvarnished human misery the gods will splash all over the front page."

Addison grinned and reached into a desk drawer for her lighter. She carried cigarettes everywhere, even if she couldn't smoke them, like some nicotine-filled safety blanket. Although the Journal-Gazette had been a non-smoking workplace since before I got here, my boss regularly skirted the regulation by going back into her private office at the rear of the newsroom and opening the back window.

I dreaded opening her office door and being surrounded by the stench of blue cigarette smoke.

"Oh, don't be an idiot. It's been so damned quiet, I'm about ready to run a headline about the grass in the courthouse lawn growing a whole quarter inch this month."

"Be careful what you wish for." Dennis pushed a button on his computer, sending a completed page down to the pressroom, where it would be printed out on thin metal plates and placed in readiness for tomorrow's edition. "You may get it."

Hovering over my keyboard, I hoped he was right.

Chapter 2 Addison

The sun was just barely rising Friday morning when the phone rang in the milking parlor. I was in my farm wife gear: dirt-brown Carhartt overalls, steel-toed boots and a ratty tee shirt. I looked up from the back end of a cow, whose udder I was washing before attaching the inflator cups for the automated milking system.

Duncan and I milked a small herd of Holsteins twice a day on our Plummer County farm. Most mornings, I tried to help out before I went to work. My job at the *Jubilant Falls Journal-Gazette* may not have paid as much as my compatriots earned at larger papers, but it did provide cash and medical insurance for our family, allowing Duncan to keep the family farm and run his own graphics business from the renovated hen house just beside the barn.

Duncan, attending the cow beside me, jerked his head toward the phone as he worked. "You get it. It's probably for you anyway."

I picked up the phone, a convenience I'd insisted on when our daughter Isabella got her driver's license in high school. "Hello?"

"Addison," Elizabeth Day's voice whined through the line. "Addison, I'm sick as a dog. I can't make it in today."

"What's the matter, kiddo?" I watched as Duncan continued to wash udders.

"I went out with some girlfriends after work to the Mandarin Moon restaurant and I think I got some bad sweet and sour shrimp," Day moaned. "I've been up all night puking my guts out."

"Good God. Remind me never to eat there. Sounds like you need to stay home. What have you got going today?"

"Just that interview with the Bolodenka woman, the fiber artist, at two. I have a couple other features already in the can that are ready to edit, too." Day groaned again.

"Don't worry—I'll cover it for you. Take some Pepto and go back to bed, OK? We'll see you when you feel better." I replaced the phone.

"Another late night?" Duncan began moving down the line of cows, attaching the teat cups to udders. His words were terse, as if he'd had to deal with too many of my interruptions over the years.

"Nah." I watched as he flipped a switch above each milking stall to begin drawing the sweet milk into the clear pipes overhead. Those pipes rushed the white liquid to the stainless steel cooling tanks housed in an old stone milk house built on to the side of the barn, holding it there until the refrigerated tanker from the dairy in town came to pick it up later that morning. The system was nearly thirty years old, but it beat the hand milking that Duncan remembered from his own high school days. "One of my reporters is calling in sick—she's got food poisoning. She's got an afternoon feature story I said I'd cover for her. I should be home in plenty of time for dinner."

"Famous last words."

"What? Between you and Dennis—" I playfully shoved my husband, who at six foot three towered over me. "He thinks I'm going to bring the wrath of God down on us by talking about how slow it's been. Honestly, I'm kind of enjoying it."

Duncan gave me a quick squeeze around the shoulders and a kiss atop my head. "I just wish I had more time like this with you."

A cow mooed, reminding us of the task at hand. Whatever was going on in the outside world didn't matter. Right now, only milking did.

***

By seven, chores were complete and I'd showered and changed into my work clothes. I had just a few minutes before the race toward deadline started in the newsroom at seven-thirty. I poured coffee into my outsized plastic travel mug, ready to begin the day at the newspaper.

I was a rarity in Plummer County these days. Jubilant Falls born and raised, I returned to my homey little Ohio town, leaving a better job at a bigger paper when Duncan had decided to take on the family farm. Most of my graduating class had left town, finding jobs in and across Ohio or out of state. Just a few of us elected to stay in town.

I was born Penny Addison, daughter of Walt Addison, the commander of the local Ohio State Highway Patrol post. I was six when my parents divorced and my mother left town.

I never saw June again.

Dad and I moved in with his mother, who I called Grandma Ida, in Jubilant Falls' historic district, just blocks away from the downtown. He still lives there, bad knees and all. He's made the place into the centerpiece of the Plummer County Historical Society's Christmas home tours. Although he never remarried, he's getting to the age where he's enjoying the attention of more than one widow at the senior center.

I always wanted to follow in dad's footsteps, but back then, girls didn't become cops. Instead, I went to Ohio State and majored in journalism, thinking if I couldn't work in law enforcement, I could certainly write about it with the knowledge that came with growing up a cop's daughter.

No such luck: my first assignment was what then was called "Women's News," soft features about home, fashion and children, none of which I knew anything about. After Duncan and I got married, I started sending out my résumé under a new name, Addison McIntyre.

One crusty editor liked my stories and hired me sight unseen, assuming I was male. The day I showed up, he told me he thought I didn't belong in the newsroom. As a test, he sent me out on a fatal accident just to see if I'd fold.

Instead, I flourished. I came back with a story about a young man and his date on their way to the high school prom with another couple. The foursome would never see their graduation as a result of fast cars, wet roads and beer purchased with fake IDs.

I still had that story tucked away in a box in the attic. It ran with my picture of a sequined high-heeled shoe lying in the middle of a rain-soaked road as state troopers measured skid marks leading straight to a tree.

I'd stayed a couple years, covering everything from highway deaths and murder to the scourge of drugs, every conceivable inhumanity man chose to practice on his fellow man. The editor conceded that I'd done a good job, but didn't deserve the same pay as the other men in the newsroom since "most of them had a family to support, after all."

That old-school editor was the first to test my ability to cover crime, and he wasn't the last. Folks change jobs frequently in the newspaper business: Whenever the next news editor thought that my possession of a uterus meant an inborn inability to cover trauma, it only took one story to set him straight.

Soon after, Duncan's parents announced they wanted to retire from farming. I knew it was time for us to return to Jubilant Falls. I found a home at the *Journal-Gazette* and never looked back.

I've been at the *Journal-Gazette* longer than Isabella has been alive. I covered everything from cops to courts to city hall, county government and schools, before taking the managing editor's position.

Now, as I headed into the city, I stopped for a traffic light, taking time to light a cigarette and slurp my coffee before the light turned green.

I never wanted to do anything else. I was lucky and knew it. Most folks never got to pursue their passion.

Traffic began to move and I thought briefly about Elizabeth's interview with Ekaterina Bolodenka. Maybe this Bolodenka woman was one of those people. She could take her passion for weaving and color and turn it into beautiful works of art.

Maybe that's the tack I'll take with this story, I thought, pulling into the newspaper's parking lot. *Maybe this is a woman who has followed her passion and it's led her to Jubilant Falls, too.*

Chapter 3 Graham

"You need to see a doctor." Standing outside my bathroom, I called through the door to Elizabeth Day.

I heard her flush the toilet, then the sounds of her teeth being brushed. Wrapped in my robe, she opened the door. Her eyes had dark circles underneath and her face was pale.

"I'm not going to any doctor," she said. "I know what this is."

She picked up her purple wig off the floor and ran her hand across the sparse stubble of her naked head, evidence of the autoimmune disease alopecia. It wasn't contagious or fatal, Elizabeth explained the first time I'd seen her adjusting her hair from side to side in a mirror. Her immune system for some reason turned on her hair follicles, leaving circular, hairless patches across her head. When her hair got exceptionally thin, she'd just started shaving it off and wearing wigs. It began when she was halfway through college, she told me, and although she was used to it, other people could get weird about her baldness.

I was the only one she allowed to see her like this. No one in the newsroom knew her violet hair was a wig, or if they did, they never said anything. With Elizabeth's quirky style and vintage clothes, the purple hair was her signature look. It wasn't the only wig she had. There were other Kool-Aid colors: red, orange and Kelly green, as well as a conservative brunette wig, which made it easy when we ventured out to dinner in Columbus or Cincinnati.

We'd been seeing each other for about a year, successfully hiding the relationship from anyone else in the newsroom and hopefully, everyone in Jubilant Falls. As connected as our boss was in the community, it wouldn't take long for the information to get back to Addison.

I pulled her close, wrapping my arms around her.

"Listen, don't you think I hear you in the mornings puking in the ladies' restroom?" I asked softly, kissing the top of her patchy, balding head. "You're doing it two or three times a week lately."

She didn't answer, but wrapped her arms around my waist and buried her face in my chest.

"You lied to Addison, too."

"Oh, like you never have," she said, into my chest.

"You've got me there," I answered. "I still think you need to call a doctor." I let one hand slide down to her belly. "Just in case."

Elizabeth stiffened and pulled away from me. "Oh, don't even go there. I'm not pregnant."

"I didn't mean—"

"Don't go there, Graham. Just don't go there." She stomped into my bedroom and slammed the door.

"Elizabeth? Beth?" I knocked on the door.

"Go to work, Graham," she said, through the door. "I'm going to go back to bed for a while, then I'm going home. Oh God…" There was the sound of retching again.

"You OK?" Thank God I lined my bedroom trashcan with plastic bags. I hoped she'd made it there.

"I'm fine. Go to work."

"OK, if you insist. I'll call you later to check on you." She retched in reply.

I turned and walked through my tiny kitchen to the only door of my attic apartment, grabbing my keys from a hook on the doorframe. I stopped in front of the last kitchen cabinet and opened the small drawer below the countertop. Opening the drawer, I removed a small blue velvet ring box, put it in my pocket and went to work.

***

I twirled the small ring box with my right hand as I gripped the steering wheel in my left, pulling onto Detroit Street and heading south toward downtown and the *Journal-Gazette*. Before I got into the newsroom, I would stop at the police department to pick up the reports from overnight, scanning through them for anything story-worthy. If there were, I'd spend a few minutes with Assistant Chief Gary McGinnis getting the details.

Maybe I shouldn't have bought this ring, I thought. Maybe that was impulsive.

Something about Elizabeth pushed me beyond my personal comfort zone into an exhilaration I'd never felt before. We'd never said, "I love you" to each other, but I was confident in my love for her. I just knew she felt the same way about me.

Being in love was different from what I did at work, where risk and confrontation was commonplace — I got paid for that. At work, it was all about the story, finding the truth, backing up your sources and getting it in print. The story was right or it was wrong, even though what happened in it could be black, white or a hundred shades of gray. As long as it was factual, as long as it was true, that was what I got paid for.

I could take the easy way out and just write up the facts. Or I could look a little deeper, into the depths of nuance and distinction below every story's surface, if I wanted to dig.

I looked at it this way: A guy setting out to rob some pizza joint would be wrong. But finding himself on the other end of the owner's 12-guage, what would he be then? He might be robbing the place for reasons ranging from drugs to joblessness to just the thrill of taking something that isn't his. He might be dead or wounded as a result of the confrontation, but he is not blameless and he definitely didn't think about the possible consequences of his actions.

But he's still a victim.

The guy behind the counter is a victim, too. Maybe it's the third time this month somebody's robbed him. Maybe the next time his cash register gets cleaned out, he won't be able to make a payment on his business or his house, so he decides to do something to make sure that doesn't happen. He buys a gun and it sits beneath the counter and one night just before closing, some asshole comes in and says four words that change both their lives forever: "This is a robbery."

He's stood up for himself and his business, and odds are, he's not going to be charged with anything, but he's got to live with the consequences of what two deer slugs do to a human body late on a Saturday night. And all that makes him a victim, too.

I could do a routine pizza joint robbery story in four to six paragraphs — and most reporters would. The bigger story behind that could be the collapse of a neighborhood, the collapse of a family due to drugs or whatever, or the collapse of a whole economy. That's the story I want to do.

What I said in my story, how I covered that shooting, it had to be right. I had to be careful. I couldn't assume anything and I had to check my facts.

But love… and Elizabeth: That was something else.

We started seeing each other after a boozy night following the Associated Press Awards in Columbus. My story on a major fire at one of the county's industrial egg farms won a first in Best Breaking News; Elizabeth won for her feature writing. There were some other awards for sports coverage and for our special sections, projects we'd had no hand in but accepted on Addison's behalf.

After the banquet, we decided to celebrate.

I still remember what she wore as she walked to the front of the room to accept her award: That purple wig, a full-skirted, vintage red-flowered dress right out of the costume department of *Mad Men*, denim jacket, orange tights and black, steel-toed work boots. She was a few years older than me, a real woman with her swelling bosom and ample hips. Vintage fifties clothing suited her well.

After several drinks, we found ourselves outside the bar, leaning up against her car, staring at the full moon. I reached for her hand and she let me take it, giving me an odd look as I did.

"I'd like to see you again," I said.

"You're drunk."

"No, I'm not. I'm serious. Can I take you out to dinner?"

"Is there a policy on inter-office dating?"

"Probably."

"Then no."

"We'll go out of town when we go out. Nobody will ever know."

"No."

"C'mon, why not? We've had a great time tonight. Why not see if we can keep having a good time together?"

She shrugged. "OK. If you want to—just this one time."

The next weekend, we had dinner and drinks on a Cincinnati riverboat, cruising up and down the Ohio River for four hours under a full summer moon.

"So the big deal about you, Kinnon, is that nobody knows anything about you," she said, slicing into her piece of rubber chicken breast.

"Nobody's ever asked," I answered.

"I am."

"OK, here it is: I spent my high school years at a Jesuit boarding school, and I went on to a Jesuit college."

"Boarding school? That's pretty hoity-toity."

I didn't tell her that my mother lost me to foster care when I was six, thanks to drugs, and when she showed up on my tenth birthday, she'd not only cleaned up, but she'd reinvented herself. By then married to a wealthy Indianapolis industrialist, Mom looked like a queen in her rose-colored silk suit as she sat in the courtroom, explaining why her parental rights should be restored.

Before that courtroom appearance, my last memories of her had been as she was led off to jail, wearing torn jeans, a ripped Led Zeppelin tee shirt, stringy hair and the hollow eyes of a woman beaten by her addictions and the men in her life.

She met Bill, my new stepfather, when she was a waitress — or at least that's what she told me. I was a freshman in college before I found out the truth: it was a topless bar and she was a dancer. When Bill rediscovered the Catholic faith of his childhood, he foisted that religion on my mother and together, they thought there was nothing better than the rigid education of Jesuit boarding school for a rambunctious boy.

For me, family time was Christmas in Bermuda and summers at Bill's sprawling home in a gated community outside Indianapolis. The rest of the time I spent at boarding school.

"Yeah. I guess it was pretty hoity-toity," I said to Elizabeth as the sound of the paddlewheels sloshed rhythmically in the moon-drenched Ohio River. "What about you?"

"Oh, nothing much. Suburbs. Picket fences. A dog, a cat, a brother, two parents who teach at the high school," she said. "Good folks. I just went another direction from my parents, but they were cool with it. Tell me more about you."

"There's not a lot about me, either," I said. "I edited the college paper, interned at the *Indianapolis Star*, and ended up in Jubilant Falls."

What I didn't tell her then: Two younger brothers, Jackson and James, soon supplanted my place in the family and as they were groomed by Bill to take over the family factory, I was relegated more and more to the background.

Bill gladly paid for a year-round apartment beginning in my sophomore year of college. As long as my grades stayed up and my record stayed clean, or maybe because I stayed gone, the tuition and rent checks kept coming.

I found I liked the thrill of the chase in journalism, and probably, as a byproduct of my Jesuit education, the search for justice, with its the moral absolutes of right and wrong. As long as Bill knew I could support myself he didn't care what I majored in.

"At least it's something that will get you a real job," he said. "Not like philosophy or pottery." To help me on my way, he said he pulled a few strings for the Indy *Star* internship.

My mother, the former crack whore and stripper, wore a Chanel suit to my college graduation, looking ever the part of Indianapolis's best-known philanthropist and social diva. Bill endowed a business management scholarship before we left. I started at the *Journal-Gazette* two weeks later.

Mother and Bill each sent big checks on my birthday and Christmas and postcards from wherever they and my little brothers were vacationing.
I made sure I worked a lot of holidays. It was easier for everybody that way.

But Elizabeth, my Elizabeth... That first Cincinnati riverboat dinner-cruise led to another date, then another and another. The night I caught her adjusting her wig in my bathroom mirror was the first time we made love and all the walls came down.

I told her the truth about my family. She told me about the struggles she had with her alopecia and, with the love and support from her family, how she finally embraced it with the multicolored wigs and funky style.

I actually begged off working this last July 4th weekend. Addison was surprised I wanted a holiday off, but admitted I probably deserved it.

"Whatever you're doing, God knows you've earned it. Have a good time." Addison said. "Duncan and I aren't doing anything at home. I can catch whatever news breaks."

I never told her why I wanted the time off — Elizabeth and I went to Shaker Heights to meet her family.

Two weeks after we visited Shaker Heights, I'd bought the ring, a simple quarter-carat solitaire. I was just struggling to find the best time to ask her — and when to take her to Indianapolis to meet my family. I wasn't sure how somebody as plainspoken and grounded as Elizabeth would fare in the self-rarified air of Bill's new money.

But what was going on with Elizabeth? Was she pregnant? We were smart enough to use birth control — she'd made it clear she wasn't going to end up with a baby before she was good and ready. Had something happened?

I pulled my battered Toyota into one of the parking places in front of Jubilant Falls' City Hall, where the police department took up the entire basement floor. I opened the glove compartment and pulled out a reporter's notebook. I placed the blue velvet box next to the notebooks. I couldn't think about Elizabeth any more.

It was time to go work.

***

"Chief G wants to see you in his office."

The dispatcher, a tiny blonde with big blue eyes, pushed the photocopied stack of yesterday's reports across the tray beneath the bulletproof glass. Without waiting for my response, she buzzed me through to the police department's offices.

I already knew my way through the basement's labyrinth to the small room that housed McGinnis's metal desk, city issue chairs and the bookshelf where his gun belt, his Kevlar vest and pictures of his wife and kids sat among his case files.

Assistant Chief Gary McGinnis was the second in command at the Jubilant Falls Police Department, behind his brother Marvin, the chief, and the department's most prominent face. Half the force had the last name of McGinnis, so the two were identified as Chief G and Chief M — or, behind his back, The Big M, because of his creeping obesity.

As I entered, Chief G was sitting behind his desk and stood to shake my hand.

"Good morning sir," I said as we sat down. "What's up? I haven't had a chance to look at the reports."

McGinnis took a gulp of coffee from the FBI mug on his desk before answering.

"Nothing you'll find in there." He nodded at the stack of paper in my hand.

"Oh?"

"Have you been watching the news reports out of Collitstown?" he asked.

Collitstown was a medium-sized city about twenty miles down the road from Jubilant Falls. It was the home of the area's largest employer, Symington Air Force Base. Like the rest of the area, it was struggling with the decline of manufacturing; the crash of 2008-2009 hit particularly hard.

"Only when I think they may have beat us to something."

The assistant chief cracked a smile, probably his first this morning.

"Then you may not have noticed there have been a number of incidents that could likely be characterized as hate crimes occurring there. We have reason to believe the groups may be migrating here and organizing in Plummer County."

"Not to be snide, but I'm surprised Plummer County doesn't have its own homegrown hate groups."

"We have had some small wanna-be skinhead groups, idiot teenagers generally. This is the first time we've had any indication something serious is about to develop."

I flipped open my notebook and clicked my pen with my thumb. Chief G held up his hand to stop me.

"This is strictly off the record for now. I just want to give you some background. This is a joint operation with the sheriff's office, so when we are ready to move on these guys, I will let you know."

Flipping my notebook closed, I nodded. "Do you have anyone in particular you're watching? Off the record?"

Chief G opened a manila folder and slid two photos across the desk. "There are two. One we know, one we hope you'll know."

One was a Jubilant Falls resident and long-time small town crook, whose face had often been on our front page.

The other was an older version of me.

Chapter 4 Addison

Even by Jubilant Falls' Midwest standards, the woman standing at the door of the Lunatic Fringe Farm was striking.

Tall and lithe, Ekaterina Bolodenka was dressed in slim jeans and worn brown cowboy boots. The manure clinging to her boot heels and soles told me this woman was a real farmer, not like so many of the suburbanites who came out from the adjacent, more urbanized county seeking to play farmer by raising miniature horses or heirloom tomatoes, whatever the hell those were.

Bolodenka's western-style denim shirt highlighted a thin waist and full breasts that looked like the work of a very competent surgeon or the decision not to have children. A green John Deere baseball cap covered dark hair that peeked out from the back of the hat in a ponytail of tumbling curls.

Standing in front of her, I felt even more self-conscious about my squat boxy frame. God, I'm built like a damned fifty gallon drum, I thought to myself.

"Hi, I'm Addison McIntyre," I said, extending my hand.

The Russian woman's accent was thick and hard to decipher, despite her slow, careful speech and tentative smile.

"Hello, I am Ekaterina Bolodenka—call me Katya. Welcome to my farm. I call it the Lunatic Fringe. Come inside. We talk there."

Stepping inside from the bright sunshine, it took a moment for me to adjust my eyes to the darker living room. The room was filled with worn overstuffed furniture that looked like cast offs from a closed-down motel rather than imports from Mother Russia. The coffee table had deep angular scratches marring each leg, exposing the particleboard heart.

There were a few hints of Bolodenka's heritage, however. Here and there, small reproductions of medieval Russian icons sat among family photos on the cheap knock-off side tables, next to several sets of nesting dolls. A picture of a young woman holding a baby girl in front of the colored onion domes of St. Basil's cathedral on Moscow's Red Square caught my eye.

I pointed to the picture. "Your daughter?"

Bolodenka was quiet for a moment, her graceful smile replaced by a cloak of sorrow. "The woman holding the baby, she is—was—my sister, Svetlana," she answered, softly. "The baby girl is her daughter, Nadezhda. We called her Nadya."

"Are they still in Russia?" I picked up the frame.

Bolodenka shook her head.

"No. They are dead."

"Oh. I'm so sorry." I sat the frame down and pulled a pen and reporter's notebook from my purse.

Bolodenka wiped a tear from the corner of her eye. "Yes. I-it is very difficult that I talk about them." Even in sorrow, her grace suffused the odd little room.

"I understand. Let's talk about you winning 'Best of Show' at the Ohio State Fair instead. Is this your entry here, above the couch?"

Hanging on the wall above the stained plaid couch was an abstract tapestry done in brightly colored yarns. The yarns, warm browns and grays mixing with lighter colors of reds and blues, cascaded from a large circle in the upper left corner, rolling and tumbling like water escaping a rocky riverbed and filling the canvas with exploding colors before seeming to fall invisibly off the edge of the canvas.

The effect was elegant and abstract, very much at odds with the cheap, tarnished furniture and Russian knickknacks.

"Wow," I said.

Bolodenka seemed to relax. A tentative smile came across her face. "Yes, yes. This is it. All of the fiber comes from my herd. I shear each animal. I card the fiber, spin it and dye it. Then I weave on tapestry loom."

"It's beautiful."

"Here. Touch." Bolodenka reached out and caressed a corner. "It's alpaca."

"Oh my God, that's softer than any wool I've ever felt! What's an alpaca?"

Bolodenka's smile grew more confident. "Come. I show you."

We walked through the living room and out the front door. A short walkway led back to a new metal pole barn and long lines of pristine white fence.

Beside the barn, just a few steps from the main farmhouse, sat a small pre-fabricated house, a cross between a hunting cabin and a cottage, the kind that some of my father's friends put up at the lake for their retirement fishing trips.

"You've done a lot with this place," I ventured, trying to keep up with Bolodenka's long strides.

"Yes. I rebuilt the barn that used to be here and added that house for my farm manager. " She pointed at the small cottage. "You have been in Jubilant Falls long time, yes?"

"All my life. In fact, I was here the night the original barn burned."

The barn had gone up in flames along with a series of other area barns that summer. Some started when the green hay stacked inside caught fire spontaneously; others, like the one that happened here, were arson, set in an attempt to cover a murder.

Before Bolodenka moved here, the farm belonged to Larry and Denise Jensen, long-time friends of Duncan's and mine. After the fire, Larry found work at the new Japanese auto parts factory; they gave up farming and moved to town. Both Duncan and I mourned the loss of yet another Plummer County farm.

My thoughts about the Jensen's must have shown on my face.

"Everything OK? Yes?" Bolodenka asked.

"Yes, just thinking about some things…"

"Ah. We all have those things that never leave us, yes?" Bolodenka nodded sagely and began walking again toward the pasture gate, where a tall, young black man leaned on his forearms against the fence, his shoulders hunched and his hands clasped in deep thought. He turned and nodded at us as we approached the fence.

Bolodenka introduced him. "This is Jerome Johnson, my farm manager."

"Addison McIntyre, *Jubilant Falls Journal-Gazette*." I extended my hand. I caught a sharp look that passed between the two before he returned my handshake. "I'm here to do a story on Ekaterina winning best of show at the state fair."

"Just a local story?" Johnson asked sharply, again shooting Bolodenka a hard look.

"Well, yeah. Why would anyone outside the county care?" I asked.

"No reason. Just asking." He slipped his long, thin fingers into the front pockets of his jeans and leaned against the fence.

This Johnson guy certainly is a bit protective to be just an employee, I thought.

"Jerome, please," Bolodenka touched his arm gently. "I was going to introduce her to the girls."

She stopped at the fence gate and climbed up a couple rungs. Leaning forward so that her thin legs balanced her against the gate's top rung, Bolodenka cupped her hands around her mouth and called "Llama, llama, llaaaaaama girls!"

From the far corner of the pasture came a herd of long-necked graceful animals, each one a different shade of brown, gray, white or black.

Their faces seemed almost camel-like, except smaller, and unlike any other livestock I'd seen, they had two toes, not hooves. Their ears stood at attention, listening attentively to their owner's call. Some of the animals looked fuzzy, an odd cross between teddy bear and a giraffe, while still other others had wool that hung in flat curls that floated gracefully from their necks and backs like yards of rope with each step they took.

In the center of the herd was a larger animal, black and massive, with ears that hooked above its head like two bananas. A huge black ruff hung from its neck to its chest, down the massive shoulders to the front legs. The midsection was shaved around the back and belly, but the same heavy black fiber was allowed to grow at a sharp angle along the lower part of the back legs. Beside it skipped a smaller version of itself, simultaneously lifting all four little feet off the ground with each bouncing step.

"Oh my God, is that a llama? She's gorgeous!"

Bolodenka smiled as the llama pushed her way through the smaller animals and nuzzled her chin. Bolodenka returned the affection by burying one hand in the deep black ruff and scratching the animal's neck. "Yes. She's my favorite llama. I call her Dolly. This is her baby, Ramsey. Jerome, he calls him Rama."

I rolled my eyes and laughed. "Rama Llama and Dolly Llama?"

"One is American rock and roll and the other is Tibetan religious leader, yes?"

"Yes. What are these critters here, though?" I nodded toward the smaller animals. They seemed to be miniature versions of the llama, with spiked rather than banana-shaped ears. There were two kinds of wool that hung on their bodies.

"These are alpacas. They come from South America and have been in U.S. since the 1980's. The fuzzy ones are called Huacaya—"

"What? Say that again."

Bolodenka smiled. "I know my accent strong and my English bad. Jerome, you tell her."

Johnson seemed to relax. "The first one is pronounced *wha-ki-uh*. The others, with the long dreadlocks, those are suri alpacas. Both are raised for their fiber, like sheep."

"Are they related to llamas? They look like they could be."

Bolodenka stopped scratching Dolly's neck and climbed down from the gate. "They are all what is called camelids. Camels, llamas alpacas, guanacos and vicuñas are all camelids." The softly flowing Spanish sounded rough and choppy with her Russian accent.

I reached to caress one of the alpacas' backs, but it shied away.

"They're not real friendly," Johnson said. "They're pretty stand-offish if they don't know you."

"Are these the only animals you have on the farm?" I turned to Katya.

"No, we also raise cashmere goats," Johnson continued to answer. "We also have a few Blue-faced Leicester sheep as well."

Crunching gravel sounds made us turn toward the driveway. Recognizing the pale blue aging Subaru, I waved.

"That's Pat Robinette, the *Journal-Gazette's* photographer," I said as the tall pony-tailed man stepped from the small car.

Jerome shot another disparaging look at Katya. "I don't have a good feeling about this," he said.

"Don't be in picture then," she said shortly. "Is there something else you need to do? Clean barn, maybe?"

Without speaking to Robinette, Johnson spun on his heel, and marched back toward the small modular cottage.

"I'm sorry for Jerome. He can be difficult," Katya smiled. "He means well."

I introduced Pat and quickly explained the idea behind the story.

"Would it be possible to include the animals in the shot?" Pat asked. "How about we include your loom?"

"Oh, no — the loom is almost six foot tall. I have spinning wheel," Katya said. "I can bring that out and we can set it near fence?"

"Perfect!" Pat exclaimed.

Within a few moments, the photo was set up. Katya sat sideways by the fence; the wheel of her spinning wheel turning as Dolly Llama looked over the fence and the alpacas poked their heads through the slats.

Pat shifted into gear, switching lenses, shooting the scene from various angles as Katya began to spin. There was peace on Katya's face as she worked. Drawing long strands of carded alpaca fiber, called rovings, from a basket at her feet, she held the end of the stranded fiber in one hand as she began treadling the pedals on the spinning wheel.

Magically, the fiber attached itself to the yarn, twisted by the turning of the wheel, and wrapped itself onto the bobbin.

As I watched, Bolodenka's hands moved back and forth, pinching to pull the carded fiber almost apart, letting it loose for a millisecond for the flyer to twist it into yarn and wrap it around the bobbin. With Zen-like calm, she repeated the process over and over, turning the fiber magically into yarn.

"So, how did you end up in Jubilant Falls?" I asked, continuing to make notes. I could tell she would reveal more as she spun yarn, relaxing as she moved her hands back and forth from the bobbin.

"Mainly because my business. It needs land and Plummer County has land," Katya said. "The farm house was perfect for my home and my studio. The land was wonderful for all animals, the alpacas and the llamas, the sheep and the goats."

Mesmerized by the wheel and the sound of Pat's clicking camera, I listened quietly as Bolodenka began to tell her story.

"I was born in Moscow. My parents and my sister, Svetlana, came to this country when I was five and Svetlana was seven. We lived in Chicago and we attended St. Volodymyr's church in the Ukrainian Village neighborhood. The church and her daughters, those were the center of my mother's life.

"She never let me and my sister forget Mother Russia. We only speak Russian at home, English only when we are outside of house. That is why my English still so bad. I fall in love with the great medieval tapestries of the Orthodox Church, so I study art at the Art Institute of Chicago. Svetlana, she fell in love with Alexis—he was majoring in political science at University of Chicago. They get married, have baby Nadya and return to Moscow so Alex can do dissertation on the fall of communism. I follow six months later to do my own thesis on church tapestries."

Katya's voice fell to a low, sad pitch. "We should have never left. Six months later, a cab driver, drunk with too much vodka, drive up on sidewalk as Alexis, Svetlana and Nadya are walking home from market. All are killed."

"Oh, how awful!" I looked up from my notebook.

Katya nodded. "The news kills my mother. She has heart attack and dies two months after we bury Svetlana and Nadya."

"Is your father still living?"

Katya shook her head. "No. He died from lung cancer while Svetlana and I are in Moscow."

"So you're all alone, then."

"I could not stay in Chicago."

"So how did you end up with these llamas? Growing up in Chicago doesn't seem like it's much preparation for farm life."

Katya smiled. "You are right. I wandered for a bit after my family died. I taught art history in Cleveland and saw my first alpaca and llama while I was driving through the country one afternoon. I bought a few animals, learned to spin my own yarn and decided to put my art background to good use. I learn about the animals, I buy more alpacas, I buy cashmere goats and sheep and then I need farm. Here is perfect farm for me." She smiled and shrugged. "I make tapestry and decide to enter it in fair. That's my story."

"I got all the shots I need." With a flick of his wrist, Pat removed the long lens from his Nikon and placed it in his backpack, smoothly switching the camera back to a smaller lens.

"Well, that's all my questions. I guess we're done here." I reached out to shake Katya's hand. "I'll probably put this story in sometime in the next couple days, depending on what the other news is. Can we help you take your stuff back inside?"

"Oh, no. I can get it." Bolodenka seemed not so much to stand as to unfold, swanlike, from the small stool she'd been seated on. "Thanks for coming."

We exchanged goodbyes. Pat and I walked back to our cars parked in front of the farmhouse, close to Jerome Johnson's cottage.

"That sure is a sad story, isn't it?" I scuffed gravel from the driveway in front of me with each step.

"If you believe it, yeah. It's pretty sad."

I looked up sharply. "What's that mean?"

"Turn around. Slowly."

There in the front window stood a hard-eyed Johnson, his fists jammed hard into his jeans' pockets. A small 35-mm camera hung on a thin back strap from his left shoulder.

I waved and nodded, then turned back to Pat.

"He's watching us. That bastard's been spying on us!"

"Yup." Slowly, Pat opened the door of his Subaru and slid his backpack onto the front seat beside him. His movements were slow and certain and his eyes never left the black man in the window. "There's something creepy about this guy, Addison."

"I'm getting the hell out of here and I'm calling Gary McGinnis the first chance I get," I said. "I've got to find out what this SOB is up to."

Chapter 5 Katya

We Russians are a dark people, down deep, deep in our soul, but still the picture on the front page made me smile. I spread the newspaper across the tousled bedclothes.

"Look! Isn't this wonderful picture?" I asked in my bad English. The newspaper article on my farm took up half of Saturday's front page. I grinned broadly and pointed at the llama that dominated the photo. "See? Doesn't Dolly look beautiful?"

"This is the kind of stuff that makes my job difficult. You know that, don't you?" Jerome slipped a hand inside the loose gray tee shirt I wore, running his fingertips across the small of my back.

It was Saturday morning. We were in Jerome's single bedroom in his home behind the barn. I smiled knowingly and pushed the newspaper to the floor. I slipped off my cotton pajama shorts and slid underneath the covers next to him, kissing his bare bronze chest and wrapping my arms around him.

"The picture or me?"

I knew the answer. I was temptation for him and he was for me. I couldn't help it — and neither could Jerome. For once, I felt safe with a man. I knew I wouldn't be struck, and I wouldn't live in fear — mostly.

Jerome understood me. He spoke my language, understood my culture and my people. I could talk to him and he could talk to me.

I knew about the Moscow prostitutes where he sometimes found comfort as a young Marine, stationed at the American embassy. They cost him little more than a few American dollars and some vodka, but brought comfort to a lonely young man in a strange new country. When his commander caught wind of a possible romance, Jerome was sent back to the States before it could hurt his military career.

So women were his downfall. So what? Isn't that true of most men? It was for all the men I had known. I didn't care. We were together now and that was all that mattered, despite the professional relationship we were supposed to have and the difference in our skin color.

Jerome arrived on the farm the same time I did. I'd been so afraid to be alone that first night. The sounds of that old house creaking, the wind across the fields, they were new sounds and they terrified me. It was late at night when I knocked on the door of his little house, my eyes red with tears and vodka, still mourning the loss of little Nadya and the pain of yet another move under cover of darkness. He'd pulled me into his arms, meaning to be comforting, and a friend. We made love on his worn living room couch that night.

Jerome hated himself in the morning, and he promised me it wouldn't happen again. I replied by pulling him back to the bedroom.

Right now, that first long ago night was far from our minds. I slid one leg across his naked body and nuzzled my face into his neck.

Before Jerome could speak, I slid on top of him, pinning his arms down and playfully biting his neck, then his shoulders and his chest, casting playful glances up at him. He moaned as I moved further down his stomach, kissing, then licking his skin, loosening my grip on his arms as I came closer to his tightly curled pubic hair.

Jerome groaned as he cupped his now-free hands around the back of my head as I took him briefly in my mouth. I sat up and straddled him, taking him inside me.

The crescendo built and built in the tiny room as our pleasure exploded together.

"Oh n'da, n'da, n'da!" I moaned in Russian, collapsing against Jerome's chest. He wrapped his arms around me and held me close.

"Mmmmm," I purred. "Kolya..."

I gasped and rolled off of him, horrified at what I'd just said. Jerome clenched his fists and stared at the wall.

"I'm sorry," I whispered. I laid my hand tentatively on his shoulder. "I'm so, so sorry."

Pushing my hand away, Jerome sat up and reached for his bathrobe, folded precisely on the chair beside him. "I've got to get down to the feed store," he said through clenched teeth. "I'm going to go take a shower."

"Jerome, please—I'm sorry."

"We've got a lot to do today. I suggest we get started."

Chapter 6 Addison

"Oh for Christ sake, Penny, you're supposed to put your cigarette out when you get a massage." I propped myself up on Suzanne Porter's portable massage table which this Saturday afternoon, was set up in her dining room. I drew deeply on my cigarette then ferociously stubbed it out in the green Melamine ashtray Suzanne held indignantly in front of me.

"There. Happy now?" I exhaled toward the ceiling, and then lay down flat on my stomach again, my face resting in the massage table's circular headrest.

"Yes." I heard pages turn as Suzanne consulted the massage technique textbook on the dining room chair beside me and began to work the tension from my shoulders. "Now doesn't that feel better?"

I grunted in reply.

"I appreciate you letting me practice on you like this. John and the boys won't."

"Ouch! Ease up, there, Brunhilda!" I said sarcastically. "I can't understand why!"

Suzanne and I had been friends since childhood, back when my father could give me a quarter, and send my tall, skinny friend and me downtown on our bicycles without worrying if I didn't come home until dinner.

We'd wander the downtown, walking our bikes along Jubilant Falls' thriving Main Street, staring in the windows of Gabriel's Jewelers or at the fancy women's clothing and kitchen appliances in the window of Hawk's Department Store. For a quarter, we could stop at Sven Olin's drug store, scramble up onto the tall black metal stools at the soda fountain in the back and combine our quarters for a sundae or an order of French fries.

Much to Suzanne's disgust, the bike ride home always had to include a stop in the shaded stone courtyard between the county jail and the tall Plummer County courthouse, so I could see the prisoners being escorted to court by sheriff's deputies, or lawyers consulting with their clients.

Sometimes, I saw the men who worked for my father at the State Patrol post coming to testify in court in their sleek gray uniforms and wide-brimmed hats. They'd stop and pat me on the head.

I also watched the local newspaper reporters who congregated along this same stone walkway to get that one perfect quote from defendants on their way to face justice or newly-convicted felons, walking with shackles and handcuffs, back to jail, then, in a few days, into Ohio's penitentiary system.

As a young girl, I wasn't sure which of those scenes I enjoyed most, to Suzanne's chagrin. Nearly forty years on, she was still my best friend.

"How are things between you and Porter?" I asked.

"He's still coming home to me every night, and we've got everything we need and more," Suzanne said, a lilt in her voice. "Can't ask any more than that."

Just a few years ago, Suzanne's husband John Porter was the *Journal-Gazette's* philandering court reporter. I fired him for screwing up stories, but he'd come up smelling like a rose, as he always did, landing a job as the vice president of public relations at the new Japanese auto parts plant.

Now he made enough money for Suzanne to work part-time as a cosmetologist at the Clip-N-Curl Salon and attend massage therapist training in the afternoons because she wanted to, not because she had to.

Since he'd managed to "get a real job," as he'd snidely told me, after his unscheduled departure from the Journal-Gazette, there was plenty of money to let the five Porter boys join the YMCA swim team, play youth football in the fall and soccer in the spring.

Suzanne's mother didn't raise a fool. That was enough for Suzanne to keep the home fires burning.

"You two still as disgusting as ever?"

Suzanne giggled like a teenager; I rolled my eyes, my face hidden in the massage table's headrest.

"That's all I need to know," I said.

I was silent for a few moments as Suzanne's strong hands began to knead my calf muscles.

"You usually don't ask about John or my marriage. What's going on?" she asked.

"Suzanne, I hate to bring up bad times, but how did you know something was going on with Porter?"

Suzanne stopped working, her hands, coated in fragrant massage oil, rested on her bony hips. "Don't tell me Dunk's got some sort of middle-aged insanity going on. Not the last loyal husband in Plummer County."

Clutching the bed sheet against myself, I rolled over and sat up.

"I don't know what it is, Suzanne. I've been thinking about how much stress my job has placed on our family and, oh, I don't know…"

"You don't think he's fooling around on you, do you?"

"No, but I wouldn't blame him if he did."

"The day Duncan McIntyre steps out on his wife is the day the world comes to an end," Suzanne arched an eyebrow at me. "Don't go jumping off that bridge before you come to it. You tell me all the time how tough things are on the farm. Didn't you just tell me he's got to sell some more heifers?"

"Yes."

"He's probably sick to death about that, Penny. Even I know how much he loves those cows. Can you look any further than the end of your own nose to see when somebody else is hurting?"

I sighed. "I suppose so."

"Don't think that man's running around on you," Suzanne said, shaking a fragrant finger at me. "Is he gone late at night?"

"No, but I can be sometimes."

"When he is gone, does he come home smelling like someone else?"

"No, but he could, considering my job… I'm gone so many hours… He could be cleaned up long before I ever get home."

"Oh, like every single woman in Plummer County is going to go search out some farmer up to his knees in cow shit for an affair. Be realistic, Penny, for God sake. Unless he's meeting some honey at four in the morning inside the milking parlor, you've got nothing to worry about. I can't call your house after ten without waking somebody up!"

"I guess so." I slipped off the massage table, clutching the sheet firmly in front and behind me. Outside, an old truck pulled up to the curb in front of the Porter's and cut its rackety engine. Suzanne looked outside.

"It's Isabella," she said.

"Yeah?" I moved toward the half-bath off the hallway where my clothing lay in a pile. "She was going to drop her dad off at the feed mill and run some other errands while you abused me. I didn't expect her back so quickly."

As I slipped into the half bath, I caught a glimpse of my tall redheaded daughter as Suzanne opened the door, giving her a quick hug and kiss as she entered.

"Aunt Suzanne, where's my mom?" Isabella's sounded panicked.

"Hey baby," I heard Suzanne say. "She went to get dressed. What's wrong?"

"It's Dad. There's been a big fight down at the feed store and the police have Dad in the back of a squad car."

***

"I swear to God, Duncan, I never thought I'd see you here, of all places."

I opened the back door of the police cruiser and leaned inside. Holding a blue reusable ice pack against his left eye, Duncan shrugged hopelessly.

"Dad! What happened?" Isabella peeked into the cruiser to look at her father. "Are you in trouble?"

"He's not under arrest, Penny." Jim McGinnis, youngest of the four McGinnis brothers on the Jubilant Falls Police Department, stepped away from a knot of men in the parking lot to call out this vital information to me. "We're just asking a few questions."

There weren't very many officers with the JFPD who didn't know me. I grew up with all four McGinnis boys and they, along with Suzanne, were among the few who still called me by my given name.

Chief Marvin was the oldest of "the McGinnis boys," as locals still called them. A few years ahead of me in high school, Marvin was the star of the football team's defensive line, glorified in the way that small towns glorify each fall's young gridiron warriors, before an on-duty knee injury and a desk job turned his corn-fed muscular frame fat, sloppy and soft.

Gary, the assistant chief, graduated in my high school class. It was often Gary who provided my reporters and me with the information we needed to cover Jubilant Falls' crime. Chatter from those in the know said when Marvin retired Gary would assume the police chief's job.

Harold, a year younger than Gary, was next and one of the JFPD's three detectives.

Seven years younger than Marvin, Jim was the youngest and the only one still on the beat.

"Duncan took a punch from that guy over there—" Jim used his pen to point toward the other squad car, where a gangly, young man I recognized as Doyle McMaster sat in the back seat. "We're filing assault charges against him."

McMaster's green John Deere hat, its bill bent into a half-moon and smeared with black grease, was pulled low over his face as he slouched down in the back seat of Jim's cruiser.

"You know how to pick 'em Duncan," I said softly as I leaned into the cruiser.

"I'm sure you can tell me why, too," Duncan answered.

"Doyle McMaster has been on the front page for everything short of homicide," I whispered. "He's a Class A creep with a record a mile long. The women who work at common pleas court even call him a frequent flyer."

"Well, he certainly established that."

"What's that mean?"

"We were talking about how hard it is to run a dairy farm when McMaster starts shooting off his mouth about how the Mexicans are coming in and the blacks are taking all the jobs at the auto parts plant," Duncan continued. "I guess he works for that big commercial hog plant east of Longfellow. He was pissed because he got his hours cut and he's losing his house. Anyway, just as he's starting to rant and rave about the blacks—and of course, he didn't use that word— and this guy comes in—" Duncan jerked his thumb at the knot of men still telling Jim McGinnis what happened.

In the center of the group stood Jerome Johnson.

I gasped.

"What?" Duncan asked.

"Remember when I went over to the old Jensen farm yesterday and interviewed that Russian woman? That black guy is her farm manager!"

"Great. I get in a fight and my wife knows more about the participants than I do."

"No—you don't understand! As Pat and I were leaving the farm, we pass a little house she's built on the property and this Johnson guy is standing there staring at us. It was like he thought we were trespassing or something. He had a camera, too—he'd been taking pictures of us. It was weird."

"Well, Doyle was being a jerk and he called Johnson a nigger and Johnson threatened to hit him and Doyle swung and I stepped in between them, then all hell broke loose." Duncan took the ice pack away from his eye and gazed at me. "How bad does it look?"

I grimaced. "Doyle did a good job. You've already got a shiner."

Duncan groaned, sliding from the back of the police car. He handed me the ice pack. "We ought to do something nice for Jerome. He's new in town, and he's certainly not seen the best Jubilant Falls has to offer."

"I'm not cooking dinner, not if you want to ever talk to them again."

"I can fix steaks on the grill, baked potatoes are easy, and you can get some salad or something at the market."

I rolled my eyes. My idea of entertaining involved beer and popcorn, maybe cards, and even that could be done badly enough to assure company wouldn't come back.

Popcorn could be burned. Beer could be flat. And the jack of hearts could be missing from the euchre deck in the kitchen junk drawer. And who knows—the phone might ring in the middle of the evening and I'd have to leave my guests to go chase some story.

It would be easier if we went out to a restaurant. That way, at least the bad food wouldn't be my fault.

I was also a little uncertain about inviting someone into my home who'd been surreptitiously photographing me.

Duncan walked into the knot of men around Johnson and extended his hand.

Behind me, Isabella sighed. I turned to see her standing with her hands on her hips.

"What is it?" I asked, exasperated.

"I guess this means we're not going to go looking for a car for me today, then, huh?"

I stared at my daughter, incredulous. "Who said anything about buying you a car?"

"Dad."

***

Silent on the ride home, I lit a cigarette as soon as the truck came to a stop, tossing the match into the gravel driveway. I let Isabella walk into the house before stopping Duncan on the porch.

"Can you answer me one goddamn thing?"

"What? I got you out of cooking. Jerome says he doesn't feel much like going anywhere after this morning. I did invite him over Sunday afternoon, though."

"That's not what I'm talking about."

"What?"

"Why the hell did you tell Isabella you were going to go out and buy her a goddamned car? We've got bills, Dunk! We can't turn around and buy Izzy a car! Why did you promise her that?"

Duncan placed a hand on my shoulder and sighed. "I know things have been crazy and I'm sorry. I got the bill paid today at the grain elevator and everything else is caught up. I'm not going to have to sell those heifers."

"But, Dunk, a car?"

"This isn't our cash. This is the money she's put back from her fair animals every year."

Like most Plummer County kids, Isabella was a member of 4H through school and, each year, raised one of the farm's Holstein bull calves, along with a meat goat, to sell at the end of the county fair.

She'd scrupulously put the money aside since she was ten. That money ranged each year from a couple hundred to the several thousand the year she'd won reserve grand champion feeder calf.

"I thought that money was for college!"

Isabella appeared at the kitchen screen door.

"Mom, I'm in my second year of college. I'm living at home, commuting to community college. Grandpa's old car is falling apart. I'm just asking to spend a little of my own money!"

She flapped her arms against her sides in exasperation. I caught a glimpse of the star tattoos that circled both wrists, covering scars from a suicide attempt in high school and stopped cold.

"I'm sorry baby. You're right. Go ahead. It's your money."

"Thank you," she said.

Inside, the kitchen phone rang. Duncan picked it up and handed it to me. It was Graham Kinnon.

"Hey, Addison, everything OK?"

"Yeah, we're great. What's up?"

"I was listening to the scanner and thought I heard Duncan's name come across on an assault."

I rolled my eyes. Figures Kinnon would already be on top of the story. He really needed to get a girlfriend or a hobby or something.

"Yes, just a little discussion of race relations down at the feed mill this morning," I said. "Duncan ended up with a black eye."

"Is that why I heard Doyle McMaster's name?"

"Yes. You know all about him, I'm sure."

"Yeah, McMaster is one of the jail's more frequent guests, but there's something else you need to know about him," Kinnon said. "He's being investigated for some possible hate crimes. The police and the feds think he's up to his knees in some suspicious activities in the next county. Gary McGinnis told me about it Friday morning."

Chapter 7 Graham

I hadn't seen that face since my mother went to prison.

On Sunday morning, I sat in my boxers at my small round table in my attic apartment with a coffee mug, staring at the photo I'd gotten Friday morning from Chief G.

It was a little older, a little more battered, but it was still the same face that showed up periodically with whatever drug du jour he and my mother would ingest. That would be followed by what I realized now was rough sex behind her bedroom door. Late in the morning or early in the afternoon, they would awake from their mutual stupor and argue.

Then he would beat her as I cowered behind my bedroom door, hoping the violence wouldn't extend to me.

Abuse-worthy crimes included making weak coffee, a TV that was too loud or no food in the fridge. Then she would cry as she bound up her wounds and he would leave—until the next time when he returned with whatever illegal substance he'd scored and the whole cycle began again.

One day during a visit with the social worker, I peeked inside my file on my social worker's desk and saw my mother's occupation listed as 'unemployed/prostitute' and the sentence: 'Mother likely trades sex for drugs, possibly in child's presence.' By the time Mom brought me home from court on my tenth birthday, I was too thrilled to have her back to ask her where she'd been and how she'd changed.

Then I was shipped off to boarding school and other things took precedence. After I'd started covering crime here in Jubilant Falls, I sure knew the meaning of hookers and junkie mothers.

That face on the photo always denied he was my father, even though his name, Benjamin Thomas Kinnon, was listed on my birth certificate. By the time the court decided my mother wasn't fit to keep me, finding who my daddy was didn't seem to be a big concern. So Benny Kinnon vanished into the Indiana sunset, only to show up twenty years later, here in Jubilant Falls.

"We weren't sure if you were related to our suspect," Assistant Chief McGinnis said. "But with the same last name, we had to ask. We believe he could be tied up with a group known as the Aryan Knights, an off-shoot group of the KKK."

"The Aryan Knights?" I asked. "I don't know anything about them."

"They are primarily white supremacist, anti-African American, anti-Mexican, and very violent. They espouse strictly traditional male and female roles, which are often enforced through domestic violence. Not surprisingly, many of them are fundamentalist Christians with extremely right-wing views." Chief G. took another sip from his coffee.

"They recruit primarily via word of mouth and hold recruiting meetings in member's homes, which make them difficult to track. We'd heard through some confidential informants that meetings have been held at Doyle McMaster's place out in the county."

Doyle McMaster was a well-known thug and all-around asshole. If he punched Duncan, it would be a misdemeanor assault, another in a long list and wouldn't amount to more than a short item in the police blotter. I intentionally hadn't mentioned Benjamin to Addison when I'd heard her husband Duncan's name come over the scanner Saturday. No sense adding fuel to the fire on that story.

And, truth was, I didn't think I wanted to answer any of her questions. Benjamin Kinnon wasn't anybody's business but mine.

I left the photo on the table and went into the bedroom. I got down on my knees and pulled out a small battered shoebox, the one containing all my worldly goods while I was in foster care.

Mother asked that it be thrown out soon after I came home from court with her. I begged our maid to let me keep the little box, which held yellowing photos of Mother holding me as an infant on her lap, a small metal toy truck with chipped red paint, a bright blue rabbit's foot charm and a small teddy bear with an arm nearly ripped off, the stuffing falling out like so much white, puffy muscle. The box's corners were duct-taped together and at one point, someone strapped clear packing tape around the box to keep the lid on. At the bottom of the box, I found what I was searching for: my kindergarten photo, the only professional photo I would have taken until I came out of foster care.

I was wearing a striped navy and green shirt that day. My hair was tousled and I had a bewildered look on my face, like the picture had been snapped before I knew what was going on. I walked back to the table and laid the picture next to Benjamin's.

I shivered at the resemblance: We were both tall and lanky, our faces were thin, and we shared prominent cheekbones and Adam's apples. *No doubt, I was Benjamin Kinnon's son.*

Across the room, the police scanner crackled to life:

"Engine 26, Medic 26, Rescue 26, Technical Rescue Team—report of a hiker falling off the path at Canal Lock Park and into the gorge. Victim is located about four hundred feed off main path on a rock ledge. Victim is a 21-year-old male, possible broken leg. He is conscious and in contact with friends at the top of the gorge by cell phone."

Sounds like a story to me.

I grabbed a napkin, scribbling notes on it as the fire chief requested the medical helicopter from the trauma center in Collitstown be put on standby.

Canal Lock Park was the historic reminder of Jubilant Fall's founder McGregor Shanahan, who tried and failed to turn the creek now named for him into a canal connecting it to the Ohio River, giving merchants and farmers in Jubilant Falls a way to get their goods to market.

I jumped into a pair of jeans, slipped on a shirt and put on a sturdy pair of boots, grabbing my camera as I ran out the door.

Driving toward the park, I called Addison to let her know what was up, and that I'd get photos.

"Thanks, Graham. I appreciate it. I've actually got company this afternoon," she said.

Once at the park, I parked among the gaggle of fire trucks and ambulances. Volunteer firefighters, light bars atop their pick-up trucks, filled about half the parking spaces. I grabbed my press pass from its weekend post, hanging from my Toyota's rearview mirror. It was more a precaution than anything else; I'd been here at the *J-G* long enough that most everybody knew who I was, but it never hurt to have it with me.

I smacked the glove box door with the base of my fist to pop open the broken lock. The door swung down, revealing the stack of reporter's notebooks and the ring box I'd left there Friday. Gently, I picked up the box and held it in the palm of my hand.

Elizabeth.

After she felt better on Friday, she went home to Shaker Heights for the weekend to celebrate her mother's birthday. She was due back home this evening and was supposed to stop by.

Maybe her mother would talk her into seeing a doctor. I know they didn't have a lot of secrets between them. They did things together—lunches, shopping, weekend girls' trips where they got their fingernails and toenails painted. Surely she had told her mother what was going on. And what else could it be except pregnancy?

If it was, I had to make it right. I would ask her to marry me tonight. I was not going to be the kind of father Benjamin Kinnon had been to me. My child was going to grow up with a mother and a father, knowing what it was to be loved.

The story was waiting; I stuffed the ring back in the glove box and slammed it shut.

I walked down the path near the gorge to get as close as I could to the scene, snapping photos whenever I could get a decent shot. Within an hour, a team of paramedics had rigged a system of pulleys and ropes around the trees and lowered a paramedic in a harness, along with a stretcher, down the side of the gorge.

Within another half an hour, as I shot video with my smart phone for the website, the victim, strapped into the stretcher with his left leg in a splint, was raised up the side of the gorge with the same ropes and pulleys. With my SLR camera, I got another shot of the victim being loaded into the medical helicopter and another as it took off from the wide field next to the parking lot.

Provided my photos were OK, this would likely be our main art for Monday's paper, unless someone else covered something I hadn't heard about.

I got a quick interview with the incident commander, who explained the finer points of gorge rescue techniques to me. I also spoke to the victim's friends, who were crying happy tears that he had gotten out alive. Before I left the scene, I made sure of the details. Names spelled right? Check. Age? Check. Victim's hometown? Check. Transported to what hospital? Got it. Were the injuries life-threatening or not? Got that too.

Shortly thereafter, I was walking into the newsroom to write up the story and upload my photos.

Assistant editor Dennis Herrick was already there. A Reds baseball game was blaring on the newsroom television. A half-eaten burger and a paper cup sweating with condensation sat at sports writer Chris Royal's desk, which meant he was probably out back in the employee lot, talking on his cell phone to his girlfriend and smoking a cigarette.

It wasn't unusual for any of the newsroom staff to wander in and out over the weekend. It was easier to get things done without the pressure of Addison breathing down our necks about a ten-thirty deadline and the phone ringing incessantly.

Dennis and I nodded at each other in greeting and I explained what my story was about.

"I'm just uploading Saturday's stories to the Website," Dennis said. "I can upload this rescue story and photos for you when you get it done. Did you happen to get video?"

"Yeah I did—on my phone. I'll e-mail it to you in a second." I sat down and flipped on my computer.

"Did you see Saturday's paper?" Dennis asked.

"Yeah. Awesome shots Pat took of those llamas or whatever they're called," I answered without looking at him. I already had my lead halfway written: *A Jubilant Falls man is recovering at a Collitstown hospital, following a fall into the gorge at Canal Lock Park Sunday...*

I needed to bang out the story so I could be back home by the time Elizabeth got there.

The phone at Dennis's elbow rang. He picked it up on the second ring.

"Hey, Addison. Yeah, he's here," he said. "Yeah. He just came back from Canal Lock Park—he's got photos. No, I haven't seen them yet. Yes, he got video. He's working on the story right now. All of Saturday's stories are uploaded, by the way. I put your llama story on the home page."

I tuned out the rest of their conversation as my writing picked up steam. Elizabeth would be back in town in just a couple hours and I had to make things right. If I could help it, another Kinnon child would never wonder where or who his real father was.

Chapter 8 Katya

"You have lovely farm, Addison." I stepped from Jerome's Jeep Cherokee and shook Addison's hand, then the hand of her husband, Duncan, who had the black eye. "Thank you so much for inviting us."

Jerome shook Duncan's hand but only nodded sharply at Addison. I would have to say something to him about his rudeness when we got home.

"I appreciate what you did for me yesterday, Duncan," he said.

Duncan shrugged. "The folks here in Jubilant Falls aren't all like Doyle. That's why we wanted to have you over. I hope you like steak."

Jerome nodded and smiled, rubbing his hands together. "Sure do."

Duncan McIntyre led us over to the maple tree in front of the old white farmhouse.

A grill and a picnic table sat beneath the rustling leaves. A blue and white cooler sat at the base of the tree, filled with beer and soda. Paper plates and plastic silverware were held in place by a large ceramic bowl filled with salad and covered with plastic wrap. A plastic-wrapped plate held brownies; another bowl contained baked beans.

I heard a cell phone ring. It was Addison's; she stopped walking with us to answer it. Keeping myself safe is an old habit, so I stopped to listen, pretending to examine the flowers around the front porch.

"A hiker fell? At the park?" She was silent for a few moments. "Thanks, Graham. I appreciate it. I've actually got company this afternoon."

I relaxed. Maybe one of these days I could hear phone conversations without fear, but not right now.

Maybe later today I could make up for yesterday with Jerome. After what I'd said in bed Saturday morning, he left angrily.

"*Za bazár otvétish,*" he said in Russian as he slammed the door. "You'll pay for those words."

What did he mean by that? For the rest of Saturday morning, I sat in my house, rocking back and forth on my bed as I cried and worried. I don't know where Kolya's name came from, or why I said it. Once again, I was thoughtless, stupid. Here I am, beginning again, with wonderful man in my life — of all things to say! Would Jerome leave me because of my stupidity? Would we become two people living just feet apart, yet strangers? A few hours later, he was home and angry at something else, not me — a fight at the feed store. Jerome let me comfort him and my intimate indiscretion was forgotten.

Now, here we were enjoying an outdoor barbecue on a Sunday afternoon as if nothing had come between us.

The four of us chose beers from the cooler and sat down at the picnic table.

"So, how did you end up in Jubilant Falls?" Duncan asked.

Jerome shrugged and his words came easily. "Katya hired me away from a farm up near Ashtabula."

"So you're from Ohio?" Duncan asked.

"No, Virginia. I served in the Marine Corps for a while—"

"That was where he learned his most excellent Russian," I interjected in my bad English. "He was guard at embassy in Moscow."

"Virginia to Moscow to Ashtabula to Jubilant Falls? That's quite a trip," Duncan said.

Jerome shrugged again, looking sideways at me. Once again, I revealed too much.

"I hire him because he can speak my language," I said, trying to cover my tracks. "It makes it easier for me. Can you imagine me finding farm manager who speaks Russian? I am luckiest woman on planet!"

"We should have included his story in the piece we did for yesterday's paper," Addison said. "It would have made it so much better."

"Oh, no, I couldn't." Jerome shook his head humbly, but his eyes were sharp. Addison's eyes were just as hard, neither she nor Jerome trusting each other.
In my position, you catch these things, the looks, the funny glances and the words with two meanings.

"So you were a guard at the American embassy? Does that mean you have a law enforcement background?" Addison asked. "I know the sheriff's office is always looking for new recruits. Prior military service puts you a few steps further up the hiring ladder."

Jerome shook his head. "Thanks, but no thanks. I enjoy what I'm doing."

Duncan smiled. "There's nothing like working the land, is there? My wife tells me you've got llamas and alpacas. What do you use them for?"

Jerome began to talk about the animals and I relaxed. Duncan opened the grill; potatoes wrapped in foil already sat on the hot coals. As he and Jerome talked, Duncan laid four pink steaks on the grill, their juices sizzling. The sun was warm and I heard cows mooing in the distance. Beyond the cornfield that stood between the old white farmhouse and the road, cars drove by only occasionally.

When the steaks were done, we filled our plates and chatted as a warm breeze made the green cornstalks sway.

For the first time in a long time, I felt safe. Jerome and Duncan were talking American football now—Jerome was actually laughing. Addison listened as I told her more about how I made yarn and how I dyed it. We ate our meal, good, simple farm food, and when our plates were clear, Addison passed around the plate of brownies.

I helped her bring the paper plates and bowls back into the old kitchen, putting the bowls in the sink to soak. Addison wasn't so different from a lot of the women I'd grown up with, even though she was older than me. She had a husband, a daughter, a home to be proud of, and she was a professional. Her husband was a nice man. He stood up for Jerome, didn't he?

Was this what it was like to have a home? A community? I hadn't felt this way since I was little girl. Maybe Jubilant Falls, this funny little Ohio town, would be where I could put down roots, maybe I could even...

No, I told myself. Stop thinking like that! It could never happen.

The table was clear and the afternoon lunch was over. Duncan reached out to shake Jerome's hand.

"Thanks," Jerome said. "Thanks for everything."

"I just wanted you to know that not everybody in Jubilant Falls is like Doyle McMaster," Duncan said. "What he called you is not acceptable here. We're a small town, but we don't accept small minds."

Jerome looked Duncan straight in the eye. "I'd be lying to say I'd never been called a nigger before. I'd also be lying to say I didn't beat the shit out of the white man who did it—and I'd do it again. It's not often that a complete stranger steps in like you did. I appreciate that."

"I must thank you for your kindness, too," I said. "We must have you over for dinner. I cook you complete Russian meal."

"That would be very nice," Duncan said. "We'd love it."

As Jerome drove us back to the Lunatic Fringe, I laid my hand on his muscular thigh.

"They seem like nice people," I said tentatively. "It would be nice to have friends here."

Jerome nodded. "I'm sure they are, but we've got to be careful. They can't know the truth."

"Is that why you don't like Addison?"

"I don't trust anyone who could possibly blow the lid off our situation. It's too dangerous."

I sighed as Jerome turned the Cherokee into the drive. "Jerome, wait! Stop!"

I pointed to the pasture where the llamas paced nervously up and down the fence line, making their odd, rhythmic, high-pitched alert sound, one they made only when they sensed danger.

Jerome slammed the car into park. He pulled a handgun from the holster around his ankle as we both jumped from the Jeep and ran toward the fence. Jerome got there first.

"Oh God." He knelt on the ground. It was dark, but I could see the carcass just outside the fence line.

It was Dasha, my cashmere ram. His throat was slit, nearly severing his magnificent head. The wound continued down his gray belly, his intestines spilling onto the grass, dyeing the dirt beneath the green grass a dark, dark red. Sobbing, I sank to the ground.

"He's still warm," Jerome whispered. "This just happened. Who ever did this knew we were gone and knew when we were coming back. Katya, we're being watched."

Chapter 9 Addison

"Goo-ood morning, darlin'!"

I don't know what the hell time Earlene Whitelaw got into the office in the morning and I still wasn't convinced she did anything but delegate, but I had hopes I'd be able to get my first cup of work coffee poured before I had to deal with her. *So much for my luck.*

Figures. It was Monday.

Sliding into the employee break room just outside the pressroom, I mumbled my morning greetings.

"Penny — Addison, I was just thinking..." Earlene probably wasn't that tall, but with Miss Texas pageant hair sprayed high above her head and her insistence on wearing six-inch stilettos, she towered over me. She clenched her hands together and smiled hopefully at me, like a recalcitrant four-year-old, looking for forgiveness.

"What, Earlene?" I wanted to pound my head against the coffee machine.

"I was thinking about bringing a group of residents together, in a-a—" Her Texas accent was thicker than most natives'.

"Focus group?"

"Yes. A focus group."

Oh, Jesus. Don't do this to me, I thought. As the newspaper business continued to limp along, I heard stories from other editors at chain newspapers about how head office bean-counters who had never spent a day in a newsroom suddenly decided it was a great idea to bring in folks from the community to find out what they thought of the news coverage. The suits would sit and listen to what people thought, nod sagely, promise the moon and then dump the responsibility on the newsroom, which was already trying to do twice as much with half the staff.

The *Journal-Gazette* struggled ever since the economic crash, with outdated computers and a second-rate website that crashed on a regular basis. Advertising revenue was slowly coming out of the tank, but the days of a twenty-eight-page, two-section hometown paper were long gone, thanks to the Internet and Craigslist.

"What exactly do you think you'll get out of a focus group?" I poured my coffee and started toward the narrow stairs that led to the second-floor newsroom, knowing she'd follow me, teetering on bright yellow stilettos with turquoise flowers on the toes.

"Well, I believe we'd hear what the community thinks."

I stopped half way up the stairs and turned around. "Earlene, I can tell you what the community thinks: They want more local news coverage. That takes a bigger staff. They want a bigger paper. That takes more advertising. They say they want more good news on the front page, but the truth is nothing, nothing sells better than sex offenders, fatal car crashes or homicides.

"The day I have a story where a sex offender is shot, or where a pedophile dies in a car crash, the circulation department practically pees themselves with joy over the jump in single copy sales. You can only put so many stories of Happy the Clown visiting a kindergarten class on the front page!"

"I just thought—"

I turned and started back up the stairs, then stopped. *After all, she is your boss,* a little voice said. These last eight months since she'd taken over for her father had been tough, but she was learning. She'd also brought a large pile of cash from her fourth divorce settlement that staved off further staff furloughs or cutbacks. There was even talk of new computers in the newsroom.

"All right Earlene, I'll tell you what," I said, clutching my cup handle so tight my knuckles hurt. "If you want to put together a group of community members for a meeting, I'll sit down with them and I'll listen. I won't promise any more than that."

Earlene clapped her hands, like she'd just been promised a trip to the zoo.

"I have some folks in mind for the group. Let's meet this afternoon." She turned and, steadying herself with both railings, headed back downstairs to her office.

I sighed, knowing I'd just been railroaded. *Kill me now, God. Kill me now.* At least the meeting was after deadline.

Once in the newsroom, I flipped on all the lights and turned on the police scanner. Dennis Herrick usually got here right after I did. Photographer Pat Robinette, and reporters Marcus Henning and Elizabeth Day would be in momentarily. Graham would follow them about fifteen minutes later, after he'd stopped at the police station for morning reports.

I stared up at the white dry-erase board on the newsroom wall, where reporters listed their upcoming stories. So far, the front page would have Graham's gorge rescue story from Sunday with photos, and Marcus had an update on the city swimming pool. Since she hadn't been here on Friday to update me on Monday's stories, Elizabeth hadn't updated the board. I knew she had two stories ready to go—a profile on the new principal at Jubilant Falls High School and the story of a Golgotha College sophomore who just returned from a mission trip to Romania. The one that fit would be the one we used.

I walked into my office just off the newsroom and flipped on the computer. As everyone got settled in, I perused the Associated Press wire, looking for national and state stories of interest.

Right on schedule, Graham wandered into my office doorway, holding the weekend police reports.

"So how's Duncan?" he asked.

"He's got a lovely shiner, but he's fine," I answered.

"How do you want to handle this?"

"We don't make a big deal of any other minor assault. Just because the victim is my husband doesn't mean we should change policy. List it in the blotter."

"Already got it written out for you." Graham handed me a sheet of paper.

I took it from him and began to read: *"Doyle McMaster, 31, of Jubilant Falls, was arrested Saturday about noon following an assault at the Grower's Feed Mill. According to police reports, McMaster got into a physical altercation with the victim after McMaster reportedly used a racial slur. A second man was also struck when he tried to intervene in the altercation. McMaster was charged with misdemeanor assault; both victims' injuries were minor and were treated at the scene."*

"It's not a 'physical altercation,' it's a fight. You also didn't include McMaster's address or the feed mill address," I said, handing the story back to him. "Change those and it's fine. Didn't you tell me McMaster was possibly involved in some hate crimes in the next county?"

Graham nodded. "Assistant Chief McGinnis said the police there are watching some suspicious activity, but there's nothing local yet. He said he'd let me in on anything when it happens."

I nodded. "Anything else going on?"

Graham shuffled through the reports. "Not really. This is mostly blotter stuff—a couple public intox charges and a teenager took his mom's car without permission. Stupid stuff."

"OK. Well, write them up as briefs for the public records page. By the way, did Gary say anything about Jerome Johnson to you? The black guy McMaster hit?"

"No, why?"

"Just asking." I waved him out of my doorway. "No big deal. Go get started. Keep an eye out on that hate crimes thing, though—if McMaster gets nailed on anything out of town, we need to do a story."

Graham nodded and headed back to his desk.

With Graham's story on the gorge rescue, the front page came together easily that morning. We only had to use a small amount of wire copy, a short story about a tropical depression threatening to turn into a hurricane in the Gulf of Mexico. After catching what few errors there were, I sent the last page down to prepress nearly twenty minutes early. I ducked back into my office and closed the door: I had a few phone calls to make.

Whoever Jerome Johnson was, I didn't trust him. We may have all sat beneath the tree in my front yard yesterday and shared a meal, but that didn't mean I believed his story about growing up in Virginia, or joining the Marine Corps or living in Ashtabula. Something about that man pegged my bullshit meter and I was going to find out why.

I punched Gary McGinnis's number into the phone. He picked it up on the second ring.

"Hey Penny. How's it going?" Gary and I had known each other since high school. We were comfortable with each other, the kind of ease that comes from working together for years, building trust, but knowing where the boundaries between a cop and a reporter lay. If he could tell me, he would. If he couldn't, I knew when and how to push.

"Not bad. Hey, I need a favor. You know the deal Saturday where Duncan got hit in the eye by Doyle McMaster?"

"Yup. What do you need?"

"I need information on the other victim in that mess, Jerome Johnson."

"What do you need it for? A story?"

"No, not really." Briefly, I explained about seeing Johnson taking photos of Pat and me on Friday afternoon, his odd hostility at our doing a story at Katya Bolodenka's farm, and his story on Sunday about meeting her in Ashtabula. "I just don't trust him, Gary, and if Duncan is going to be inviting this guy over to my house on a regular basis, I'd sure as hell like to know who I'm dealing with."

"Let me see what I can do. I'll call you back later this afternoon."

***

"Hi Penny! Ya'll come on in!" Earlene had her back to the open door when I knocked. Her elbows were planted on the Queen Anne credenza behind her matching writing table. She recognized me by my reflection in the makeup mirror she held in one hand; the other was carefully outlining her lips with a red pencil.

She smacked her lips together, blending the liner with her cherry red lipstick, and turned around, clicking her matching nails on the desk surface.

Following her father's retirement, before she even knew what the word deadline meant, Earlene's first project had been to remodel the publisher's dark masculine office. She pulled down the knotty pine paneling, and had new drywall hung in its place. Baby-chick yellow paint now covered the walls. She'd also replaced her father's desk with the more feminine Queen Anne writing table and credenza, but kept the towering bookshelves that lined two walls.

She'd also replaced the two Morris chairs in front of the two desks with more feminine upholstered chairs in matching yellow striped fabric.

Behind the desk, above the credenza was a six-foot tall self-portrait of Earlene herself in full English equestrian apparel, mounted on a sleek black thoroughbred. She appeared considerably younger; her hair was still platinum blonde and her waist was thin and trim—whether that was fact or the painter's doing, I couldn't tell. She cupped her riding helmet under one arm and held the reins with the other hand. Her jacket was royal blue and her light tan jodhpurs slipped into the tops of black knee-high riding boots. In the background, a large barn sat at the end of a long line of oak trees.

Her third husband had the portrait painted at the beginning of their short-lived marriage. It hung in the foyer of their palatial Fort Worth home and when they split up, it had been the one item he had gladly given her. Everything else had been bitterly debated, but in the end she'd walked away with half his oil money and all of his Porsche. It was parked next to my Taurus in the employee parking lot with the vanity license plate 'WAS HIS.'

"So, let's get started. I have a bunch of people I'd like to include in this little focus group." Earlene ruffled through the papers on her desk. "Oh wait—here's the list."

"Before we get started, I want you to know that I have some fundamental problems with letting a focus group dictate our coverage," I began.

"Oh, no—don't you worry about that, darlin'! I just want to get the pulse of the community, hear what people are thinking. These are folks who have come by my office and introduced themselves to me and I thought they'd make a good sounding board. The first name is… let's see… Reverend Eric Mustanen."

"He's pastor at the Lutheran Church," I said, nodding. "He comes to the newsroom every year during the week before Ash Wednesday with his annual listing for mid-week soup suppers and Easter services and again at Christmas. He seems like a reasonable guy."

"Angus Buchanan?"

"Hmm. He might be a problem."

Redheaded and beefy, Angus Buchanan was the local car dealer and reminded me more of a polled Hereford bull than someone who spent thousands upon thousands of dollars in advertising with us each year.

I had to remind him periodically that he might have the right to determine what goes in his ads, but he couldn't influence my newsgathering. He snorted like a Hereford bull, too, when he stomped out of my office.

"But he spends so much money with us!"

"That's the ad department. That's not the news department!"

"He did say something about a story that ran last year that he wasn't happy about."

"One of his mechanics was caught selling meth. He was selling it from his apartment, not out of the dealership. We never identified him as one of Angus's employees, but he took offense that the story ended up on the front page."

Earlene cringed. "Oh. That is unfortunate."

"Earlene, the last thing I'm going to do is to temper my news coverage to suit our advertisers. This guy was caught with a meth lab in his living room, for god sake! It's not my fault he decided to sell to an undercover cop! We only reported it. Am I supposed to know the name of every Buchanan Motors employee?"

"Well, that is true," she said slowly. "Here's a couple more names: Naomi Callum and Hedwig Ansgar."

"They are both presidents of the area's two garden clubs," I said. Retired teacher Naomi Callum was the leader of the upstart Plummer County Peonies, which had been founded in the 1950s.

Hedwig Ansgar, another retired teacher, presided over the older, more sedate and prestigious Garden Club of Jubilant Falls, which had been founded during the town's golden age in the 1890s. Hedwig was nearly as big and beefy as Angus Buchanan, but better dressed. I privately referred to her as The Dowager Empress.

While anyone with an interest in getting dirt beneath their fingernails could join the Peonies, those who wished to join the Garden Club had to be nominated by a current member, vetted by the membership committee and approved by a two-thirds majority. Many of the ladies who belonged were married to Jubilant Falls' old guard business and themselves tottering toward decrepitude, but they managed to have their finger on the social pulse of the city.

"They seem to be delightful little old ladies, I thought." Earlene looked at me over her list, hopeful I wouldn't object to them.

"They're not bad," I shrugged. "I do think they probably have a vision of our business that is about thirty years old, but I think they are big supporters of a hometown newspaper."

"OK, what about Melvin Spotts?"

"No. Just flat out no."

"Why?"

"Do you have any idea what a crackpot he is?"

"He seemed rather, well, intense when he came to my office."

"Intense?" I asked. "At least twice a month, he leaves a nasty message on my phone or sends an e-mail accusing me or my staff of covering up the real corruption he feels is going on in Jubilant Falls. It's everything from crooked cops to upper level federal cover-ups and unidentified flying objects landing outside the city. You know he told me that he thought the federal government was hiding barrels of radioactive waste in the old landfill? It took me two weeks to convince him that wasn't true. I'd take him seriously if his voicemails didn't have a parrot squawking, "Don't tread on me!" in the background."

Earlene's eyebrows knit together in confusion. "Oh, dear."

"You didn't promise him a place on the focus group, did you?"

She grimaced.

"You didn't."

She nodded. "I thought... he seemed to have so much valuable information."

"Oh Jesus, Earlene."

"I've scheduled a meeting for next week with these folks — next Monday at two o'clock."

I stood up and closed my eyes, resisting the urge to blow up at her. Maybe she would see what a disaster this group could be after one meeting. I could only hope.

"OK," I said, gritting my teeth and gathering my cell phone and notepad. "I'll be here."

My phone's voicemail light was blinking when I dragged myself back to my office and shut the door. I shook off my need for a cigarette and punched in the password to listen to the message: "Penny, this is Gary. I looked into your buddy Jerome Johnson. I don't know what to tell you, but the guy doesn't exist. Neither does Ekaterina Bolodenka. Outside of a social security card and an Ohio driver's license, neither of them has any records of any kind. Anywhere."

Chapter 10 Graham

"You didn't come over Sunday night."

I took my chance while the newsroom was empty except for the two of us and made a beeline for Elizabeth's desk.

For once, everyone else scattered. Addison came back from lunch and disappeared into a meeting with Earlene. Dennis slipped down to advertising to flirt with Jane the secretary, and Marcus was scouring the halls at city administration office for a story. Pat was down at the high school, getting photos of the high school football players at practice.

"I got into town late. I'm sorry," she said. She didn't look at me as she pulled a plastic container with her lunch salad out of her bottom desk drawer.

"I called your cell phone a couple times. You never answered."

"You know I don't use the phone when I'm driving. Traffic was awful."

"Everything OK? You feeling alright?"

Her brown eyes met mine.

"I'm fine." Her tone told me not to ask again.

Last night, awaiting her arrival, I'd set my table with flowers and the two dishes I could find without cracks in them. Elizabeth's favorite marinated pork chops still sat in the fridge, along with baking potatoes and fresh green beans. I bought a chocolate cake from an out-of-town baker with the words 'Will You Marry Me?' written in frosting across the top with the blue ring box embedded in the center. After eleven o'clock and no return phone calls, I put everything away, turned out the lights, and sat in my darkened apartment, alone.

"Would you like to have dinner tonight? My place?"

Before she could answer, I heard a woman with a heavy Russian accent speak.

"Can someone help me, please?"

We turned to see a tall slender woman with curly black hair standing in the entranceway. She looked like she'd been crying.

"Yes?" I asked.

"Is Miss Addison in office?"

"No, I'm sorry, she's in a meeting. Can I help you with something?"

"I have farm with llamas—"

"Oh!" Elizabeth spoke up. "You're Ekaterina Bolodenka—Addison did the story on your animals and your fiber arts for Saturday's paper."

"Yes. Someone is killing my animals. Last night it was my cashmere ram—this morning it is female cashmere goat." She stopped to wipe her eyes. "My farm manager, Jerome Johnson, he find dead goat on doorstep this morning."

"Jerome Johnson? Is that Jerome Johnson the same man who was assaulted this weekend?" I asked, directing her to my desk.

Nodding, Bolodenka pulled a wadded tissue from her jeans pocket and wiped her nose.

"Why would someone do that to my animal?" she wailed. "Why?"

I pulled a notebook and a pen from the piles of paper on my desk. "Tell me what happened."

"Yesterday, we have picnic with Addison and her husband," Bolodenka began. "Wonderful, relaxing picnic on front lawn. We come home and find my Dasha, my ram, dead by fence." She stopped and shuddered before continuing. "Someone cut his head off and—" she made a slashing motion from her throat to her belt and began to cry quietly.

"I'm so sorry," I said. "What happened this morning?"

"Today, I am fixing coffee when Jerome comes in, with hands covered in blood. He has found another dead goat on his doorstep, the small house near barn."

"I know it's hard to talk about it, but what happened to this animal?" I asked.

She made the same slashing motion and once more burst into tears.

Elizabeth came over with a box of tissues and handed her one, patting her on the shoulder.

"I just never expect this to happen to my animals!" she said. "Me, it's one thing—animals, it's another."

"Have you filed a report with the sheriff?" I had a fairly decent relationship with the new sheriff, Judson Roarke. He'd replaced the old sheriff, Ernest Boderman, who retired after nearly thirty years in the position.

Roarke had been Boderman's chief deputy and my go-to source for any information for crimes in the county, since Boderman had a chip on his shoulder regarding the media and seldom returned anyone's calls.

Boderman was the reason why I began carrying a police scanner wherever I went, since showing up at the scene was just about the only way I would get information.

"Jerome, he was going to do that. I thought Addison can help us, so I came here."

"Why did you need to talk to Addison?"

"Her husband Duncan said she knew who punched Jerome, Saturday."

I lay my pen down on my desk. "Miss Bolodenka, the man who struck Jerome Johnson may have some connection to hate groups. It's possible that Doyle McMaster is killing your animals to intimidate Jerome."

Her eyes widened, but she didn't speak.

"Let's go talk to the police. Maybe they can give us some other information."

***

Chief G was finishing a phone conversation when Ekaterina Bolodenka and I walked into his office a few minutes later.

"Yeah. Whatever you can find out let me know. Great. Thanks," he said as he hung up. "Hi, Graham, what can I do for you?"

"Chief, this is Ekaterina Bolodenka, and she's having trouble with someone killing her livestock."

"I'm sorry to hear that," he said. "Anybody who hurts an animal is special scum in my book." Chief G's face betrayed nothing as he reached out to shake Bolodenka's hand.

"Thank you," she answered, wiping her eyes.

"I told her that McMaster might be a likely suspect, if he's doing what you think he's doing," I said.

"That's entirely possible." Chief G indicated we should sit down in the chairs in front of his desk. "Tell me what happened."

Bolodenka repeated the story she had told me as the chief took notes, interjecting an occasional "Uh huh" as she talked. She was crying again by the time she finished; it was difficult to pull the facts from beneath her heavy accent and her sobs.

"Can you tell me a little bit about yourself?" he asked. "What is your relationship to Jerome Johnson?"

"He is farm manager," she said. "I am born in Moscow. I come to this country when I am five and my family we live in Chicago. I also lost a sister and a niece in car accident. Her husband died too. I studied art and taught art history before coming here to Jubilant Falls." The story was automatic, like the recitation of the lines from a play. She'd probably been asked those questions so often it just ended up sounding that way.

"You're not employed now?" Chief G looked up from his notebook.

"My farm and my art are my income. I have rented out several hundred acres to other farmers for their crops."

He nodded.

"It's entirely possible that Mr. Johnson is being targeted by Mr. McMaster as part of a hate crime," Chief G said. "We have reason to believe that McMaster is part of a group from the adjoining county that may be coming into Plummer County and organizing more hate groups. The problem is that your farm is not in my jurisdiction, since you live out of the city. You need to report this to Sheriff Roarke."

"Jerome, he is reporting to sheriff."

"Good. Sheriff Roarke is aware of the same facts that I just told you. I will tell him that we spoke and what I told you. He may want to take other steps, but you'd have to talk to him about it."

She nodded.

We stood and shook hands.

"Graham, I need to speak to you about something else. If you would wait here, I'll walk Miss Bolodenka to the elevator."

"I can find my way back to newspaper and car," she said. "Thank you so much for helping. I feel better now."

Chief G led Bolodenka from the office and I sat back down in my seat. Within a few minutes, he was back, with a file folder in his hand. He handed me another copy of Benjamin Kinnon's picture as he returned to the seat behind his desk.

"So, is he any relation?"

I studied the picture silently as I thought about my answer. What would happen if I revealed what I knew?

At boarding school, the Jesuits taught us to be open to God's directions, to discern God's will for ourselves, not an easy concept for a dorm full of hormone-poisoned boys to consider, to conquer ourselves and to regulate our lives in such a way that no decision is made under the influence of anyone or anything else.

I had no emotional connection to Benjamin Kinnon. He was only a name on my birth certificate. Yet, I hated what he had done to my mother and, with the situation with Elizabeth, on some level I now realized the damage of his abandonment.

I also sensed his evil.

"Yes, I know him." I handed the photo back to Chief G. "He's my father."

"You're kidding me, right?"

I shook my head. "Nope. Sperm donor is probably a more appropriate term." Briefly, I briefly filled him in on my past: Mother's connection to Benjamin Kinnon, her drug use and rehabilitation, my time in foster care and what amounted to our dual transformations into the wife and stepson of one of Indianapolis's bright lights.

Chief G leaned back in his chair when I finished speaking. "Wow. I was figuring maybe an old drunk uncle, idiot cousin or something like that—everybody has one like him in the family, right? But your father?"

"I never had any relationship with him. He disappeared a long time ago."

"Well, he's back. Like I told you the other day, he's moved to Jubilant Falls."

"Where is he living?"

"He's out in the west end, right now living out of an old motel there. We've got our eye on him."

"Do you think he and McMaster could be behind these animal killings?"

Chief G nodded. "I think they put him at the top of the list."

My stomach dropped. "What are you going to do?"

"Right now, all we can do is watch. People have a right to their opinions, however ignorant and ill informed. These folks also have the right to meet with other ignorant and ill-informed idiots, but they don't have the right to do anything like this. If we can confirm that these two assholes have anything to do with these animals being killed and they are part of a pattern of intimidation, there will be consequences. They will be swift and they will be serious. The problem is, guys like this are like bloodhounds when it comes to sniffing out an undercover cop."

"What can I do to help?"

Chapter 11 Addison

No, I'm sorry. I have been the priest here for many years." The priest at St. Volodymyr's church spoke slowly and thoughtfully at the other end of the phone. "I don't know of anyone named Bolodenka who attended here, or lived close to here."

I pushed for a little more information.

"She had a sister named Svetlana, who had a daughter named Nadezhda—they called her Nadya," I said. "She died, along with her husband Alex and the baby in an auto accident in Moscow. Would there have been a memorial service here for them?"

"Well, it's entirely possible that a memorial service could have been held here, but as I said, I don't know that name and when an entire family is killed like that, our whole community would grieve. We haven't had a service for a circumstance such as that since I've been here. Is it possible Bolodenka is her married name?"

"I don't know if she was ever married. Her mother and father are both deceased, though."

"Hmmm... Is it possible that she attended another church?"

"How many St. Volodymyr's churches are there in Chicago?"

"There are a couple, actually. This church is Eastern Orthodox. There is a St. Volodymyr and Olga Catholic Church and, to confuse you even more, a Saints Volodymyr and Olha Ukrainian Catholic Church. Maybe you could try there."

"OK, thanks." I hung up the phone, chewing pensively on my thumbnail. Had Katya Bolodenka fed me a line? And why would she do that? What point did it serve? What were she and Jerome Johnson hiding? And why couldn't Gary find anything?

I really didn't like the idea that a story I'd written could be blatantly false, but I didn't have any proof of that. How important was it that a priest in a large city like Chicago couldn't remember one parishioner? Did that mean anything at all?

Most importantly, what was the point of her secrecy?

I picked up my phone again and began to dial the numbers of the next church the priest suggested. There was a knock on my door and Elizabeth Day peeked her purple head through.

"Hey Addison, you got a minute?"

Elizabeth stepped into the office. By her body language, I could tell what she wanted. After while, an editor knows when this conversation is coming: over the years, I'd had enough staff come through my office to know when a reporter had grown enough professionally to want to leave the nest.

The first few months Elizabeth was here at the *Journal-Gazette*, she would go cry in the ladies' room every time I made a serious criticism or structural change to one of her stories. She'd come a long way, though, and while I don't ever think she'd make a good police reporter, her skills at everything else had stepped up. She could take criticism now, she could write a hell of a lead and she could bang out a story like there was no tomorrow.

"Sure, kiddo. Come on in," I said, hanging up the phone. "Have a seat."

"Can I talk to you about something?" she asked. "Something personal?"

Chapter 12 Graham

It was nearly eight in the evening before Elizabeth got to my apartment. I wrapped my arms around her and hugged her tightly in the doorway.

"C'mon in," I said. "I can start dinner."

From the kitchen, I watched Elizabeth flop on the couch, where she began to unlace her black military boots and pull off her socks, her face pensive. I pulled the pork chops and the green beans out of the fridge and began cooking, the marinated meat sizzling as it touched the preheated pan. Once the chops browned, I would turn the heat down and begin to sauté the green beans in olive oil. I wasn't a great cook, but I could find my way around a cookbook.

"Can I get you a glass of wine? How was the school board meeting?" I asked as I stirred.

"God, yes, please." Elizabeth sighed. "The meeting was boring as hell. It's the last meeting before school starts, so it was all about setting the cafeteria lunch prices, approving changes to the student handbooks, crap like that. I don't even know if it is worth a story."

I reached into the fridge again, behind the cake with the engagement ring on top, and pulled out a bottle of red wine.

"Did lunch prices go up? That's what usually happens this time of year," I suggested, hoping I wasn't grinning like a fool.

"A quarter at the high school and twenty cents at the middle school."

"If you don't do a story, then every mother in town will blame us for her little darling missing lunch on the first day of school because he didn't bring enough money." I uncorked the wine and poured two glasses, handing one to her. "So how was your visit with your mom this weekend?"

She took a tiny sip of wine before she answered. "Fine. She's fine."

"What did you guys do? Anything special?"

"Not really." She drew up her legs and tucked them beneath her round bottom.

"Did you feel OK this weekend? No problems with your stomach? The wine isn't bothering you, is it?"

She sighed, this time in exasperation, and took another sip of wine. "Why are you so worried about it?"
"Because I worry about your health!"

"I'm not pregnant, OK?" she retorted sharply. "I don't know why you're suddenly so worried about that. I throw up a couple times in the morning and you just go all baby daddy on me!"

"You've been throwing up a couple times a week for three weeks! What do you expect me to do—or think? I'm allowed to care about you, aren't I?"

"Worry all you want, but I just have other things on my mind—and it's not a baby."

"So what is it? There's not anything else wrong, is there?" This wasn't the way I wanted tonight to unfold, not with an argument about a possible pregnancy. I turned the heat down on the pork chops and covered the pan. In two steps, I was beside her on the couch. She leaned up against me and was silent for a moment.

"Ever wonder what you're going to do next? I mean in your life, not just during an ordinary day," she said softly.

I wrapped my arms around her and pulled her close, the hair of her purple wig beneath my chin. "Sometimes. What do you mean?" What happens next just might depend on you, I thought.

"How long do you want to stay here in Jubilant Falls?"

I shrugged, still holding her tight. "I hadn't really thought about it. Why?" What did she mean? Did she have any inkling of what I was about to ask?

"Some days I just can't stand this place. These meetings just made me think, 'Here I am starting another school year again, with all the same stories and all the same crap.' There are times when I think I've written every story there is to write, I've taken every picture of every damned cute kid in Plummer County that needs to be taken."

I shrugged. "Sometimes I think the same thing: 'Haven't I written this story before?' It happens."

"I'm just bored out of my mind and I'm bored with my job. Do you ever get bored, Kinnon?"

"Sometimes. Like right now, when the news is slow, I can't stand it." I returned to the stove to check on the chops and dumped the green beans into a separate pan to sauté them. "Maybe we could go someplace next weekend. What do you think?"

She didn't respond to my question.

"Maybe something will come of what that Russian woman told you this afternoon," Elizabeth said, instead. "Maybe they'll catch the guy who is killing her animals. That would be a great front page."

"I hope so." It was my turn to shrug. I couldn't let Elizabeth know yet about Benjamin Kinnon or what Chief G and I had discussed. I couldn't even do a story about the conversation I had with Ekaterina Bolodenka this afternoon until I had a chance to talk to Sheriff Roarke and see what kind of report had been filed.

"Let me help you with dinner," she said. "I don't want to talk about this any more."

"No, this meal is on me — my treat. You've had a lousy day. Just sit there." I smiled at her and this time, she smiled back. She's going to say yes, I thought to myself. She's got to.

Within a few minutes, the microwave beeped, signaling the baked potatoes were done. A quick check of each pan showed the meat was cooked through and the green beans were tender. I loaded everything onto a platter and carried it to the table.

"Dinner is served," I said.

"My God, Kinnon, you've outdone yourself," she said, settling into one of the dinette chairs. She reached over to the platter and picked up a green bean with her finger, snapping off a bite of it in her sweet red lips.

"I wanted tonight to be something special. Be sure to save room for dessert."

She arched an eyebrow. "Oh, we can make it special. Trust me."

I reached across the little table, lacing my fingers through hers and smiled. *Yes. Yes, we will.*

Conversation turned casual—work stuff, programs we watched together on television. I hoped she couldn't sense the nervousness building in me. Soon, our plates were empty.

"Kinnon, you did a good job," Elizabeth said, pushing back from the table.

"We're not done yet." I stepped over to the fridge and, drawing out the cake, began my carefully rehearsed speech, the one I'd stood in front of the bathroom mirror and repeated over and over:

"Elizabeth, we've been seeing each other for almost a year now. I just want you to know I love you, like I've never loved anyone before. You brighten my world like no one else ever has and I don't ever want to lose you."

I set the cake in front of her and opened the blue ring box in the center.

"Elizabeth, will you marry me?"

Her face was ashen as horror rose in her eyes. Maybe she was just surprised, I thought. Maybe she didn't hear me right.

"Elizabeth? Will you marry me?" I asked again.

"Oh God, I was so afraid you'd do this!" She jumped up and, gagging, pushed me out of her way. The door to the bathroom closed and once again, I heard her vomit.

This time, I didn't hover outside the door, begging her to call a doctor. I sank on the couch and stared into space as my world came to an end. I waited until I heard the toilet flush and the sound of running water as she brushed her teeth.

The bathroom door finally opened. Her eyes were red and her purple wig slightly askew.

"You want to tell me now what's really going on?" I asked softly.

She leaned against the bathroom doorframe.

"I got a new job, Kinnon. I'm going to write features for the *Akron Beacon-Journal*," she said softly. "I told Addison this afternoon while you and the llama lady were at the police station. She's going to announce it tomorrow at the staff meeting."

"You weren't going to tell me first? You were going to let me get blindsided at a staff meeting?" I asked angrily.

"Kinnon, I'm—"

I didn't let her finish. "You didn't think I would be happy for you? That I'd be proud somebody at a big metro thought you were good enough to write for them?"

"Kinnon, I'm sorry. I'm so, so sorry."

"So your trip to Shaker Heights wasn't for your mother's birthday."

"Well, yes it was. We also looked for an apartment in Akron."

We were both silent.

"Find one you liked?" My voice was barely above a whisper. I felt beaten, like I'd just taken a punch to the gut.

She nodded, a tear running down her cheek.

"How long have you been looking for a new job?" I asked.

"A couple months. I wasn't sure how you'd take it or how Addison would take it," she said. "It was the stress of applying for a job and then worrying if I would get it or if I wouldn't. I was thinking all kinds of crazy things: What if somebody called for a reference before Addison knew I was even looking? What if I gave my notice and she fired me for some reason? And us—I wasn't sure how you'd react."

"Guess you know, now."

She sat down next to me, wrapping her arms around my neck. "Yeah. They told me Thursday I'd gotten the job."

"So you woke up Friday morning with me, in my bed, knowing you were leaving, and started throwing up."

"I didn't know what to say! It's not that I don't love you, Kinnon—I do," she said. "It's just that I'm not ready. If we got married now, I could see us settling down in Jubilant Falls and never leaving. I'm not willing to do that. Not right now."

"I'm not planning on staying here at the *Journal-Gazette* forever either," I said. "I don't know what I want to do next. I just know I want you in my life forever, whatever comes next."

"Kinnon, please—"

I pulled her arms from around my neck and looked her in the eye. A note of desperation crept into my voice. "Listen, Beth, why can't we see each other, even after you go to the *Beacon-Journal*? On weekends, I could come up to Akron, or you could come down here…"

"And what happens if there's some breaking news story? I'm going to sit here while you go chase it?"

"And you don't think you'll have some assignments that interfere when I come up to see you? That's the business we're in! Nobody else is going to understand like I do. I understand about the crazy hours, the lousy pay, how frustrating it is when your sources don't call you back and the story is due in twenty minutes. I understand that, but there's one thing you need to know. Nobody else, Beth, will love you like I do. Nobody."

She pulled away from me and reached for her socks and boots.

"And I must be the dumbest girl in the world for turning you loose, Kinnon, but right now, I think it's the best for both of us." She kissed me on the cheek and slipped out the door.

I waited until I heard her car pull away from the curb then hurled the cake against the door.

Chapter 13 Katya

"You did what? You dumb *súka!*" Russian profanity spit from Jerome's mouth. "Why did you do that? Why did you think the editor of the newspaper, of all people, could help you?"

I tossed my hands in the air. "She knew who struck you. She knew he was bad man! I thought I could find out more to help you!"

We were standing in the feed room of the barn. Bags of grain were stacked on pallets along two walls. On a third wall hung kitchen cabinets with vet supplies like worming medicines and bandages. Beneath them was a small sink in the center of a small counter. Jerome's desk was along the fourth, looking out the one window onto the front pasture and driveway.

Jerome picked up a fifty-pound bag of feed and heaved it angrily into the wheelbarrow just outside the entrance to the barn's interior.

"I told you to stay here!" He picked up another bag of feed. "I told you I would take care of it!"

"But Jerome, I—"

"No! You listen to me!" The second bag landed in the wheelbarrow with an angry *thunk* and his voice got louder and louder. "You have made this detail harder than any other job I've ever been on. You continually step outside the boundaries of what you have been told more than once are in place to keep you safe. You keep doing these things you don't think are dangerous — like the state fair and the newspaper article—but they are!"

"What the hell am I supposed to do?" I screamed back at him. "Sit here and do nothing? Twiddle thumbs until it's time to move on to next place? Do you know what is like to try to talk to people and everything that comes out of your mouth is a lie? I have never taught art history in my life! I can't talk about my mother, I can't talk about my sister—"

"What don't you understand?" The veins stood out on his neck. "We're trying to keep you safe until the trial, Katya!" Grunting, Jerome angrily yanked a third bag of feed onto his shoulder.

"And then what? I disappear again?"

He stopped, the bag of feed on his shoulder, and sighed. "No. Not this time. Not if your identity wasn't compromised. Since this town is so far off the beaten path, the plans were to let you stay here, once we were sure you were safe. I mean, who the hell would come looking for someone in a town called Jubilant Falls?"

"So now the truth," I said. "I have blown our cover?"

The feedbag slid from his shoulder into the wheelbarrow, more slowly this time. Jerome pulled his smart phone from the holder on his belt and, after touching screen a few times, turned it so I could see: It was the photo of me from Saturday's newspaper article, smiling into the camera, seated at my spinning wheel surrounded by llamas and alpacas.

"Where is that?" I asked.

"It's on the newspaper's website. Anybody looking for you can do an Internet search and find it. That story was posted Sunday while we were at McIntyre's house having lunch."

I covered my face with my hands. "And when we come home, Dasha is dead, then today, Zaneta, " I said softly. "I am dumb *súka*."

"What happened when you went to talk to Addison this afternoon?"

"I started to tell you — she wasn't there. So I talk to reporter, his name is Graham Kinnon," I began. "He said the man who hit you might be doing other things, bad things."

"Like what?"

"A 'hate crime' was what police chief called it."

"You also talked to the fucking police?"

"I didn't tell them anything except that my animals were dying! Graham Kinnon, he tells me the police are watching this man and police chief might have more information for me, so we walked down there to talk to him."

"Oh, Jesus, Katya."

"I told him you were talking to the sheriff."

"I didn't just talk to the sheriff, Katya."

"Who else did you talk to, then?"

"Who do you think?"

I closed my eyes.

I knew the answer.

"I have to protect myself, too, Katya. I can't let another detail like this go south. I screwed up once and it cost me my career in the Marines. I'm assigned to protect you, but you're not making it easy on me," he said. "I have to tell my superiors what you are doing and how that compromises your safety. It doesn't make it any easier that we are sleeping together."

"Oh, and I'll bet you were completely honest with them about that, weren't you?" I snapped. "I'm tired of hiding everything in my life. I want to be able to live the kind of life everyone else lives. I'm tired of being everyone's dirty little secret."

He sighed. "You won't be a secret forever. I promise. But I had to let my superiors know what happened."

"What did they say?"

"The trial is next month. You are the lynchpin of the entire federal case, the prosecutor's main witness. We have to keep you alive, but you have got to follow the rules. They were adamant about that."

"What if the person killing our animals is this bad man, this Doyle McMaster? What if it's not—?" I couldn't even say his name.

"It doesn't matter, Katya. If you're dead, you're dead and the case is over. I'm out of a job—and Kolya Dyakonov goes free."

Chapter 14 Graham

After deadline Tuesday, Addison gathered us all together in her office for a staff meeting. Most of it was plans for the upcoming Labor Day weekend: Who would cover Monday's parade, how much time Pat could give to that weekend's festival, Canal Days, for front page art, coverage for the first day of school, crap like that. I doodled aimlessly on the notebook on my lap.

"And I have one more announcement." I looked up as Addison smiled at Elizabeth. "One of our own, Elizabeth here will be moving on to bigger and better things. She's accepted a position at the *Akron Beacon-Journal.*"

Addison led the congratulatory applause as Elizabeth blushed; Marcus, Dennis and Pat all joined in. It was difficult, but I managed a smile.

"That's great news!" Marcus Henning said. "When's your last day?"

"I start September fifteenth in Akron, so whatever the Friday before that is," she answered, glancing at me.

"Let's go out to dinner that night for an official send-off then," Addison said. "Sound good?"

Everyone around me nodded.

"You available that night, Graham?" Addison asked.

"Sure. I'll be there." I tried to sound pleasant. *Maybe I'll get lucky. Maybe there will be a four-alarm fire.*

There were a few other items Addison needed to go over, but in a few minutes, thank God, the meeting broke up.

"I'm heading down to the sheriff's office," I called out, heading for the door.

"Kinnon, let me walk down there with you — I need to go to Aunt Bea's to get a soda," Elizabeth said.

I didn't answer.

"Hey, Kinnon! Wait up!" Elizabeth grabbed her purse and followed me down the stairs, out the front door and onto the sidewalk. At the corner, she grabbed my shoulder. "Graham, hang on! Quit walking so fast!"

"What do you want?" I stopped abruptly.

"You're going to make these next two weeks a living hell for me, aren't you?"

"No, I think you did that all by yourself."

I turned away and started back down the sidewalk, heading east on Main toward the Sheriff's Office, a block past the big stone courthouse.

"Graham, wait, please!"

"I've got work to do, Elizabeth. I'm supposed to meet with Sheriff Roarke in about five minutes," I called over my shoulder. I didn't look back. I just kept walking.

Chapter 15 Addison

After Tuesday's staff meeting, everyone scattered.

"I'm heading down to the sheriff's office," Graham Kinnon called out.

As slow as it's been, maybe he can dig up a story, I thought to myself, closing my office door. Before I checked on tomorrow's advance pages, I needed to touch base with Gary McGinnis. In a moment, I had him on the phone.

"Hey, it's me, Penny."

"So what's up?"

"I called the church Katya Bolodenka told me she attended as a child in Chicago and the priest there hadn't heard of her," I said. "I even called two other churches with the same name and they never heard of the family either."

"I didn't dig up anything on her on my end either," he said. "No previous tax records under that name, no credit rating anyplace."

"I looked up the deed to that farm on the county Website," I said. "She paid cash for it. There's no mortgage."

"Where would anybody get that kind of cash to buy an entire farm? When I asked her yesterday what her income was, she told me her art and the farm were her only income."

"You saw her?"

"Right after I left that message on your phone yesterday, she and Graham walked into my office."

"Really? Nobody said anything to me that she came here."

"Apparently someone slaughtered two of her cashmere goats—one Sunday night and one early Monday morning. Graham thought that it could be tied to Doyle McMaster, so he brought her to my office to talk about it. "

"But you can't help her with that, since she lives in the county," I said.

"I know. She originally was looking for information from you about McMaster. Apparently her farm manager was at Sheriff Roarke's office filing a report while she was talking to me."

"What did you tell her?"

"Just what I'd told Graham the other day—that we suspect McMaster may be involved with a hate group that could be moving into this area."

"Considering the fight he got into with Duncan and Jerome, that wouldn't surprise me. And there's another one—that guy Jerome Johnson. You couldn't find anything out about him?"

"Nope. You said he'd lived in Ashtabula? I sent his BMV photo to the chief of police in Ashtabula and he's never heard of him."

"Maybe he just didn't have a record."

"The Marines have no record of him either, Penny. I should have been able to find something there and I couldn't."

"So the story she fed me about him being a guard at the embassy in Moscow was a load of crap."

"Looks like it."

"Then they're both lying. I didn't find Katya in any school records. She told me she studied at the Art Institute of Chicago. They have no record of any female student under that name. What do you think is going on?"

Gary was silent for a moment.

"Russian organized crime is known for trafficking in heroin and women," he began slowly. "We've had a hell of an increase in heroin use, just like everybody else. The location of that farm, not far from the highway like it is, could be a perfect drop spot. Drugs or women or both could be moved in and out of there without anyone knowing."

"You think so? I thought the Russian mob was centered on the east coast. You think they would move this far west? Are there any Russian crime families headed by women?"

"Anything is a possibility." Gary shrugged.

"What about protective custody of some sort? Witness protection?" I asked.

"If they were under federal witness protection, we'd know. Besides, some of the stuff she is doing could be considered pretty conspicuous — I read that story you wrote on her farm. Protected witnesses are generally told to keep a real low profile. A story like that could get her thrown out of the program."

"Would the feds normally have a handler like Jerome Johnson living on the property?" I asked.

"Witness protection can involve twenty-four-hour security, if someone is supposed to testify in a federal trial of some sort, for example. And you're assuming Jerome is the federal agent."

"She's too tiny to be his protection," I said dismissively.

"Penny, I've seen some little females who could kick ass up one side and down the other. That kind of a story would be a good cover — the poor little Russian lady who can hardly speak English and needs a big, strong man to help her run her farm. The same could be said if she's running drugs or a prostitution ring out of that farm. Johnson could be her enforcer in that situation."

"But the only suspicious person I saw there was Jerome Johnson. He creeped me out."

"No one else? Women or men?"

"Just livestock — llamas and alpacas. And I was inside the house, too."

We were both silent.

"I don't think she's in protected custody," Gary said. "I don't know what's going on, but it's not that."

I sighed. "There's something going on there that we don't know anything about and I don't like it. I mean, what if the story I wrote on her is a complete fiction?"

"What if it is? That doesn't make you look bad — it makes her look bad. Would that be a story? So what happens then? You can't do a story on any suspected illegal activity until an arrest is made. Besides, who is going to believe that a yarn-spinning llama farmer is also a drug dealer? I don't think it fits together. Let the police look into what may or may not be going on at that farm."

"Yeah, that's true. I just don't like being fooled by somebody."

"That's our business, Penny—you and me both, we get lied to on a regular basis. At any rate, whatever is going on, their livestock doesn't deserve to be killed like that. I'm strongly leaning toward McMaster being stupid enough to keep harassing Jerome Johnson by killing his animals. I'd bet the rent that Judson Roarke does too."

"We'll have to see what Graham comes back with. He was on his way over there when I called you."

"Keep me in the loop," Gary said. "I'll talk to you later."

The rest of the afternoon was routine. I sent Earlene an e-mail telling her about Elizabeth's new job and letting her know I'd like to fill the position as soon as possible. After that, I checked tomorrow's advance pages for content and errors; finding only minor tweaks, I shipped them downstairs to pre-press and sent Dennis home for the night. Marcus came back from city hall with a story about a street department employee who was retiring after twenty-five years; Pat was getting the photo. Elizabeth's story on the new principal was still in the queue, so that could run in Wednesday's paper.

God, I need some unvarnished human misery, I thought to myself. How much more boring can a page one get?

"Hey, Addison, can we talk for a minute?"

I turned around to see Graham looking somber. "As long as you're not giving notice, too," I said, smiling.

"No, ma'am. Can we talk in your office?" As usual, Graham's face betrayed nothing.

"Sure."

"I got a call from my mother this afternoon," Graham began as he took a seat in one of the office's old wingback chairs. "I need to take some time off."

"I'm sorry to hear that," I said. "You've never spoken much about her. I hope she's OK."

"Yeah, she and my stepfather live in Indianapolis. She's fine—my stepfather has had a slight heart attack, nothing serious, but she wants me to come home for a few days."

"Well, we still have Elizabeth and as slow as it's been, there shouldn't be any problem. I can catch whatever breaks," I said. "How much time off have you taken this year, outside of holidays?"

"None."

"Why do I even ask? Go down to see Peggy, get me a vacation form and I'll sign it before you leave tonight."

"Yes, ma'am."

"So anything happening at the sheriff's office?"

He shrugged. "Not really. They got a few grants for some DUI checkpoints for the holiday weekend. I can write that up before I leave this afternoon."

"I talked to Gary McGinnis. He said Katya Bolodenka was here to see me yesterday and you took her down to see him about her goats being slaughtered."

Graham nodded. "Her farm manager Jerome Johnson was supposed to be filing a report with the sheriff, but when I checked on it this afternoon, they didn't have anything. Sheriff Roarke said Johnson didn't want to file a report, but just wanted extra patrols around the farm."

"Hmmm. That's interesting." I wasn't going to spill what Gary had told me, since we didn't have any proof of anything—including their real identities. And if they were involved in something illegal, like Gary said, it wasn't a story yet. I was just being nosey and I knew it—all because I just didn't trust Jerome Johnson.

"See if you can get either one of them to go on the record about it. If there's someone out there targeting animals, others might want to know that."

"I checked. There have been no other reports of any other farms being targeted." He stood up. "I'll get that form and then I'll run out to their place to see if they'll talk to me."

My desk phone rang—it was Isabella's cell phone number. I waved Graham out of my office.

"Hi, Mom!" Isabella sounded excited.

"What's up, baby?" Since her suicide attempt in high school years ago and her diagnosis of bipolar disorder, I never could quite take a situation at face value when she sounded overly excited or overly sad. She was good about taking her Lithium and submitting to the frequent blood tests that monitored her medication levels, but I still worried.

"Dad and I are down here at Buchanan Motors and I've found a car that I like. Could you come down and look it over? Please-please-please-*pleeeease*?"

I relaxed and smiled. "Why do you want me to look at it? Your dad is the mechanical member of the family."

"I know, but it's so cute! Dad says it drives OK. He got under the hood and said the engine looks fine."

"Sure. I can come down for a little bit, but I've got to come back to work afterwards."

Down at Buchanan Motors, Isabella and Duncan, with his black eye just beginning to subside, were standing beside a little two-door Ford, painted candy-apple red. It was third in a row of used vehicles on Buchanan Motors' lot. It was an automatic, with an AM/FM radio. It would get her through the rest of college and be reliable transportation to her first job, whatever that would be.

"Do you like it, Mom? Do you like it?"

"It's cute, yes," I said.

"It will eat up about half of her savings," Duncan said. "But it looks like it's a good car. I told her she made a good choice."

Out of the corner of my eye, I saw Angus Buchanan sauntering toward us.

I nodded at Duncan and waved at Angus. "I don't have any complaints, then," I said to Duncan. "Go ahead and get it. Hello, Angus!"

The car dealer reached out with his thick hand to shake mine.

"Hello, Addison," he said. "You guys decide on a car?"

"Yes," said Isabella, clapping her hands. "I want this one."

"Good choice. Need financing?" He began to steer us toward the showroom.

"Nope," Duncan said.

"Yeah, you farmers always pay cash, except when it comes to equipment," Angus joked as he opened the glass door with one hand and pointed toward a corner desk. "You can just head over there to George—he's my business manager and he'll take care of the paperwork for you. I need to ask Addison about some other business."

"What's up?" I asked as Duncan and Isabella headed inside.

"I just want you to know that I really like this new publisher, this Earlene."

"Well, thank you, Angus," I said. "I'll tell her that."

"I really like the idea of this editorial board, too," he continued.

"Editorial board?" I asked. A focus group was bad enough, but an entire editorial board? I shivered at visions of weekly meetings where I defended my front page to people who had no clue about newspapers.

"She called it a focus group, I guess," Buchanan went on. "Anyway, I think it will be good for members of the community to have input on the newspaper."

"The community has always had input into the Journal-Gazette," I said, defensively. You'll have less input than you think, Angus, I thought. You won't dictate my news coverage.

"Well, you and I may have to disagree on that, Addison," Angus gave me his best used-car dealer smile. "I'm looking forward to tomorrow's meeting, though."

"Excuse me?"

"She didn't tell you? I just got an e-mail saying she's set up a meeting for two o'clock tomorrow afternoon."

I gritted my teeth. "I didn't think we were meeting until next week."

Angus pulled his Blackberry from his shirt pocket. "Nope. This e-mail just came a few minutes ago. We're meeting tomorrow. I guess I'll see you then, huh?" Angus shook my hand and headed toward another couple looking at used vehicles.

"I guess so." I tried to sound pleasant, but somehow, the only thing I really felt was aggravation.

Shake it off, Penny, I told myself as I went into the dealership to find my husband and daughter. *Earlene's your boss now. Things are bound to be a little different.*

Once the papers for Isabella's car were signed, and the check written, she and Duncan headed back home. I headed back to my office.

Graham's vacation form was on my desk; he'd requested the rest of the week off. Beside the form was a page from a reporter's notebook, scrawled with Graham's handwriting:

Addison — KB and JJ don't want to go on the record about the slaughtered goats, so no luck there for a story. The story about the DUI checkpoints is done and in the system. I'm on my way to Indianapolis. See you next week — Graham.

"Well, shit," I said to myself. "I can't make up the news. Maybe something else will happen while Graham is gone."

Sighing, I tied up a few more loose ends, found and responded to Earlene's e-mail about tomorrow's focus group meeting, and submitted the ad for Elizabeth's job to an online journalism job board. I turned off the computer and, slinging my purse over my shoulder, shut off the lights as I closed the office door.

As I turned around to lock the door, I heard the sound of a sniffle. It was Elizabeth, wiping tears from her eyes.

"You OK, Elizabeth?" I asked.

"I'm fine," she said, wiping her nose. Her purple hair made her eyes look that much redder. "I guess I'm going to miss this place more than I thought."

"We're going to miss you, too," I said, patting her on the shoulder. "You've done a good job here. You've grown a lot professionally and you're going to do a great job in Akron."

"Thank you."

I patted her shoulder again and headed down the back stairs toward the pressroom and the employee parking lot. As I left, I caught a quick glance of Elizabeth holding a toothbrush and sobbing.

Chapter 16 Graham

Bill didn't really have a heart attack, but Addison didn't have to know that.

The ruse got me to get out of the office for a few days, enough time to do a little digging.

I also wouldn't have to look at Elizabeth for her final two weeks in the office. Before I left town, I dropped the toothbrush she kept at my apartment on her desk, along with some other personal belongings.

The drive to Richmond, Indiana, took me slightly over an hour from Jubilant Falls — about the same time it had taken Mother to get there from her gated community outside Indianapolis. Enough time to think about the questions I wanted to ask her about Benjamin Kinnon.

The restaurant was dark and Mother was waiting for me in an inconspicuous corner. She was impeccably dressed, as always, in a pair of slim black pants and a short-sleeved, pale pink blouse. Shiny black sandals encased her painted toenails; pearls hung from her ears and around her neck. Her subdued makeup was flawless. A wide-brimmed summer hat and large sunglasses sat on the seat next to her purse.

The dinner crowd was beginning to filter in. She twirled the stem of her martini glass between her fingers as we looked over our menus. She ordered a salad. I chose crab linguini—this meal would be on her tab.

I started by asking about my two younger brothers.

"So how are Jackson and James?"

"They're fine. They're spending the week at soccer camp. Jackson starts his freshman year in high school this year."

"So where's Bill?" I asked.

"He's in Florida this week, on a golfing trip. We bought a condo outside of Boca Raton last year and he takes clients down there for golf outings."

"Sounds pretty fancy."

"You know, only the best for Bill. So what did you want to ask me about?"

"Tell me about Benjamin Kinnon."

She sighed and cast her eyes toward the ceiling. "I knew this was coming. I just didn't think it would take so long."

"So is he my father?"

"You have to understand, Graham, I was going through some hard times then—I'd made several extremely poor decisions..."

"Yes or no, Mother. Is he my father?"

"The social worker at the hospital kept pushing me to name someone as the father on the birth certificate. Benny Kinnon was around the most, so I wrote down his name. There were..." She paused, took a ladylike sip from her martini, and looked across the room at the other diners, no doubt checking to see if anyone might know her. "...A lot of men in my life at that time. I don't know if Benny is really your father or not."

I pulled Kinnon's folded police photo from my shirt pocket and took my press pass from around my neck. I laid the two of them side by side on the table. She flinched.

Sarcasm seeped into my voice. "Looks like you guessed right."

"Graham, please. You don't understand—"

"No, you don't understand," I snapped. "I have spent my life as the dirty little secret from your past. You were a drug-addicted hooker when I was a kid. You were a topless dancer when you met Bill and after you married him, I became a painful reminder of everything you wanted to forget!"

"That's not true! We always gave you the best of everything!"

"As long as it didn't involve anything more than writing damned checks! You and Bill shipped me off to boarding school the first chance you got—and kept me away as long as you could pay my tuition!"

"Graham, that's not fair!"

"I remember the day you were arrested, Mother. I still remember your torn tee shirt and the ragged jeans. I can still see your busted lip and the black eye Ben Kinnon gave you. You've got fancy clothes and nice jewelry today, but I know the truth about you."

"Lower your voice!" She hissed, leaning across the table. "People will hear you!"

I complied, but anger still came through in my words. "I want to know how much you know about Ben Kinnon."

Mother gripped the stem of the martini glass and continued to speak low.

"Sometimes he had a job, but mostly he boosted cars, then sold them to chop shops. When he couldn't steal cars, he stole credit cards then sold what he bought with those cards. When he got some extra cash, he bought drugs and brought them over to share with me."

"Like what?"

"Graham, do we have to go through this? Really?"

"What kind of drugs did you do with Benjamin Kinnon?" I asked again.

She sighed. "Heroin mostly. I used to shoot it between my toes so no one could see the needle marks. Sometimes we did crystal meth."

"When did you last see him?"

"He was arrested the same day I was arrested. I haven't seen him since."

"You were charged with heroin possession, right?"

Mother looked around, hoping no one was listening. "Yes, Graham. I was."

"What was he charged with?"

"Distribution. He had a lot more heroin on him than I did. We were both high on smack and got into a fight. The neighbors called the police and they found the heroin."

"The neighbors weren't the only ones to call the police, Mother. I did."

"Oh my God."

"What did you expect? You were getting the shit beat out of you! Where did you meet Benny, anyway?"

Mother took another genteel sip of her martini. "Junkies always seem to find each other. I was his lookout when he stole cars."

"Did you ever work with him on the stolen credit cards? Like when he tried to buy stuff?"

"Sometimes, if it was a female name on the credit card…" Mother's voice trailed off, then turned whiney. "Graham, you have to understand that those were different times for me. I met Bill and he really was a savior for me, for both of us. You understand that don't you?"

"I understand that I spent four years in foster care while you spent two years in prison and then took two more years to get yourself together. I understand that you stopped doing drugs and married a very rich man who wrote a lot of checks to keep me out of his hair."

"Don't look at it that way, Graham," Mother wheedled. "You couldn't have had the things you had if it wasn't for Bill."

"I also understand that you had all your Indiana court records sealed right after you got married. Was that Bill's doing, too?" A quick online search before I left Jubilant Falls confirmed that for me.

"He understood that I'd made a few mistakes and deserved a new start."

"Including hiding a son by a known heroin dealer and thief."

"We never hid you! That's not fair!"

"No, but after Jackson and James were born, I certainly wasn't made to feel part of that family."

"Oh, Graham, I'm sorry. You have always been my son and I have always loved you." She reached over and patted my hand and I dropped the interrogation bit, despite the anger I still felt. She was my mother, after all. She had come a long, long way from what she had been and, however poorly she may have handled the situation, she took me along for the ride. "I just have one question, Graham. Why ask about Benny Kinnon and why now?"

I took a deep breath. "My girlfriend and I—we had a little pregnancy scare. It kind of got me thinking."

"Oh! You have a girlfriend! How wonderful!"

"*Had* a girlfriend. We broke up."

"I'm sorry to hear that."

I shrugged. I wasn't going to go into the details with her. Instead, I changed the subject. "Do you know where Benny Kinnon is now? What he's into these days?"

She looked shocked. "No. Why would I?"

"No reason, just asking. We never talked about it before and it wasn't until this other... mess... that I even thought about him."

The waitress brought our meals to the table and the conversation changed: Bill's golf habit, the boys new private school, Jackson's newly discovered fascination with girls, the death of an aged Yorkie I never met, and where James was considering going to college. She never asked about my job and I never volunteered anything. We shared a piece of cheesecake, she paid the bill and we got up to leave.

"I know I made a lot of mistakes, Graham, and I'm sorry about that," she said as we hugged. "I'm sorry to hear you and your girlfriend broke up, too."

I shrugged. "Can't do anything about it now—about either situation."

She ran a manicured hand through my short brown hair, no doubt a show for those around us. "I know. I love you Graham."

"I love you, too." I turned to leave, heading toward the door and the parking lot. We wouldn't walk out together— we never did. As I pulled out into the street, Mother was standing at the restaurant's front door, hiding behind the large floppy summer hat and big designer sunglasses.

That's OK, Mother, I thought. *I won't tell anyone we met, either.*

***

"Hey Kinnon, where are you?" It was Elizabeth calling on my cell phone. I was back on the Ohio side of the state line, driving down the highway and contemplating what I was going to do next.

"I'm on my way to the hospital in Indianapolis. My stepdad had a heart attack," I lied. "I'm off for a couple days."

"Yeah, that's what Addison said."

"So why are you calling me?"

"Because I don't believe her—or you."

"Well, that's your problem, isn't it?"

"Kinnon, c'mon. Do you have to be such a prick?"

"You don't tell me you're leaving to take a new job, you let me make an ass of myself proposing to you and I'm the prick? Tell me how that works."

"Kinnon, please."

"What do you want?" I slid my Toyota into the exit lane. It would take me down another interstate through Collitstown; midway through the city, I'd take an exit for the two-lane state highway that would bring me back to Jubilant Falls in about forty-five minutes.

"I want… I want to explain myself. I want to say I'm sorry."

"I think you pretty well did. You're bored with your job, you're bored with me, you got a new job and you're moving to Akron."

"Graham, it's not just that—"

"Yeah, it is Elizabeth. Yeah, it is. I gotta go." I disconnected the call with my thumb and tossed the phone into the passenger seat.

Her sudden need to apologize surprised me. It could make what I was about to do a little more difficult, I thought to myself. I probably couldn't go back to my apartment now. She'd see the car, know I wasn't in Indianapolis, and come knocking at my door. Knowing Elizabeth, she would be insistent enough to drive past my place over and over again until she found me and pushed her reasoning why she wouldn't marry me down my throat. I couldn't afford a hotel room; maybe a rental car would be enough to throw everyone off.

The next exit took me to the Collitstown airport. I pulled off and drove into the airport garage. Parking my car in the last spot on the top level and stuffing my press pass into my pocket, I went in search of a rental counter. Half an hour later, I was back on the highway, this time driving a black Mustang and on my way to taking down Ben Kinnon.

Chapter 17 Katya

We are fire and gasoline, Jerome and I. When we fight, it's an explosion. When we make up, it is again an explosion. This time, the explosion happens in my house, in my bed, at night.

We fell apart, breathing heavily. I rolled on my side toward him and lay my hand on his cheek. He pulled me close and pressed his lips against my forehead.

"Katya," he whispered. "Oh, my Katya."

"After trial, Jerome, what happens to us?" I asked softly.

He sighed, kissed my forehead again, but didn't answer.

"Can we stay here? I love my farm and I don't want to leave it."

"It depends on a lot of things— how the trial comes out, for one. You know that." His words were soft.

"You will stay with me?"

"Always."

I wrapped my leg around his strong, brown thigh. "*Ah-byet,*" I whispered into his ear in my native tongue. "Promise."

The sound of car wheels on gravel stopped him from answering. Jerome jumped from the bed to the window, pulling on his jeans as he peeked through the curtain.

"I don't know who this is — they've got their headlights turned off," he hissed, reaching for his gun on the bedside table.

Dressing frantically, I peered over Jerome's shoulder, trying, as he was, to see who was coming up my driveway.

It was a big car, what they call sport utility vehicle. I couldn't tell the color in the dark, but there were two people in the front seat. The car stopped and the passenger, a big burly man stepped out, an automatic rifle in his hand.

"Quick! You know where to hide!" Jerome ordered sharply, poking his gun barrel between the windowsill and the curtain.

"Jerome," I whispered touching his shoulder. "I love you."

His brown eyes moved from the window to mine. Handing my cell phone to me, his words were quiet. "I love you, too. You know who to call."

I ran to the closet, and, pushing my hanging clothes to one side, found the pocket door that opened into the old walls of the farmhouse. Inside the walls, against old plaster and wood, my protectors had nailed a hand-made ladder, which led to a panic room in the attic.

From the outside, the room looked like a row of old antique dressers and trunks, fronted by a large wardrobe, piled against a wall. The wardrobe was attached to the false wall and had a false back, like the closet, for escape from the front.

The panic room walls, and the wardrobe, built a few feet away from the real wall, were bullet proof, reinforced with metal.

I was supposed to hide here if someone suspicious came to my farm.

As the front entrance burst open downstairs, I pulled the closet's back door closed behind me and scrambled up the ladder.

Crawling from the ladder into the panic room, I slid the door behind me closed, my terror growing. Kneeling in the dark, I scrolled through the numbers on the cell phone's dim screen with my thumb.

"Where is it? Where is it?" I whispered in Russian. To protect me, in case I lost my phone, the emergency number for the Witness Security Program (or WITSEC as Jerome called it), the one to call in case we were discovered, had been entered on my cell phone as a fake pizza place, but what was the name? What was the name?

Furniture crashed on the first floor and two men's voices echoed through the floorboards of my panic room as their heavy steps pounded up the stairs.

"Where are you, bitch? Where are you?" I knew that voice: It was Luka Petrov, one of Kolya's thugs. Luka had been an enforcer for Kolya for many years, collecting his debts, silencing those who would oppose my husband, the man I was to testify against.

"Stop or I'll shoot!" Jerome shouted.

I dropped the phone as gunshots rang out, pushing myself with my legs, crab like, into a corner. Jerome cried out—bullets must have struck him. I covered my mouth with both hands, digging my nails into my cheeks to keep myself from screaming.

"Where is she?" Luka demanded.

I imagined him standing over Jerome—I know how Luka works. Kolya taught him well. Like Kolya, Luka doesn't kill on the first shot. Kolya's first shot would have wounded, enough to get the victim—like my sister as she held her baby daughter, or now, Jerome—to understand what he wanted.

There was a thud, probably a kick. Jerome moaned.

"Where is she? The woman you call Katya—where is she?" Luka screamed. Another thud, another moan. "You have her hidden in this house, yes? Perhaps upstairs?"

Bullets ripped through the attic floor outside my panic room. Still tight against the wall, I bit the palm of my hand to keep the screams from coming. The floors beneath me, like the walls, were reinforced to keep bullets out, but because the farmhouse was so old, the room was not soundproof. Had I fallen, or screamed, they would know where I was.

"Maks," Luka said to another man. "We must take our guest downstairs and show him why it is better to cooperate."

No, Jerome! No! I wanted to scream. I knew what came next—more kicks, more punches. First one ear would be cut off, then the other. Luka's bare hands would pull out teeth, twist private parts, until he got the answer he wanted. Then he would place the barrel of his gun against his victim's forehead and pull the trigger.

There was no doubt Luka had learned Kolya's ways well. I'd seen photos of Alexis' body, my sister's husband, after he refused to tell Kolya's thugs where I went. Next, Kolya had them hunt down Svetlana and baby Nadezhda and kill them in cold blood.

I'd seen those photos, too. A U.S. marshal had shown them to me when we had to leave my last hiding place, the hills of Virginia's Shenandoah Valley.

I'd broken rules by keeping in touch with them and they paid terrible price. Now, I'd broken rules again and someone else who loved me would also suffer and die.

No one was would be able to find me here in Jubilant Falls, they said. You'll be safe here in Jubilant Falls. Until once again, I broke the rules and once again, someone suffered.

I slid one foot across the floor, trying to bring the phone closer to me. I had to call, to save Jerome's life. In the bedroom beneath me, Jerome screamed in pain as he was dragged to the stairway. More screams as they pushed him down the stairs and he landed with a thunk at the bottom.

A thick, sickening silence settled upstairs. Was Jerome talking? If he was I couldn't hear him. Were Luka and his goon torturing him? Was he already dead?

I reached for the phone and began to scroll through the numbers again— there it was! The name of the fake pizza parlor was the last number in my phone: Zapponelli's Pizza. I pressed the number, but all I heard was a weird electronic sound. Did the call go through? What was happening? Did the heavy metal walls that kept out bullets also keep my phone calls in? I'd never had problems making cell phone calls before. I tried again, then again. Why wouldn't the call go though?

Heavy footfalls thudded up the stairs to the second floor, then up the attic stairs. Luka was coming for me, roaring, screaming, like an animal. Had Jerome told them where I was?

Panicked, I dropped the phone as I scrambled back to the ladder in the wall, sliding the wall panel closed behind me. I climbed down into the space between the walls and waited for death.

Chapter 18 Graham

By the time I pulled up to the curb in the rented black Mustang, darkness had fallen. The only light shining on at the Plummer County sheriff's offices came from Judson Roarke's office. It was on the fourth floor, above the first three floors that contained the jail administration office and jail on the second floor, the county's dispatch center on a windowless third floor and an entire first floor of records.

I called his personal cell to let him know I was downstairs. Within minutes, Sheriff Roarke was at the main door, unlocking it to let me in. I followed him to the elevator and we rode up to his office. Neither of us spoke until we were seated.

Roarke's office was very different than Chief G's city-issue metal chair and desk. Portraits of previous Plummer County sheriffs circled the room. Each portrait had a small brass plate with their names and dates they served, nailed into the bottom of the wooden frame.

His desk and chair were heavy wooden relics, ornate with scrollwork, from those previous men's administrations, but clearly, there had been funds through the years to keep them polished and in good condition. Despite the heavy air of history, the office had an atmosphere of accessibility, maybe because Roarke was just starting the first year of his second term and hadn't settled into the permanence of the last sheriff, a throwback to a time when becoming a deputy was a matter of patronage and old boy networking, not professional law enforcement abilities.

Roarke had done a lot to change that perception.

He'd worked himself up from road patrol to chief deputy over his career and he'd seen the department from the inside out. He worked well with the press — I cringed at some of Addison's stories she told about how inaccessible the office had been, particularly to her — and cleaned out any old guard who didn't see his vision.

Right now, he had other things on his mind. Sheriff Roarke looked over his reading glasses at me.

"You don't have to do this."

"I know."

"Does your boss know what you're doing?"

"No. I'm officially taking vacation time because of a family health crisis."

Roarke nodded.

"I'll remember that. Chief McGinnis knows what we're doing — this is a joint operation. We're not going to have you wear a wire, just yet, but that may come in the future."

"I figured."

"Right now, we just want you to get to know him, get him to trust you and find out what his activities are. If he's seriously involved in any white supremacist activity, we need to watch that. If he's just a blowhard, running his mouth, then he's not a lot unlike his buddy Doyle McMaster. Either way, most likely he'll end up here as one of our taxpayer-subsidized guests."

"OK." My cell phone, the ringer turned off, vibrated in my pocket. I pulled it out and glanced at it: it was a text from Elizabeth. Without reading it, I stuffed the phone back into my pocket. I had more pressing things to worry about.

"You understand the risk you could be taking," Roarke was saying. "These guys are violent and if they think you are not trustworthy in any way, they'll hurt you — or worse."

"Yes."

What Roarke didn't understand was my need to look Benjamin Kinnon in the face, find out what he was about and then exorcise him from my life, no matter what it took. I'd come through an essentially rough start just fine, rose up from drug addicted parents, came out of the foster care system and got an excellent education — thanks, whether I wanted to admit it or not, to Bill and his money.

My fears over Elizabeth's possible pregnancy made me think deeply about the relationship a son should have with his father. Except for contributing half of my DNA, Benny Kinnon had been only a small part of my life. There was something else about this man I needed to know, though. What made him the way he was? Why did he turn to a life of crime and drugs? And most importantly, might I become like him?

A long string of men wandered in and out of my mother's life on an hourly basis in my young life. Benny Kinnon's connection had been only slightly more frequent: apparently, he used my mother when he needed laid, a lookout or a fence and he paid her back with drugs or violence.

He never claimed me as his son. In that way, he wasn't much different from Bill. Both kept me at a distance: I was an inconvenience, an obstacle standing between them and my mother. Benny used drugs and violence; Bill used a checkbook.

Roarke slid a piece of paper scrawled with Ben's west side address on it across the desk.

"When are you going to meet him?" he asked.

"Probably not until tomorrow — Wednesday. If he's a junkie, I figured he probably wouldn't be coherent much before lunch."

Roarke stood and extended his hand. "There's not many people who would take this kind of risk, you know."

"I know." I shook the sheriff's hand. He escorted me back down the elevator and to the front door. Neither of us spoke until Roarke opened the door.

"Be careful."

"I will." I slid into the front seat of the Mustang and pulled my cell phone out to see Elizabeth's text message.

Where R U, Kinnon? Don't believe Indy, she'd texted.

U R right — not Indy, but out of town. Don't believe? Check airport garage 4 my car, I texted in reply.

It's easy to lie to someone who breaks your heart. Maybe more lies would come as easily tomorrow when I knocked on my father's door.

Chapter 19 Katya

Cringing behind the safe room wall, I hung on the ladder inside the wall, listening in terror as Luka, roaring outside wardrobe door, tried to break through the reinforced back.

He threw himself against it over and over, shaking the walls of the old farmhouse. The marshals assured me I wouldn't be hurt behind the wall of the safe room, but that didn't mean I wouldn't be scared. I know what Kolya's thugs could do. If he broke through, my death would be slower and more painful than Jerome's.

The metal held. Terrified, I flattened myself against the back wall as, with a roar, he pulled the wardrobe's front door off in frustration, the hinges groaning.

"I know you're in there!" he raged in Russian.

A hail of bullets sank into the reinforced wardrobe back—and stayed there. Luka roared again in fury.

I exhaled as his footsteps faded into the distance. He was leaving—but was he leaving the house? If I went downstairs, would I find him sitting on my couch, waiting for me? Had my call to the emergency team gone through? Were they on their way to save me? I couldn't take the chance.

Carefully, I slipped down the ladder, back into my bedroom closet. Stepping away from the false back door, I peeked out of the closet. The room was empty. On tiptoe, I went to the window and moved the curtain aside to look. The big SUV still sat in the driveway.

Were Kolya's thugs still in the house? Were the marshals on their way? Who knows? I slipped back into the closet and up the ladder, back into the panic room.

Stepping across to the wardrobe's reinforced back, I ran my fingers across the raised metal lumps and shivered. *I must leave. I must get out.*

I opened the false door and slipped outside. In a few steps, I was at the attic's rear window.

I stepped out onto the roof and shimmied down rain gutter to the rear porch roof until I felt safe enough to jump to the ground.

A siren echoed in the distance, blue and red lights lighting up the night. Was it the marshals? Were they coming down my road? Had the call gone through? Were they coming here? Would I be safe now? The sound of footsteps pounding up the stairs told me I couldn't wait to find out.

I jumped from the porch roof to the ground and, as bullets rained around my feet, ran into the night. Once again, I was escaping, running in terror for my life.

Chapter 20 Addison

Away from work, my taste in books tended toward something I could quickly get lost in. Maybe it was the snail's pace in the newsroom that was drawing me toward the lurid true crime story that I held in my hands.

I was reading in bed when Duncan, wearing a pair of pajama bottoms, entered the bedroom, fresh out of the bath and rubbing his wet hair with a towel. I looked up at him and smiled. The hair on his chest was dotted with silver now. The six-pack he had when we first married was a little less defined and had a little more of a paunch, but with his wide shoulders and narrow hips, after twenty-five years, he was still the man of my dreams.

Tossing his towel across the back of a chair, Duncan flipped back one of Grandma McIntyre's Depression-era quilts and slid into our antique Jenny Lind bed.

Our bedroom was basically the front half of the old McIntyre farmhouse's second story. It was a large but narrow room, with a small closet, like many other houses from the 19th century.

We'd never updated the house since taking over the farm from Duncan's parents, so Isabella's bedroom was at the back of the house, next to a small bedroom we sometimes used for guests, but which was used mostly storage for out-of-season clothes. The three of us shared the single upstairs bathroom with a claw foot tub.

Because of their large family, Duncan's parents turned a downstairs back parlor into their own bedroom. That parlor now did double duty as the farm office and a seldom-used formal dining room.

"So it looks like Izzy's happy with her new car," I said, laying my paperback in my lap.

"Yes, I think so." Duncan leaned back onto a wall of pillows propped behind his head, and with the remote, turned on the TV atop his dresser. "It looks good mechanically and I think she's going to enjoy it for a long time."

We were silent as the ten o'clock newscast's opening theme song played and the program began.

Truth be told, it wasn't until after those first few news stories that I could really relax and think about something else other than the *Journal-Gazette*, knowing that no one else had beaten me to a story.

The opening segment was a young male reporter standing in front of yellow crime scene tape. There were police cruisers and a fire truck barely visible in the back of the dark shot.

"Police are investigating what they are calling a hate crime, after someone set fire to a car parked at a local volunteer's home," he began.

"Duncan! Turn that up!" I pointed at the screen as the camera panned to the burned-out frame of a small car.

"The owner of this car is an African American, who declined to appear on camera, but he is a volunteer at a local community center," the reporter droned on, staring into the camera. "He told police that he had a confrontation with a young white man last week at a local mall when he and two teen agers, members of the community center's Black History Club, were selling candy as part of a fund-raising effort."

"Oh my God," I said. "Graham Kinnon told me that Gary McGinnis suspects the guy that hit you—Doyle McMaster—of being involved in hate crimes. You think he could be behind this car fire?"

"Wouldn't surprise me a bit," Duncan said.

"This is the third such incident to occur here in Collitstown and police believe they are connected." The camera panned from the reporter, back to the burned-out car and the police cruisers. "They have a description of the man, but are not releasing that information."

"Holy shit," I said, sinking back into my pillow.

"It's not a story until they charge him—if they charge him—so don't worry," Duncan said, patting my leg.

I nodded and sighed with relief after a few more stories played, all no consequence to Plummer County: a downtown crash between a Collitstown city bus and a motorcyclist, the opening of a new restaurant in a county further north.

My ears perked up as the scanner on my dresser crackled. A county ambulance was being dispatched for a frantic mother's call on a baby with a high fever—a family's crisis, but not a news story. I relaxed and turned back to Duncan, comfortable now that no one had beaten me on a story. I could worry about other things, family things.

"It's not going to be long before Izzy is done with college," I said.

"Yup." Duncan nodded, staring at the television, one arm slung behind his head.

"Have you guys talked at all about what she plans to do?" I asked. Since our daughter had been born, Duncan shouldered the majority of the parenting responsibilities. It made sense for our situation—he was certainly at home more than I was; my job brought the insurance benefits and cash into the family equation.

That didn't mean I didn't feel guilty about it.

More than once, I'd left Duncan with Isabella, whether she was a squalling baby or sullen teen, to go chase a story. Sometimes, I did it intentionally, when I felt I'd reached the end of my very limited parenting abilities. He'd been the one who found her when she'd tried to commit suicide in high school. It was the only time in years I'd taken time off from work.

Duncan shifted against the pillows, but kept looking at the television. "She's talked about doing more with Henhouse Graphics, building that up unto a full-time operation," he said.

Henhouse Graphics was Duncan's part-time business that he ran during the year after the crops came in and farming slowed down. He ran it exactly from where it sounded like—the old henhouse beside the barn. He took only the occasional job: yard signs and buttons during local political campaigns, logo designs or the occasional sign.

"Does she want to live here after college?"

"I think so. I don't have a problem with that, do you?" He glanced over at me. "We could sure use the help."

"No, not at all." I put the paperback on the nightstand beside me and turned on my side toward him. "I know this sounds weird, but what about the farm? Has she ever asked about running the farm?"

Duncan looked away from the television. "When did you start worrying about passing on the farm?" he asked softly.

"I don't know," I shrugged. "Just seeing Katya and Jerome here on Sunday, knowing they live in the Jensen's old place—it's been kind of eating at me that Larry and Denise had to give up that farm, even though it happened a couple years ago."

He patted my thigh. "We haven't ever really talked about passing on the farm. I wasn't really sure she was ready for that conversation."

"Are you going to bring it up?"

"Sure."

"When?"

"Not before she graduates from college. Would you want to be young and confident, with the whole world ahead of you, and have your dad hand you a bucket and ask if you want to help bail water out of the Titanic?"

"Is it that bad, really?"

"Selling a couple heifers would get us a little bit ahead, but that puts me in a position where I've got to hope next year's calves aren't all male and that there will be a female in there that will produce decent amounts of milk down the road. I mean, our bull is good, he passes on great traits, but there's always the chance when we need it most, he won't. Money's tight, but it's always tight."

Duncan sighed as he rearranged the summer quilt around himself.

"You haven't had a raise in years, and everything I do depends on milk or grain prices," he continued. "There are days I think about getting out of the dairy business and just going into grain production. We're one of the few dairy farms left in the county."

I nodded. "Do you want to keep the farm in the family?"

This time Duncan was silent for a moment. He had two brothers and four sisters, all of whom shared the three upstairs bedrooms in their childhoods and then ran as fast and as far away from Plummer County as they could after graduation. Duncan had been the only one who wanted to keep the farm.

"Yes, of course I do, but if Izzy doesn't want it, we need to talk to my brothers and sisters about it," he said. "Right now, let's not worry about it."

He reached across me and pulled the string on my bedside lamp, leaving the room bathed in the television's blue light. He drew me into his arms.

"Are we doing OK—you and me?" I asked softly, settling comfortably against his chest. "With my job and all the stress you've been under, I know this sounds strange, but, sometimes I wonder if I still make you happy."

"Always." Duncan kissed my forehead, then my cheeks, then my lips. "Always."

I reached over and took the remote from his side of the bed and clicked the TV off. Duncan raised a devilish eyebrow and smiled as the darkness enveloped us.

***

Her screams woke me before I heard the pounding on the door.

"Help me! Help me! Help me!"

Duncan and I jumped from the bed, slipping into our clothes as we dashed through the hall and downstairs to the kitchen, where the old clock above the sink read two-thirty five.

It was Katya, standing barefoot on the stoop outside the kitchen door, breathing heavily, sticks and leaves caught in her loose black curls. Her arms and bare feet were scratched bloody; one pants leg was torn.

"Help me! Help me, please!" She threw herself into Duncan's arms as I opened the door.

Together, we guided her to the kitchen chairs and sat her down. I filled a glass with tap water and set it in front of her.

"Katya, what's going on?" I asked.

"It is Jerome! They've killed him!"

"What? Who?" Duncan asked. "Doyle McMaster? The guy he got into a fight with at the feed store?"

"No, not him — someone else."

"That's it. I'm calling the cops," I said, my hand on the kitchen wall phone.

"No, no, no —" Katya took a gulp of the water. "Don't call police. We need to call someone else."

"Who?"

"Witness protection. U.S. marshals."

"Witness protection?" Duncan and I asked simultaneously.

I let go of the phone and sat down beside her. "Katya, if there's been a murder, we have to call the police."

"How do you know Jerome is dead?" Duncan asked sharply. "Did you see the body?"

"He's dead! I know, I just know!" Katya began to wail hysterically.

"I'll be right back. We need to get over there." Duncan slipped out of the kitchen.

"No! No! No!" Katya cried out. "We can't go back there — Luka, one of Kolya's thugs, he is at farm waiting for me!"

I grabbed her by the shoulders. "Calm down, Katya! Who is Luka? Who is Kolya?"

"Please, you must forgive me. Everything I tell you in story about farm, it is lie. Everything Jerome tells you, it is lie."

Before I could answer, Duncan came downstairs, his father's old double-barreled shotgun in one hand, a pair of my summer flip-flops in the other.

"Here," he said, handing Katya the shoes. "Put these on. They will at least protect your feet. You can tell Penny your story in the car — let's get over there. We can call the sheriff on the way."

"What about milking?" I looked over at Duncan.

"You want to stay here and milk those heifers while a man could be dying? They'll wait. C'mon — let's get going," he said.

I grabbed a flashlight, a reporter's notebook and a pen from the kitchen counter. We piled into the Taurus and Duncan turned the ignition, bringing it to life. Gravel spit from beneath the wheels as we roared down the drive. I sat in the back seat, the shotgun upright beside me like another passenger.

Flipping open the notebook, I leaned between the front seats as Duncan drove.

"Tell me the truth Katya. Tell me your story."

"I am not from Chicago. I am not art instructor. I have never been to Cleveland and Jerome, he is not from, how you say? Ashtabula? I am wife of Russian mobster from Brighton Beach."

"In Brooklyn? New York?" I asked as I scribbled.

"Yes. Jerome, he is—" Katya stifled a sob. "—was a U.S. Marshal, assigned to protect me until the trial of my husband, Kolya. I turn him in because he runs gang, he is using homeless people to commit fraud."

"How does he do that?"

"Kolya owns medical clinics. His doctors write prescriptions for the patients Kolya men bring in every day." Katya calmed down as she told her story. "Kolya has people like Luka round up homeless people in vans and take to clinic in New Jersey. The doctor gives them free exam then writes prescription for drugs."

"What kind?"

"Ox-ox…" Katya's thick accent made her stumble over the word.

"Oxycontin?"

"Yes. The people, they are addicted to these pills. They get the prescriptions filled and clinic bills Medicaid. The money comes into clinic and doctor sends it to Kolya."

Medicaid fraud, I thought as I wrote. I'd seen some national wire stories about how the state of New Jersey was seeing a sharp increase in painkiller abuse and how the Russia mafia was connected, but I'd never printed those stories in the *Journal-Gazette*. They seemed too far away, too foreign for my readers to care about.

The articles described a scenario exactly as Katya described: mob-owned clinics run by dirty doctors who wrote prescriptions for up to thirty patients a day, most always for the highly addictive painkillers like Oxycontin or Oxycodone. The mobsters didn't care if the clinics' patients took the drugs themselves, or sold them to other addicts.

But the flood of drugs caused an explosion, according to New Jersey officials, in prescription drug overdoses and deaths. That didn't matter—it was the easy money from Medicaid they were interested in. Efforts were underway to shut the clinics down, but as one clinic was closed, others often popped up.

"Where is Kolya?" I asked.

"In prison, waiting for trial. But that doesn't mean he can't tell the men in his gang to do something."

"And you turned him in?"

"One of the homeless men, he got off the pills and threatened to expose Kolya and his clinics to police," Katya's voice dropped. "So one day, Kolya tells me to go shopping, hands me wad of money. I never really knew what Kolya did. I was young and stupid and enjoyed his money.

"'Go get yourself something pretty. Don't come back until dinnertime,' he tells me. But I didn't listen—or this man just wouldn't die. I came home early and heard screams from the basement. Kolya was torturing the man downstairs. I saw Kolya kill him — the same way Luka killed Jerome, I know! I know!" She began to cry again.

"One more question, Katya."

"Yes?"

"Is Bolodenka your real name?"

"No," she whispered.

"I have to tell you, Katya, I've been looking into what you told me for the article." I stopped writing and laid my hand on her shoulder. "I knew what you told me wasn't true."

"I had to. You understand? I had to tell those lies."

I patted her shoulder from the back seat as Duncan pulled into the drive.

"There's no one here!" Katya said. "I heard sirens as I ran from house. I thought marshals were coming to save me, but I was too scared to stop running."

"Looks like Luka has disappeared," Duncan said, shoving the gearshift into park and stepping out of the car.

"Be careful—there's three buildings. They could be hiding on the property. The barn is big enough to pull an SUV into," I said, handing him the flashlight as Katya and I got out. I pulled my cell phone from the back pocket of my jeans, as I held the shotgun in my other hand. "I'm calling the sheriff. If Luka is here, we're going to need more than just this shotgun."

One of the advantages of growing up in Plummer County was learning how to use a gun. As the daughter of a state trooper, I'd been taught early. As a farm wife, I'd shot my fair share of coyotes over the years when they'd made it into the pasture during calving season. If someone came out of the barn, I had no qualms about firing back, but the shotgun wouldn't be any match for more than one weapon, if these guys were still on the property.

My other advantage? As the editor of the paper, I had the private numbers of the entire county's movers and shakers—and Sheriff Judson Roarke was one of those numbers. We didn't talk often, but I was impressed with the way he'd turned the Plummer County Sheriff's Office into a first-rate law enforcement organization.

He picked up on the third ring.

"Hi Jud. It's me, Penny McIntyre from the *Journal-Gazette.*"

"Hello." Judson was remarkably alert for someone, I assumed, I'd just awakened from a sound sleep. "I know you well enough to know that this isn't a courtesy call. What's up?"

"We may have a murder," I said. "On Lunatic Fringe Farm."

"Do you know who the victim is?"

"Jerome Johnson, the farm manager for Ekaterina Bolodenka." I wasn't going to go into all the details right now. "The place where those goats were tortured and killed."

"I'll be right there."

"There's a possibility the suspect may still be on the property. You might want to bring all the firepower you've got."

"Got it."

There was a scream as I disconnected. I turned to see Duncan restraining Katya as she tried to run toward the farmhouse porch, where the body of Jerome Johnson lay in a pool of his own blood and brains.

Chapter 21 Graham

I shot out of bed as the scanner on my dresser crackled to life: "All units, possible homicide at 68734 Youngstown Road. Proceed no lights, no sirens, suspects possibly still on property. Contact complainant, a Mrs. McIntyre, on scene with property owner, who speaks limited English."

I slumped back down on the mattress, realizing, for once, I couldn't cover this story. I was supposed to be in Indianapolis. I knew the property owner who the dispatcher was referencing had to be Katya Bolodenka. And what was Addison already doing there? Listening as each sheriff's deputy responded, one by one, I stood and paced the bedroom.

If someone was dead on that farm, could it be Jerome Johnson? Or was it Doyle McMaster? Had he intentionally provoked a confrontation with Jerome, or had Jerome caught him trying to kill another farm animal? Was it Benny Kinnon? Was he the type to get his hands dirty? If so, had he found himself at the end of Jerome Johnson's gun?

My pacing expanded into the living room. I wanted to grab my camera and a notebook, head out to the scene and dig into the story, but I couldn't. As far as Addison knew, I was in Indianapolis, with my stepfather and his fake heart attack.

"Unit one on scene." Judson Roarke's voice came across the scanner. "Dispatch, I need you to 10-79 Dr. Bovir. I have a visual on one victim, a black male, mid-thirties."

I stopped pacing and sighed. Dr. Bovir was the Plummer County coroner. So Jerome Johnson was dead, three days after Doyle McMaster punched him. If McMaster had anything to do with this, then Benny Kinnon also had to be involved. Roarke would want me to find that out.

"Dispatch, this is unit one—" Roarke began again. A man's angry voice drowned out his words: "Hey, that's my wife!" The radio cut off. There was silence for a full two minutes before Roarke returned to the radio. His tone was caustic. "Dispatch, we have a second agency on scene. All radio traffic on Channel Two."

Channel Two was the interoperability channel, the one they used when communicating with multiple agencies, particularly state and federal ones. Why would those agencies show up at a county homicide? That didn't make sense. Maybe it was just the state investigative agency, the Bureau of Criminal Investigation, or BCI as they were called. They had more sophisticated tools and a bigger staff for investigations and it wasn't too uncommon for them to be called in.

That was probably what happened, I thought. But who had called them in? And why?

The scanner went silent. As long as they were on Channel Two, I couldn't follow it — and Addison was already on the scene, anyway. The story would get covered just fine. I had other things to do. I slipped back into bed and stared at the ceiling, contemplating my actions earlier that evening.

After I'd left the sheriff's office — and hopefully sent Elizabeth in another direction — I drove past the west side address where Benjamin Kinnon had a room.

It was one of those old motels, built in the 1920s when motor travel was new. The bricks had been painted white at some point, but the color was flaking off and the current owner hadn't been too concerned about maintaining the property. A single light shone over a parking lot that was more packed earth and weeds than blacktop. Five rooms flanked either side of the center office, each with a bright green door and peeling white paint. The fading neon 'Vacancy' sign flickered irregularly in the darkened office window. I'd parked my Mustang close to the road, next to a wooden sign reading "Travel Inn Weekly Rooms" with the phone number of the office beneath. The sign was painted in matching green and white and stood in a circle of scraggly bushes.

There were only three vehicles — two pick-up trucks and a minivan — in the lot when I visited. Children's toys leaned against the motel room front wall where the minivan was parked, so odds were, Benjamin Kinnon was in one of the rooms with a pickup parked in front. It was too dark to see the license plates.

I'd been at the Travel Inn a couple times on other stories. The place was a known flophouse for transients and drug dealers. Meth labs had been discovered in a couple rooms once or twice and another time a woman's body was dumped in the parking lot.

I didn't stay long. I knew I'd be back by dawn.

On my way home, I drove past Elizabeth's and parked in the alley behind her apartment. Like my place, her home was part of a Victorian-era house that was broken down into separate residences; from the alley, I could see into her bedroom window. Her purple wig was off and she wore a vintage Lucille Ball-style head wrap to cover her naked head and a pair of black cat's eye glasses. She was folding clothes and placing them in a box. I watched until she taped the box closed, then I went home.

Now, in the silence of my dark bedroom, my thoughts didn't even center on the homicide at the llama farm. Addison was there—she'd get the story. I wasn't even thinking about the man I would confront tomorrow morning, the man who probably was my father. My thoughts centered on Elizabeth.

How could I have been so stupid? I thought, as I stared at the ceiling. I missed all the signs. I'd been stupid enough to buy a ring before I ever heard her tell me she loved me. I'd never said it either, assuming that she shared what was in my heart, until the night I proposed. She'd kept me at arm's length— I could see that now. I'd stupidly misread the trip to her parents' house in Shaker Heights as the next step in our relationship. *How stupid could I have been?*

It didn't matter now. We were through and she was leaving. In a few hours, when the sun came up, I would be sitting in the parking lot of the Travel Inn, waiting for Benjamin Kinnon.

I closed my eyes and went to sleep.

Chapter 22 Addison

Jud Roarke parked his cruiser next to my Taurus. He spoke briefly into his shoulder microphone before he stepped from the black Dodge Charger. A wave of vehicles followed behind, the driveway dust kicked up by their tires glittering in the headlights and taillights.

I waved with one hand, holding Duncan's double-barreled shotgun in the other.

"Hi, Penny," he said. "Wait a minute." He stopped to speak again into his shoulder mic. "Dispatch, this is unit one —"

I cried out as somebody slammed me, face first, across the trunk of the Taurus, twisting one arm behind my back and ripping the shotgun from my hand.

"U.S. Marshal, you're under arrest!" A man's voice barked.

Before I could respond, I was handcuffed and pulled back upright by the back of my shirt.

"Hey, that's my wife!" I heard Duncan cry.

"What the fuck do you think you're doing?" I demanded. "What's this about?"

My captor, a muscular man with a graying goatee, wore a black tee shirt beneath his Kevlar vest and a black baseball cap, both emblazoned with U.S. MARSHAL across the front. In black cargo pants and military boots, he looked about medium height; beneath the collar of his black tee shirt, I caught a glimpse of a heavy gold necklace. His automatic rifle was slung across his back and his utility belt carried enough weapons to start a coup. His badge, encased in leather, hung around his neck from a beaded metal utility chain.

Behind him, I counted five other marshals, all dressed in black like goddamned ninjas with badges, pointing their weapons at Duncan, Katya or me. Behind them were seven sheriff's deputies—representing three-fourths of the ten that patrolled the county at night— standing tactically behind their cruiser doors, weapons drawn.

"Stand down, everybody, stand down," Jud said, stepping between the marshals and me. His words were smooth and soothing. "Peppin, take off her cuffs. You're in my territory now. Out here in God's country, if I arrested everyone just because they held a gun, I'd have half to three-quarters of the county in jail at any one time."

Peppin growled something under his breath as he spun me around to unlock my cuffs. I rubbed my wrists as I turned to face him.

"You have the honor of arresting the person who reported this crime and who also happens to be the editor of our newspaper," Jud continued. "Addison McIntyre, I'd like to introduce you to Robert Peppin, U.S. Marshal. He's based in the Cincinnati office."

We reached out to shake each other's hands, but we weren't pleased about the introduction. Neither of us smiled.

"Our team got a call from Ms. Bolodenka's cell phone. There wasn't anyone on the other end and thought it best to respond," he said.

"So she's in witness protection?" I asked.

"Is this on the record?" he asked.

"I am looking at the dead body of a man who had lunch at my house on Sunday," I said. "I'm going to bet there's been a public radio transmission about this crime, as well as a request for the coroner. Hell yes, it's on the record." I wanted to add, you asshole, but didn't.

"No comment."

"Katya's already told me she's in witness protection and Jerome Johnson was the marshal assigned to protect her," I snapped. "I like to get two sources on my stories. I got confirmation from her— I just wanted it from you."

Peppin shot another look at Jud, who got on his radio, his smooth tone gone.

"Dispatch, we have a second agency on scene. All radio traffic on Channel Two," he said, sharply. He clicked off his microphone and turned angrily toward Peppin. "I was under the impression that local law enforcement was to be informed when someone in WITSEC came into their area." Jud Roarke's eyes were sharp enough to peel paint off a wall, even in the dead of night.

"Ms. Bolodenka's case is extremely sensitive. We thought it best to keep to keep that information confidential," Peppin answered.

"Are you two going to look to see if the guy who shot Jerome Johnson is still on the property or is this going to be an exercise in who has the bigger badge?" I demanded.

Jud nodded; Peppin and the other marshals raised their weapons again, along with the deputies behind them. With a wave of his arm and a few words, the men began to search the property. One deputy stayed behind with us.

Katya slumped into the back seat of the Taurus.

"You OK?" I asked, leaning into the car. Duncan stood behind me, hands stuffed in his pockets.

Tears rolled down her dusty face.

"No," she whispered. "No."

"Last Friday, when I showed up to do the story on you winning at the state fair, Jerome didn't want me doing the story, did he?"

Katya shook her head.

"He knew it would expose you, didn't he?"

"Yes," she whispered. "It wasn't first time either. This farm was my last chance."

I pushed a little harder. "Jerome was not from Ashtabula, was he? Or even Ohio?"

"No. Jerome came here from Virginia, where I was hidden before, but he wasn't my original protector." She sighed.

"Why did you leave Virginia?" I asked.

Katya lifted her eyes upward as the tears flowed down the side of her face. "After I left New York, Kolya was in jail, but some of his men got released on bond, I don't know why or how. I was moved to Virginia, but I couldn't abandon my sister Svetlana, or her husband Alexis or her baby Nadya back in Brooklyn. We were so close, Svetlana and me. I broke rules. I write to her when we got to Shenandoah Valley, then we start calling each other, once a month. I get separate cell phone number that only she has. Then somehow, Kolya's gang hears that she's been in touch with me and they tell him."

"Your sister and her family didn't die in a traffic crash in Moscow, did they?" I asked softly. "Kolya or his men killed them, didn't he?"

Katya nodded. "It was Svetlana's murder—and the murder of her husband and daughter— that got Kolya in trouble again, even though he was still in jail. You don't know what it's like having to live like this, knowing I am responsible for my own sister's murder. I can have friends, but I can't tell them the truth of who I am. Everything I say is story they make up for me. My husband, the man I married, he can call his family, and he can have his friends from the neighborhood visit him. *But what about me? Why should I be the one who is forced to lie? Why should I live my life in secret? I am not one who did anything wrong!"*

"What about your parents? Are they still alive?"

"No. My father dies of cancer when I am young, before we came to America. After he dies, my mother decides to take Svetlana and me and leave Petersburg. We go to Brighton Beach, where she has brothers, my uncles. It is there I grow up and where I meet Kolya."

"How did you get all those animals?" Duncan asked, leaning into the car window beside me.

"When witness protection first brings me to Virginia, I am kept at farm where animals were at to begin with. The farm belonged to dentist who got into trouble. He was also placed in witness protection, but no one knew what to do with llamas and alpacas after he is gone."

"And you did?" Duncan asked.

"No. Not any more than the marshal that protected me there. So we learn. We learn and I fall in love with them. Then Svetlana is killed and I have to leave again."

"You couldn't leave the llamas, though, could you?"

"No. So they find this farm here in Ohio and buy it and build the little house beside barn. They build safe room for me in attic. Then we move in late at night. Three trailers full of animals," Katya smiled sadly at me. "Jerome, he is assigned to me and that night he comes to live in the little house. Now he is gone and I am once again alone."

She shook her head.

"You were romantically involved with him, weren't you?" I asked softly.

"He was in my bed when the car pulled into the driveway."

Oh, God, this is getting more complicated by the moment, I thought. She's not played by the rules of witness protection. She didn't keep herself out of the spotlight, and she's also sleeping with the marshal assigned to protect her.

I looked up to see the sheriff, Peppin and all the others coming toward us from the barn, the house and the cottage.

"All clear," Peppin said, holstering his pistol.

Judson motioned to a white vehicle at the end of the driveway; Dr. Bovir had arrived in the coroner's van. He would also have investigators with him who would record the crime scene details and take photographs. As they went to work, Judson motioned Duncan and me over so he and Peppin could grill us on the details of what happened. Another marshal took Katya to the back of his black Suburban.

"So, Mrs. McIntyre, you want to tell me what you know?" Peppin asked. "I don't care what your sheriff buddy says, you're a suspect until I say you're not."

Duncan and I started at the beginning, with the original story on the tapestry, to how Duncan had stood up for Jerome at the feed store, how they'd come over for lunch on Sunday and how I'd heard from Graham Kinnon about the animals being killed. He didn't need to know Gary McGinnis and I had just about figured out everything we'd been told was a cover of some kind. Judson corroborated the story about the dead animals.

"That was probably a warning—" Peppin began.

"But from who? McMaster or the Russians?" Judson interjected.

Peppin shrugged. "Does it matter? It's not safe for her to be here now."

"The man who killed Jerome was named Luka, Katya told me," I said.

"So the Russians found her." Peppin shot me another nasty look.

I shrugged. Nobody was going to accuse me of keeping information from law enforcement.

Dr. Bovir approached, with Jerome's badge and Ohio driver's license on his clipboard. Judson waved him into our circle. Bovir handed the badge and the license to the sheriff before he spoke. I caught a glimpse of his license as it passed from hand to hand. If it was a fake like Gary thought it was, it was a good one.

"Your victim died of a single gun shot at close range to the back of the head," Bovir said solemnly.

"Any shell casings?" Jud asked.

Bovir held up an empty shell casing balanced on the end of his pen. "Investigators are picking these up now. This looks like an automatic weapon of some sort."

"Not a double-barreled shotgun?" I asked sarcastically, shooting a nasty look at Peppin.

"No," Bovir answered. "But there is also some other evidence—I would rather not go into that in the presence of the press."

I nodded. "I understand."

Duncan looked to the east, where the sun was beginning to come up.

"Do you still need us here?" he asked. "I got Holsteins to milk."

Judson shook his head. "No. You guys go on home."

"Just don't leave town. Until further notice, you're still a suspect to me," Peppin said.

Roarke rolled his eyes.

"Thanks," I said. "What about Katya?"

"She stays with me," Peppin said.

"What about the animals?" I asked. "Who's going to feed them?"

"You don't need to worry about that. We'll take care of them," he said.

"Tell her I'll be back to check on her later this afternoon," I said, walking toward my car.

"I think you've done enough, Mrs. McIntyre," he said.

I started to spin around on my heel, but Duncan grabbed my elbow.

"Keep walking Penny, just keep walking," he whispered.

We got in the car and drove back down toward the road, where television station remote trucks were beginning to gather. A female deputy sat inside a sheriff's cruiser, parked across the driveway entrance.

The story would be fodder for their morning newscasts, if Judson came out to talk to them.

If not, they would be forced to cool their heels and babble conjecture and possibilities through their segments until they got confirmation of anything.

The investigation could take several hours; the most they would have would be when the sun came up and they got shots of the cruisers and the coroner's van. I could have my story — the complete story — done and up on the website before that. Maybe that wasn't such a good idea — TV could have it then before my paper hit the streets.

The wild card would be Peppin. Would he speak to them before Roarke? What would he say, outside of 'no comment?' That would make my decision. If he said anything beyond 'no comment,' I'd be forced to put the story on the website. If he didn't I could hold it off the web until the presses ran.

I stared straight ahead as TV reporters, mikes in hand, some with cameras on their shoulders, approached the car, pummeling us with questions through the car windows. "What's happened in there?"

"Can you tell us anything?"

"Why is the coroner's van on scene?"

"Do you know who lives there?"

"How many victims are there?"

Fortunately, none of them recognized me. If they had, it would have been ugly — there would have been allegations that I got preferential treatment over and above other news outlets on the scene. That would have made my life a living hell — and made the crime scene investigation rough. I didn't want to explain how and why the property owner showed up at my house to tell me about a murder — at least until I had the chance to put it on the front page.

Hopefully no one at the TV station would see the video and recognize me.

God knows how Earlene would deal with it.

I began to consider how to place the story on the front page as Duncan nosed the Taurus through the reporters and onto the road. I didn't have any photos, but that was OK. There were shots from the original story I'd done on the tapestry, but they weren't relevant; there were no photos of Jerome. Maybe Gary would get me Jerome's BMV photo — I could always ask. What would my headline be? What else did I have for page one?

Shit, I thought to myself. *I wish I could count on Graham right now. He's in Indianapolis. Well, I've at least got Marcus I can lean on. I'll have him get the other police reports from Gary and have Elizabeth check on the court records. What other local stories do I have in the can, ready to go?*

I jerked forward in my seat as Duncan slammed on the brakes.

"Do you not hear me?" Duncan asked.

"Huh?" I cleared my head with a sharp shake.

"I've asked you three times," Duncan began. "I know you, Penny. You're the only one who knows this entire story and you're dying to get to the paper. You want me just to take you straight there? I could have Isabella help with milking this morning. We can drop your car off later."

I looked at the clock on my cell phone: it was going on four-thirty. Duncan had only half an hour before we normally started milking. When Katya had come pounding on our door, I had grabbed a pair of dirty jeans from the bedroom floor and a tee shirt — certainly not the most professional attire to wear into work and I had that stupid focus group meeting at two.

Maybe there would be time for me to run home and change, if Isabella or Duncan picked me up and brought me home after deadline.

"Let's do it," I said.

Nodding, Duncan put the Taurus in gear. He turned left at the next road, one that would lead us straight into Jubilant Falls.

Nobody was going to beat me on this story.

Chapter 23 Graham

It was nearly ten o'clock Wednesday morning when I saw movement inside the motel room where I figured Benjamin was staying.

It wasn't difficult — the other pick-up truck I'd seen the night before pulled out at six, just as I was parking beside the wooden Travel Inn sign and the minivan I'd seen was gone. That left one room with a truck parked in front, an old rusting blue and white Ford with Indiana plates that I could now see in the full light of day.

I made a note of the plates — I'd hand them over to Roarke to run them, in case he hadn't already gotten them. It was the only thing I'd done in four hours and, as the sun warmed the car, it was getting harder and harder to keep my eyes open behind my sunglasses. Then a tall, gaunt man in jeans and work boots stepped from the motel room and I sat up, suddenly alert.

I recognized him instantly from the police photo as Benny Kinnon. An unlit cigarette hung from his lips; his face was unshaven, but despite the homemade tattoos across his arms and neck he didn't look like any of the junkies I'd seen over the years. He seemed alert, sober, almost feral in his body movements.

He locked the door and, cupping his hand around the cigarette, lit it, raising his head toward the sky as he exhaled. He jerked open the truck's rusty door; the ignition made a grinding sound as he turned the key and the engine finally sputtered to life. The transmission clunked as he put the junker in gear and pulled from the parking lot, staring at me as he passed.

A shiver ran down my spine—I was that little boy again, cowering in fear behind my bedroom door, listening to my mother scream as he beat her.

No, I told myself. This all ends today. Today I get my answers.

I turned the ignition on the Mustang and pulled into traffic behind him, following him six blocks to a run-down convenience store.

Benny parked the truck, watching me from the rear view mirror as I parked my vehicle at the other end of the lot. He shook his head and walked into the convenience store, returning in a few minutes with a forty-ounce bottle of beer. He leaned through the driver's side window to deposit the beer and began walking toward me.

He circled the Mustang twice, first from a distance, then closer, running his hand across the trunk, not speaking. Sweat beaded on my upper lip as I watched him go around the rental car: knowing Benny's history, he could be armed and, here I sat, with nothing but a notebook and a pencil.

He stopped at the passenger window and inhaled on the stub of his cigarette.

"You're obviously not a cop," he said, flicking the butt into the center of the parking lot. I could see he'd lost his lower front teeth and most of his upper right molars and wondered if that happened in a prison fistfight. "A cop would do a better job tailing me."

"No, I'm not a cop."

He went around the car again. I felt like he was taking stock, appraising the car, singling it out for his next motor vehicle theft, while trying to figure out what I wanted. I took off my sunglasses as he made his way back to the passenger window and met his foxlike eyes.

"Ahhh," he said. "I see now. So the bitch finally had her fucking little whelp come find me, huh?"

"Get in," I said. "We need to talk."

"No. There's a park down the road. Meet me there." Benny pointed west and sauntered back to his truck.

***

The park wasn't much more than a metal swing-set and a couple of picnic tables that backed up to some scraggly woods before ending at a high fence that circled a junk yard. It didn't look like any of the parks the city still maintained, but no one told that to the children from the housing project next door who were beginning to wander over to play. Benny and I parked our vehicles and walked toward a picnic table. Benny carried the forty-ounce, still in the brown paper bag, in one hand, and took a swig from it periodically.

"So why did she send you?" Benny asked as we sat at opposite ends of the picnic table's top, our feet resting on the bench seat, facing the road.

"She didn't send me. I wanted to see you."

"How'd you track me down, then?"

"Does it matter?"

He shrugged. "What the fuck do you want?"

"I want to know about you and my mom."

Benny took another swig from his beer bottle and rested his tattooed arms on his knees. His knuckles were scraped and scabs were beginning to form over wounds on his fingers.

Had he been in a fight? I wondered. *Was he responsible for killing Jerome Johnson? Or the livestock on Katya Bolodenka's farm?*

"Why? She's a whore. I'm a thief. We did a lot of smack, and we got arrested. I did four years in the joint. She did two. What else is there?"

"Why'd you hit her?"

"I was cleaning my fist and her mouth went off, maybe? Junkies do a lot of stupid shit, kid, a lot of stupid shit, and your mother was the stupidest junkie bitch I ever saw."

So, the man who was reputed to be my father was an arrogant, self-absorbed bastard with no compunction about hitting women. Good to know. Bill, despite his repeated use of checkbook parenting, was beginning to look a lot better as a stepfather.

"Why was she so stupid?" I asked.

"She's a woman — they're all stupid. They all need to be put in their place, like a lot of other folks. They need to know that somebody— a man— is in charge, because they aren't smart enough to do anything themselves. Why is any of this shit important?" Benny sounded irritated.

I was a gnat flying around his face, one he couldn't swat away and he didn't like that.

"Why do you care? You've obviously done all right—you've got a nice car, you dress halfway decent. I'll bet you've even got some sort of fancy-ass job. What are you, like a bank manager? Insurance salesman? Why fucking worry about what I'm doing or where I'm living?"

"I had a girlfriend. We thought she was pregnant for a little bit, then we broke up. The whole thing got me thinking."

"About what? That I wasn't the kind of daddy you wanted me to be? That I didn't play baseball or take you to the goddamn movies?" Benny sneered. "Let me tell you, none of us get the parents we want. You waste a lot of time wanting that, kid, because that isn't ever going to happen, whoever you are. Just like your mother wasn't fucking Cinderella, I'll never be Prince Charming."

He struck a wound I hadn't opened in a long time. In my first year of boarding school, I had a fantasy of my ideal father, mostly based on television sitcoms we were allowed to watch before lights out. I would lie on my single bed in my room, wishing for a father who came to visit me on weekends like the other boys, a father who took the time to throw a ball in the wide green campus commons with me or cheered me on from the sidelines as I, the star of the football team, scored yet another touchdown.

Mother and Bill didn't seem to want me within their orbit. Why else would they send me here? Lonely and homesick for a family I never had, I'd built the dream of an ideal father who didn't exist to cover for a father who disappeared and a stepfather who wanted me gone.

As time went by and I got older, I settled into school, made friends and got used to the idea that this father I made up was just the dream of a wounded little boy.

Now that wounded little boy was back.

"So are you my father?"

"Is my name on your fucking birth certificate?"

"Yes, but I heard Mother put your name down because the social worker made her name somebody."

Benny shrugged. "You know, all these years I always denied it—I just figured I was the only one whose last name that fucking idiot bitch could spell. I can see now, yeah, you probably are my son."

So it was true.

"After you guys got arrested, I got put in foster care," I said.

"Shit happens." He shrugged and took another swig from the beer bottle, not looking my direction. "Probably the best thing for you, between your mother and me."

"You don't do heroin any more, do you?" I asked.

"No, thanks to Indiana's Department of Corrections, I was made to see the error of my ways." Benny sneered again. "Although I am not averse to the occasional economic opportunity the marketplace provides."

"Mother got clean in prison, too."

"Well, good for her. She still a whore?"

I wanted to punch him, but I sensed that was the reaction he sought. Instead I was silent.

Benny took a gulp from his beer and stood up. I caught a glimpse of a blue-black swastika tattoo beneath the collar of his tee shirt.

"I thought so. Listen kid, I don't know why you came looking for me and I don't fucking care. Just don't do it again," he said.

He adjusted the crotch of his jeans and walked back to the truck.

"Sorry, Benny," I said under my breath. "I'll be back in touch—and soon."

Chapter 24 Addison

I was still working on the murder story when Dennis came into the newsroom shortly after seven. Bleary from lack of sleep, the words just wouldn't come anymore. I'd looked at the story so long, I couldn't tell if I was finished or not.

Pulling his thick glasses down his nose, he looked at my dirty jeans, athletic shoes and tee shirt.

"How long have you been here?" he asked.

"Too damned long," I answered, rubbing my tired eyes. "Duncan brought me in about four-thirty and dropped me off."

"I'm assuming that means we've got a breaking story," he said, stepping behind me to see the screen.

"Yes. Jerome Johnson, the farm manager at the Lunatic Fringe farm was shot. The owner said the men who did it were Russian mobsters," I said. "On top of that, he wasn't her farm manager—he was really a U.S. marshal. She was in witness protection and he was assigned to protect her."

"What?" Dennis jerked his thumb over his shoulder. "Get up. You're obviously out of your mind from lack of sleep. Did you just tell me Russian mobsters murdered a U.S. marshal in Plummer County?"

"That's exactly what happened. Katya Bolodenka, the lady with the llamas from last Saturday's story, is a federal witness and she's in hiding here, of all places."

"This is what happens when you ask for some unvarnished human misery, Addison." Despite his dry tone, Dennis was just as excited as I was. He smiled at me as I stood and he slid into my seat.

Say what you will about the state of small town journalism, I knew I had an excellent crew, staff I could depend on when the news broke.

As I stood behind him, Dennis enlarged the text on the screen and began to read:

By Addison McIntyre
Managing Editor
A Youngstown Road man was shot on the front porch of a local farm early this morning in a murder that could have ties to organized crime.

Plummer County sheriff's deputies discovered the body of Jerome Johnson, 31, shot in the head, at 68734 Youngstown Road.

Coroner Dr. Rashid Bovir would not confirm any other injuries.

Johnson's death may be tied to another homicide involving an East Coast Russian mobster and a series of shady medical clinics.

According to the farm's owner, Ekaterina Bolodenka, Johnson was a US marshal assigned to the federal witness protection program, and had been protecting her.

Bolodenka, who was featured last Saturday in a story about her work as a fiber artist, told the J-G she was really in hiding from her husband, Kolya Dyakonov, a reported Russian mobster, and was slated to testify against him in federal court.

Bolodenka had previously told the J-G that she was born in Russia, but raised in Chicago where she studied at the Art Institute of Chicago. She claimed to have taught art history in Cleveland and purchased her first llamas and alpacas in northern Ohio.

None of that was true, she said.

Bolodenka said she was actually from a Brooklyn neighborhood called Brighton Beach, in New York City, and has never been to Chicago or Cleveland.

Johnson had been identified as her farm manager, but that was also a ruse, Bolodenka said. He was on the farm to provide 24-hour protection until she was slated to testify.

The couple was also romantically involved, she said.

According to Bolodenka, two Russian men broke into the farmhouse where she and Johnson were sleeping. Bolodenka managed to escape, but Johnson was taken downstairs and shot.

US Marshal Robert Peppin, along with a special witness protection response team, were also on the scene. He confirmed Bolodenka was in the federal Witness Security program, also known as WITSEC, but would not confirm the exact details of the case.

According to Bolodenka, however, Dyakonov owned a series of New Jersey medical clinics and had been accused of Medicaid fraud. Associates reportedly brought homeless people into the clinics by van, where they were promised health check ups and medication, including reportedly highly addictive painkillers, such as Oxycodone, the cost of which was then submitted to Medicaid.

With no follow up, patients were free to take the medication themselves or sell it on the street. They would also be free to return to the clinic for more prescriptions.

Bolodenka said she witnessed Dyakonov murdering a man who threatened to report the fraud. Dyakonov is also a suspect in the murder of her sister, brother-in-law and their daughter.

New Jersey authorities have long blamed unethical doctors and Russian mob-owned clinics for the state's spike in drug overdoses and deaths, according to Associated Press reports.

Bolodenka raises llamas, alpacas and cashmere goats on the Youngstown Road farm, which she purchased recently and named The Lunatic Fringe Farm, in a nod to her art. She recently won first prize at the Ohio State Fair for a woven tapestry.

Two cashmere goats were recently killed and mutilated there, but she and Johnson declined to press charges or file a report, Bolodenka said. Instead, Johnson had requested extra sheriff patrols at the property.

It was not known at press time if those livestock attacks are connected to Johnson's murder.

"Good God," Dennis said. "Where did you get all this?"

"Katya showed up on my doorstep about two-thirty this morning. Most of what I got, I got right from Katya, so the feds aren't going to be real happy with us."

"Probably not."

"Hey, what about that fight at the feed mill Saturday? Should that be included in the story?"

Quickly he typed in two sentences:

"Johnson had also been the victim of an assault last Saturday at the Grower's Feed Mill, following an argument there.

"It is not known if the events are at all connected."

I looked at it critically and shook my head.

"Take it out. Duncan told me that Doyle McMaster used the N-word and Johnson swung at him. The two have got to be unrelated—and we don't have any proof of connection. I'm no organized crime expert, but I'll bet McMaster isn't smart enough to be wrapped up with the Russian mob—and they're too smart to get wrapped up with him."

"You going to tell Earlene all this?" Dennis asked as he tapped the 'delete' key, erasing the two sentences.

It had been my habit to meet with the previous publisher and Earlene's father, J. Watterson Whitelaw, when we had a huge story break. He was an old newsman himself—he knew the value of a free press.

Whitelaw kept the best media lawyers in the state on retainer. Before the story ever hit the page and the paper ever hit the streets, I would sit down in his dark, mahogany-paneled office, and tell him what was up. He would pick up the phone and let counsel know what we were doing, what questions he had and generally, give me the thumbs up once he knew the ramifications. He had no compunction about going up against the small-town powers that be. He knew Ohio's public record law inside and out and had no problem pushing it to the limit, even when there was a possibility such action might cost him an advertiser or two.

Earlene, on the other hand, with her concern over community opinion, might put the kibosh on this story in the interest of keeping everyone — especially the feds — happy.

"I suppose I should. Is she here yet?" I sighed.

I rolled my eyes, thinking about this afternoon's focus group meeting — what I'd begun to privately refer to as the "fuck us" group. By two this afternoon, I would be running on empty and my patience would be running thin. It could get ugly — fast.

What ground did she have to stand on? The radio dispatch was public and we had to follow up on that, not to mention the fact that Katya knew she was talking to the newspaper when she was talking to me. I had my damned notebook out, for Christ sake!

"I didn't see her Porsche in the parking lot when I pulled in."

"I'll give her a couple hours and then go down to tell her about it. I need to call Roarke and Bovir to see if we have anything else from the scene that I can include before I talk to her."

"Go down to Aunt Bea's and get some breakfast. I'll handle things until you get back."

***

Gary McGinnis was just starting his second cup of coffee when I slipped into his booth at Aunt Bea's.

"You look like hell," he said, motioning the waitress over to our table. "I heard through the grapevine Johnson was murdered last night."

"Good morning to you, too," I said, nodding at the waitress as she filled my coffee cup. "Yes, he was. Everything you and I suspected was true. Katya told me on the way over to the scene — "

"What? She came to you first?"

I slurped my coffee and nodded again. "Yes. She was knocking at my door after two in the morning—she'd apparently escaped from the house somehow."

"Hey, Linda—" Gary motioned the waitress back over. "Give her two eggs, over easy, bacon and whole wheat toast with butter—to go—and put it on my bill. She's in a bit of a hurry."

Gary turned his attention back to me.

"What the hell happened that she's telling you all this stuff at your house?" he asked. "Why didn't she call the cops? Why didn't you?"

"Katya showed up at my house, like I said. She wouldn't let me call, but as Duncan and I are driving over there, she's telling us she is in witness protection and Johnson was a marshal protecting her."

Gary exhaled and shook his head. "It all fits together then. I doubt if Johnson was his real name—or hers."

"Katya told me her name wasn't real," I said. "Too bad I don't have Graham Kinnon here to help me on this."

Linda brought my breakfast over in a Styrofoam box and sat it in front of me.

"So where's Graham?" Gary asked, digging into his own breakfast.

"His stepdad had a heart attack. He took some time off to go home to Indianapolis."

Gary's voice was odd—maybe it was the mouthful of eggs. "That so? I hate to hear that."

I shrugged. "Yeah, the kid works like nobody's business and deserves the time off, but the shit always seems to hit the fan when I'm low on staff," I said. "Anyway, do you know anybody in the marshal service? A guy named Robert Peppin?"

Gary looked up at me and nodded. "He heads up the Cincinnati office. I've met him once or twice on task force stuff, like when they come through on regional drug or sex offender sweeps."

"What do you think of him?"

He shrugged. "I don't know him personally, but I get the impression he knows his job. He's a typical fed, though, really buttoned down. Why?"

"He's an ass—he slapped me in a pair of cuffs just because I was holding Duncan's shotgun."

Gary tried not to laugh out loud. "Yup, that's Peppin. He's never quite adjusted to the fact that out here in the hinterlands honest folks own guns."

"I can tell thinks we're all savages and that everything north of the Cincinnati outer belt is the Wild West. He probably wonders if we even use forks. Roarke talked him into letting me go, but he was pissed off when he found out the feds had not told him he had someone in witness protection in his county," I said.

"I can imagine. That really puts law enforcement at a real disadvantage."

"Peppin's not going to be real happy with me about noon," I said, standing. "Oh well. Hey, before I go, can you e-mail me that BMV picture of Jerome Johnson? I need it for the front page."

"Sure. And if I hear anything else, I'll let you know—or at least where to look," Gary said.

" Thanks!" Sliding out of the booth, I took one more slurp of coffee and grabbed my breakfast. Within a few steps, I was out the door on the sidewalk.

Back in the newsroom, everyone else had arrived and Dennis had page one mocked up. My reporters had been busy as well—Marcus Henning had a story from yesterday's county commission meeting and Elizabeth Day had a feature with photos about the school bus drivers running their daily routes as practice for the opening day of school.

"Marcus, I need you to pick up police reports, since Graham is off," I said.

"Will do," he answered without looking up from his computer.

I ducked into my office to finish the story.

In between bites of my breakfast, I called Bovir and confirmed a single gunshot had killed Jerome Johnson, but that was about it.

"Can you confirm any other the victim was tortured?"

"I can't say anything until the autopsy is completed later this afternoon," Bovir said.

My phone call with Roarke was less than terse—I expected that. In an open investigation, law enforcement wasn't going to say anything to the media that would tip their hand. But Roarke was tight-lipped for other reasons.

"I'm not the point man on this case any more," he said. "Peppin's going to be your contact for any other information."

"Are you saying I won't get anything else?" I asked, balancing the phone on my shoulder, my pen poised over my notepad.

"That's entirely possible. I don't know what he'll do."

"Have Jerome Johnson's parents been notified?"

"Again, you'd have to contact Peppin. Let me give you his cell. He's going to be here for at least a few days, so this is probably the best number." Roarke recited the number to me as if by heart.

I ended my phone call with Roarke and punched in Peppin's cell phone. No answer, but even his tone on his voice mail message reeked of arrogance. "You have reached Agent Robert Peppin of the United States Marshal Service. I'm not available to take your call. Please leave a message and I will return your call as soon as possible." *Beep.*

"Hi, Agent Peppin, this is Addison McIntyre, from the *Jubilant Falls Journal-Gazette* — you know, the one you slapped the cuffs on this morning. Anyway, I'm looking for some information on Agent Jerome Johnson's murder. My deadline is at ten this morning, so I'd appreciate a call back as soon as possible. Thanks."

He wasn't going to call back; down deep, I knew that. But at least he couldn't say I didn't give him a chance to speak to me. Whether or not he took that chance was up to him.

If he didn't, I would add a single sentence: "Phone calls to Agent Robert Peppin were not returned by press deadline."

I wasn't going to give him any more ammunition than what he already had.

I stepped back into the newsroom and turned on the television to see the local break in the morning network news shows. Marcus Henning and Elizabeth Day stopped working on their stories to watch; Dennis looked up from the page he was working on.

A reporter, bottle blonde and female like many of the local television on-air personalities, was standing at the end of the driveway, a microphone in hand. The sun was up, bathing the old farmhouse with its wide porch in morning light. I could see the U.S. marshals' armada of black SUVs still surrounded the house. A few sheriffs' cruisers were still there, too; yellow crime scene tape stretched between two fence posts across the driveway. The camera panned across the scene as the reporter spoke.

"Local law enforcement officials continue to be tight-lipped about a possible homicide that occurred here at this Plummer County farm overnight. Initial radio traffic indicated that a black male in his mid-thirties was the victim, however, that has not been confirmed, despite the Plummer County coroner being on scene. No explanation has been given for the presence of US marshals as well. Sheriff Judson Roarke would not comment on the situation as he left the scene about six this morning. Stay with News 17 for more information. We'll stay on the scene and keep digging for you, our viewers."

Dennis looked over at me. "We've got a hell of a lot more than that," he said.

"I know," I answered quietly.

If we ran with this story, what would happen? Would it jeopardize the case back in New York against Katya's husband? Would it put her further at risk? Her husband's thugs had already found her and Jerome had been killed. How much more trouble could there be?

And what if I went to Earlene with my story before it hit the streets? In her misguided effort to form a focus group to hear our readers' opinions, she might kill it, particularly if Peppin came in and bitched.

I couldn't let that happen. There had been a murder—I'd seen Jerome's body myself. I wasn't going to be complicit in covering it up, no matter what anyone said. Katya had also been more than willing to tell me her story, which confirmed everything.

I sighed.

"What do you want to do?" Dennis asked.

"Print it. We're going with what we've got."

Chapter 25 Graham

The headline screamed at me from its vending box across the street: **US Marshal Found Murdered on Farm**. Jerome Johnson's driver's license photo stared back at me from below the big black letters.

Jerome Johnson was a federal agent? This was last night's homicide call?

After meeting in the park with Benny, I'd stopped at a fast food place on the east end of town, near Golgotha College, the small church school that called Jubilant Falls home.

A strip of fast food joints, girly boutiques and coffee shops (no bars to entice the teetotalling Baptist student body) sprang up across the street from the college entrance over the last few years, trying to entice students to spend their money. Traffic increased proportionately, and Tony, our circulation director, never met a fast food joint that didn't need a *Journal-Gazette* vending box at front of the door.

I waited until the route driver closed the box and drove away in the J-G delivery van before I left the Mustang and, dodging traffic, ran across the road to buy a paper.

I put my sunglasses on top of my head and began to read Addison's story, my jaw hanging in disbelief.

Katya Bolodenka is in witness protection? Her husband is a Russian mobster? Jerome lived there to protect her? The story got even more incredible as I continued to read. The story didn't mention the fight he'd gotten into at the feed mill with Doyle McMaster, but did mention the goats that were killed. Was there any connection at all or was that just a weird coincidence?

A horn sounded in the traffic behind me, reminding me I couldn't afford to be recognized. I pulled my sunglasses back over my eyes, tucked the paper under my arm, and slipped back across the street to the Mustang.

I really wanted to cover this story in the worst way, but I was supposed to meet with Sheriff Roarke later this afternoon. I wanted to be there on the crime scene, digging into the background. Homicides weren't all that common in Jubilant Falls — most of the crime here was petty, personal stuff or drug-related. This story was huge — a woman in witness protection and a federal agent protecting her from a gang of Russian mobsters.

This didn't happen here.

Even knowing Addison was on it didn't satisfy me. I wanted this story, this byline. Where would I go if I were on this story right now? I'd have the federal prosecutor from New Jersey on the phone, getting his side of the story. I'd talk to the mobster's lawyer; maybe call the reporter who had done the story on the clinics. I'd get as much dark and gritty details as I could without getting on a plane and seeing it myself — even I knew the J-G budget was too tight to do that.

But I couldn't, not right now. I had one mission to accomplish and that was to find out the truth behind Benjamin Kinnon.

I started the rental car's engine and pulled into traffic, heading back to my apartment.

As I drove, I couldn't help thinking about how Benny dumped on me. Despite his crude words and ignorant beliefs, Bennie had pegged one undeniable truth: We don't get the parents we want and the sooner we accept that, the better.

My mother had come a long way from an ugly past life. She'd gotten clean—and married money. She'd developed a veneer of respectability and, with it, social standing. She worked hard to ensure no one saw that beneath her silk suits and perfect make up was a former junkie who once sold her body to pay for her habit. She had three sons, a nice house and a very cushy life. If I were she, I wouldn't want anything to get out about how I'd lived before. I'd want my court records sealed, too.

Maybe I'd been a little hard on her at that restaurant in Richmond.

And Bennie? There was only one similarity: They'd both owned up to their addictions and kicked them, but that was it. He knew he wasn't ever going to be anything other than a thief and loser.

Was he involved with the Aryan Knights, as Chief G suspected? I didn't have any proof—yet. He clearly was a racist and sexist asshole, but that wasn't a felony. It didn't mean he was recruiting for the Aryan Knights.

I circled the block around my apartment, checking for suspicious vehicles. Seeing none, I parked in the gravel lot and, with today's newspaper tucked under my arm, sprinted up two flights of stairs to the door of my attic apartment.

Sliding the key into the lock, I opened the door.

"So, Kinnon, you want to tell me the truth about what's going on?"

I gasped. It was Elizabeth, sitting at my kitchen table, holding her key to my apartment.

"What are you doing here?" I asked.

"I could ask you the same thing," she replied. "You told Addison you were going to Indianapolis because Bill had a heart attack. You told me that, too and then you told me you weren't in Indianapolis, but you'd left town. You told me if I didn't believe you to check the airport garage. Well, I did Kinnon—and I found your piece of shit Toyota. I also found the guy who waited on you at the car rental counter. You don't think that I can't finagle information out of someone just because I'm not the big bad cops reporter you are? How stupid do you think I am? And, oh, in your haste to dump all my personal belongings on my desk, you forgot to ask for this."

She shoved the key across the table. I caught it as it tumbled off the edge.

"So what's going on, Kinnon?" she repeated.

"What do you care?" I laid the newspaper on the counter and hung the key on a hook by the door.

"I know you, Kinnon. I know how you operate. I'm willing to bet you're knee-deep in something that's going to get your ass in big trouble."

"And what if I am?"

"Addison needs to know."

"No she doesn't."

"Tell me the truth, Kinnon. Tell me what you're doing."

"I think you need to leave now."

She stood up and stepped close to me. I closed my eyes to block out the sweet smell of her perfume. I wanted to take her in my arms, feel her warm soft body against me, but couldn't. Not now, knowing she didn't love me the way I loved her. I took one step back in self-protection.

She took my hands in hers. I couldn't help myself—I raised her hands to my lips and kissed them.

"Oh, Elizabeth," I whispered as my anger disappeared.

She sighed sadly and I let her arms slide around me.

"Listen," she began, her head against my chest. "You're pissed and you've been pissed because I told you no. But wouldn't you be even angrier if I divorced you five or ten years down the road?"

"We could have made it work, Beth."

"No, Kinnon. No, we couldn't. Then, I'd be the bitch ex-wife story you'd tell every one of your post-divorce first dates and I don't want to be that. We worked together for a long time before all this started and we liked each other. We liked each other a lot. I want to go back to that."

I hugged her tightly, but didn't answer, kissing the top of her purple wig instead. I didn't know if I could do what she wanted, but I would try—and she knew it. Elizabeth released me and slipped back into her seat at the dinette table.

"You gonna tell me what you're up to?" she asked.

"Are you going to tell Addison?"

With her fingers, she made a locking motion at her lips. "Not a word. Put on a pot of coffee and tell me about it. I've got all afternoon."

"How'd that happen? With me gone—"

"In 'Indianapolis'?" Smiling sardonically, Elizabeth hooked her fingers in mock quotation symbols.

I rolled my eyes, smiling sadly. God, it was hard to have her in my kitchen again, the same place where just a few days ago she'd said she wouldn't marry me, where my world came to a screeching halt.

"Yeah, there. If you're gone for the afternoon, that leaves Marcus Henning and Addison as the only folks in the newsroom in case something breaks."

"I've got a cell phone—and Addison is in a meeting all afternoon, some focus group. Nobody will miss me. I'm supposed to be burning some vacation time, packing."

"OK, here's what's going on." I turned toward the counter and began filling the coffee maker with water and fresh grounds. "Remember I told you about my mother and how I was in foster care as a kid? And how she came and got me after she'd married Bill?"

"And how they'd shipped you off to boarding school after that? I remember."

"I didn't tell you anything about the man who was supposed to be my father." I pushed the start button and waited until I saw the water begin to bubble into the pot. I pulled a couple Indianapolis Colts mugs from the cabinet.

I couldn't turn around to look at her as I began my story.

"His name is Benjamin Kinnon and he was arrested with Mother that night when I was six," I spoke slowly. "He was a heroin dealer and a junkie, just like her. He used to steal cars and credit cards and stuff like that. His name was on my birth certificate, but Mother told me she wasn't really sure if he was the father or not—she just needed to put somebody's name down. By then it didn't matter since Benny disappeared and she married Bill and we were all going to put that ugliness behind us."

"Yes."

I took a deep breath. "I spent my childhood wondering what my real father was like. When I was in foster care, I just wanted my mother back. Then when I got her back, she looked great, life was good, but I still didn't have a dad. I mean, I didn't have bad foster parents or anything like that—I was bounced around, but I wasn't ever abused. I just wanted a home, a real home."

"Like I had," Elizabeth said softly.

"When I got shipped off to boarding school, I had these fantasies that kids do, that my real dad, whoever he was, was going to come take me away from wherever I was and I was going to have the kind of life that every other kid in my class seemed to have. You know, a dad who threw the football with me in the front yard, that kind of stuff. After a while, I began to think that I wasn't ever going to have that and I just got on with my life." I stopped and took a deep breath. "So when I thought you were pregnant—I know, I know, I overreacted—it got me thinking about how someone could abandon their son, like Benjamin Kinnon abandoned me. I was determined that my child—our child—would never experience that."

"Oh, God, Kinnon!" Elizabeth rose again and stepped behind me, circling her arms around my waist.

My hands never came off the counter. I couldn't turn around. I didn't trust myself. I just kept talking.

"Then last Friday, I met with Chief G and he's got something he wants to talk to me about. There's been a number of hate crimes in the next county and he and Roarke have reason to believe the group connected to those crimes, the Aryan Knights, is trying to recruit in Plummer County. So he shows me pictures of the guys they think are doing the recruiting. One of them was Doyle McMaster."

"The guy who punched Addison's husband?"

"Yes. The other one—the other one is Benny Kinnon."

Elizabeth's arms tightened around my waist. "Oh God, Kinnon. What are you going to do?"

"Chief G and Roarke wanted someone to get close to him, figure out what he's doing. They want to know if the Aryan Knights are organizing here in Plummer County."

"Don't tell me you're helping them."

"I met Benny this morning."

"You didn't." She released me and I finally turned around.

"Yeah, I did," I said, leaning back with my elbows on the kitchen counter.

"Does he know who you are? Did you identify yourself to him?"

"There is no doubt I'm his son—he knows it, too. He doesn't know anything more than that."

"What did he say to you? What did you say to him?"

"Let's just say we had a general philosophical discussion on the value of parents. He doesn't want me to come looking for him ever again—he made that much pretty clear."

"You're not going to do that, are you?" It was more of a statement than a question.

"He's got a room at the Travel Inn. I'm going back there this evening."

Elizabeth sighed. "When are you going to stop doing this kind of stuff?"

"What stuff?"

"This dangerous, put-your-life-on-the-line shit that you do. What if he's pissed you showed up again? What if he's got a weapon?"

I shrugged. She was right. There was more than one occasion where I'd put myself in harm's way to get a story, but it was what I do, who I am.

"What if you had a wife? What if I'd said yes the other night?" she continued. "Would you promise me you wouldn't meet with this guy, even though he was your real father, if there was a chance you could get hurt?"

"Probably not. I'd still do it."

"See, Kinnon? That's part of what makes me crazy about you. You're willing to do anything to get a story, even if it means getting hurt in the process. What kind of father would that make you? That you're willing to forget your kid or your wife to get some ink across the front page? Does that make you any better than this Benny Kinnon?"

"What the hell does that mean?"

"I lied. I'm pregnant."

Chapter 26 Addison

By two o'clock, the time of the focus group meeting, I had a change of clothes and my car, courtesy of Duncan and Isabella, but I was exhausted and starved. Breakfast from Aunt Bea's had been my only solid food since being awakened by Katya's cries the previous night. Lunch was a candy bar, two cigarettes and two cups of coffee from the employee break room.

At least I wouldn't have to go to the meeting wearing the same dirty laundry I'd had on since Katya Bolodenka came knocking at my door.

Stepping out of the ladies room stall where I'd changed, I shoved the clothes into a plastic grocery bag. They smelled of dirt and sweat and cattle.

I'd yet to see Earlene — the bookkeeper Peggy said she'd had some kind of appointment and hadn't come in yet this morning — so I didn't have the chance to tell her about the lead story before the paper hit the streets.

If her dad, J. Watterson Whitelaw, was still at the helm, I'd feel comfortable calling him at home on the story. Then again, he lived and breathed this newspaper. If he wasn't in his office, he was probably in the emergency room.

I didn't feel that way about Earlene.

I hadn't felt comfortable when her father turned the reins over to Earlene. I wasn't the only one — the entire staff felt that way. Much married and very spoiled, she never worked at the *Journal-Gazette* until her father's retirement. For the first four months she'd been here, she'd called the paper the *Journal-Tribune*.

I ran my fingers through my short choppy hair in front of the ladies room mirror and sighed. Part of me was dreading her reaction; another part was filled with bravado, my balls-to-the-wall, who-runs-this-newsroom-you-or-me attitude that I knew would get me in hot water.

"OK," I said to my reflection. "Here we go."

Earlene was seated behind her Queen Anne writing table, in front of that awful equestrian portrait. Today's paper was folded on her desk and she smelled of fresh hairspray. There was a pot of coffee and a tray of cookies on the credenza.

The focus group — car dealer Angus Buchanan, Pastor Eric Mustanen, the dowager garden club queens Naomi Callum and Hedwig Ansgar and my own personal nemesis, Melvin Spotts — were seated in a circle around her desk. The only open chair was between Buchanan and Spotts; I dragged it to the side of Earlene's desk.

"I need a good writing surface for my notes," I explained.

"Thank you for joining us, Addison," Earlene cooed. Her tone had an edge to it, although her words were smooth. "I have to say, that is some front page we had today, darlin'. We can discuss that later, but right now let's get started. These folks have some very interesting thoughts on the *Journal-Gazette*."

"I'm sure they do," I answered. Shit.

Spotts didn't waste any time going on the attack.

"What are you doing about the federal government hiding hundreds of barrels of radioactive material in the old Traeburn Tractor plant? I called you about it last week. You never called me back. There have been trucks going in and out of that site at night for years."

Earlene and the other members of the focus group looked incredulously at Spotts and then at me.

"Yes, Mr. Spotts. We looked into that and didn't find anything." I tried to stay calm.

"Of course you didn't! It's a cover up! You need to do some digging— literally!"

"The old Traeburn Tractor plant has been an auto parts factory for a number of years. They operate three shifts a day, five days a week. It's not surprising that trucks come in and out of there at night," I said. "And neither I nor my staff will trespass on to private property late at night with a shovel on a rumor."

"That's because you're too close to the powers that be. You believe anything they tell you." Spotts pointed a bony finger at me. "Now we've got U.S. marshals hiding dangerous federal witnesses here and nobody seems to know about it until this poor guy ends up dead. This radioactive storage is a disaster waiting to happen! It's going to be too late when every little kid in the county starts getting cancer like that over there at that Chernobyl plant."

"We contacted the EPA at both the state and national levels, and the Nuclear Regulatory Commission. They said no such storage site exists." After they quit laughing at my reporter, I wanted to add. "And yes, local law enforcement is very unhappy that there was a federally protected witness here that they didn't know about."

Earlene looked over at me cautiously, her eyes wide. Whether that was because of my words or Spotts, I didn't know.

"What are your sources, Mr. Spotts?" she asked politely.

Spotts blinked. "Sources? You want me to reveal you my sources?"

Angus Buchanan jumped in. "Mr. Spotts, that plant makes engine hoses. They ship them out at the beginning of third shift. That's why the trucks are there."

"Well, my sources couldn't be wrong. They're very high placed government officials. But I won't reveal their names." The old man folded his arms across his chest and lifted his chin sharply at Buchanan.

"I can't do anything unless I know who to contact," I pressed. "I don't have to use their names. I just have to know how to contact them."

"Nope. Not gonna tell you." Spotts' chin went even higher.

"Uh huh." Earlene arched her eyebrows and turned to the gardening divas. "And ladies, what were your concerns?"

The Dowager Empress crossed her spotted old hands across her wide bosom.

"Well, my membership has always been concerned about why the Plummer County Peonies photo submissions are always in color and ours are in black and white," she said. "The Garden Club of Jubilant Falls keeps a scrapbook of our annual activities, which we submit for our annual convention. We have been marked down on several occasions because the pictures weren't in color."

I glanced at Naomi Callum, who was hiding a smirk behind her hand. Somehow I knew that her club's scrapbook won convention honors more than once.

Seriously? I wanted to ask. I should be digging into who shot a federal marshal and I'm spending my afternoon mediating a garden club spat over color photos?

"I'll take this one, Addison," Earlene folded her hands and sat up straighter, like a third-grader convinced she had the right answer in class. "One of the things I've learned since taking this position is that putting color on a page depends on whether or not there is color advertising on the page. The color ads depend on if a business buys them or not."

"A lot of times, that's me, Buchanan Motors," Angus interjected, pointing at himself.

"Our weekly home and garden page sometimes has color advertising and some times it doesn't," I said, picking up where Earlene left off. "Either Dennis Herrick, my city editor, or I, put those pages together and when we have color photos—"

"Oh, who wants to hear about these old biddies and their foolishness?" Spotts jumped in. "I want to know when you're going to look into the meetings that are going on in the barn next to my farm."

"What meetings?" I asked, exasperated.

"There's a group of folks, they meet in the barn at the place next to me, on a regular basis. They bring their big ole trucks and their confederate flags, they play loud music and keep me up at night."

"Did you call the sheriff and file a complaint?" I asked.

"They don't do nothing," Spotts said. "They tell me that if that nonsense lasts after midnight, I've got a complaint. But what about those of us who go to bed earlier? Don't we have any rights?"

"Who is it? Young people? Teenagers? I would bet that it's kids partying in the barn, killing time before school starts," Angus said.

A complaint about Spotts' loud neighbor wasn't going to get me interested in a story either, any more than his beliefs about buried radioactive waste. I nodded, feigning interest.

"Who lives there?" I asked, doodling on my notepad.

Spotts shrugged. "I don't know. The barn hasn't been used in years. I don't know who lives in the house anymore."

"Maybe you ought to go over and introduce yourself to the parents," Angus said. "Maybe they don't know what's going on there."

"In my experience as an educator..." Naomi droned.

I could feel the meeting getting out of control, and I resisted the desire to take my pencil and stab myself in the thigh to keep from shooting off my mouth.

I knew this was going to end up like this. I knew I'd spend an afternoon with people who had no concept of what it takes to run a newspaper, including my boss. I can't leave, because who knows what promises she'll make to these people. Earlene might have me run each garden club photo in color, regardless of advertising and chasing down every barking dog complaint in the police reports for an investigative piece. Please, God, just kill me now.

My cell phone vibrated on Earlene's desk. It was a text from Dennis, upstairs in the newsroom: "*Jerome Johnson's parents are here. They want 2 talk 2 U. NOW.*"

Earlene leaned over to read the message along with me. She nodded at me.

"Go ahead and go. I'll handle this," she whispered.

Feeling like I'd been released from prison, I shot out of her office and ran upstairs. I didn't care if Earlene promised them the moon—right now, I'd do whatever she asked. I just wanted some insight on how a black man who spoke perfect Russian ended up dead on a farm in Plummer County.

***

"Hello, Mr. and Mrs. Johnson. I am so sorry for your loss," I extended my hand to the tall somber couple standing in the newsroom. "I'm Addison McIntyre, the editor. My husband and I had your son and Ms. Bolodenka over for a barbecue on Sunday."

They were an older black couple, both rail thin and well dressed, with an air of formality about them. He was tall, with a salt-and pepper beard, dressed in khakis and a white shirt, with a red bow tie.

His dark brown skin was wrinkled and reading glasses sat halfway down his nose, beneath brown eyes filled with sorrow. Her chocolate skin was set off by the tailored blue dress she wore and matching sensible flats.

Her graying hair was bobbed at her chin and she wore round wire glasses. They looked like academics, unsure about their son's profession, one that had resulted in his death.

"Thank you, Mrs. McIntyre, but his name wasn't Jerome," Mr. Johnson shook my hand. "May we talk in private?"

I ushered them to my office, closing the door behind us and invited them to sit in the two battered wingback chairs, wishing I had something better for this elegant and couple to sit in.

"We must reintroduce ourselves," said Jerome's mother. "The gentleman in the newsroom made the assumption our names were Johnson when I introduced us as the parents of the young man who died. I'm Dr. Yolanda Simms. This is my husband, Dr. James Reed. Our son's real name was Terrell. Terrell Simms-Reed."

"I apologize for that, but you can understand his mistake," I said.

"Mrs. McIntyre," began Dr. Reed. "We hold no grudge. We just want you to know the truth behind our son's life. It's not exactly what you printed in today's newspaper."

His head sank to his chest and his shoulders began to shake. Dr. Simms reached over and grasped her husband's hand.

"We are professors at Howard University in Washington, D.C.," she began slowly. "I teach literature. James teaches political science. Terrell was our only child. We came here to Jubilant Falls to bring his body home."

"I'm so sorry. Tell me about Terrell."

"Maybe he was a little spoiled, maybe we were just trying too hard to keep him from ending up like so many other young black men, but either way, we struggled to keep Terrell on a straight path," Dr. Simms began. "Finally, after a few brushes with the law as a juvenile, his probation officer suggested that maybe the military was the best option for Terrell."

"It was not the choice we wanted for our son, but we felt we didn't have much of an option," Dr. Reed said. "We wanted him to attend college, become a professional, like us. It was very difficult to send him off to basic training at Parris Island."

"So he really was a Marine?" I asked. "Katya Bolodenka told me he was stationed in Russia, but after she said everything else wasn't true, I wondered." They didn't need to know how much effort Gary McGinnis and I had spent in trying to track down the truth about the two of them or the brick walls we hit. Of course, if he was searching for a fake name, it's no surprise.

"Yes — on both counts. The Marine Corps taught him discipline and he became an MP, a military police officer," Dr. Simms said.

"Our son has — *had* — " Dr. Reed stumbled over the verb " — a wonderful gift for languages. He learned Russian in the Marines, which is how he ended up at the American Embassy. He was going to return to the States and attend the Defense Foreign Language Institute to learn Farsi, but his assignment in Moscow was cut short."

Dr. Simms pursed her lips as she picked up the story.

"There was apparently more than one woman able to lure our son into dangerous situations," she said. "He apparently frequented prostitutes, which could be construed as a security risk. When his commanding officer found out, Terrell was sent home. While he received an honorable discharge, nothing of this incident—" Dr. Simms stepped carefully around the word "—nothing was reflected in his record, but he was not encouraged to reenlist."

"I see," I said.

"Because of his law enforcement background and his language skills, he was able to land his present, I mean, this job with the marshal service and the witness protection program," said Dr. Reed. "Many times, he was assigned to people and locations he couldn't tell us about. Many of those he protected were Russians and involved in organized crime. He said that knowing where he was or whom he was protecting would put us in danger, so we just had to trust what he told us. He said he would often have new identities as a way to protect these people as well. We knew he was assigned to protect a number of Russian mobsters, but often we couldn't know where he was, such as this situation with Miss Bolodenka."

"Were you aware they were romantically involved?" I asked.

Dr. Simms pursed her lips again and looked sharply at her husband.

"Not until I read it in your newspaper," she said flatly. "If this woman is the reason my son died—"

Dr. Reed patted her knee. "Ssshhh. I'm sure there will be an investigation."

"You may want to trust what they say, but I'm not entirely sure I believe anything anymore!" she shot back at him.

"Have you spoken to her?" I asked.

"No, I haven't spoken to her and at this point, I doubt if I would!" Dr. Simms's anger broke through her reserved exterior. "We went over to the farm to get some answers and she refused to come to the door!"

"Who answered the door? Did anyone?" I couldn't imagine these two walking up on that front porch to ring the bell, knowing their son's body lay there just hours before. I imagine Peppin and his ninja feds probably already had the scene cleaned up and repainted, but still…

"No one answered at the farmhouse," Dr. Reed said.

"What about the animals? Did you see any animals in the pastures?" I asked.

"The animals were still outside, grazing," he said. "We walked around the back of the house and knocked at the door, but no one answered, so we walked into the barn. There was no one there, either."

If Katya were relocated again, they wouldn't leave those animals, would they? I wondered.

"Then we walked back toward this little house, between the main house and the barn—" Dr. Simms began.

"I know the building—your son lived there," I interjected.

"Well, we knocked on that door, but no one answered there, either," she said. "Even though we could hear two people arguing inside."

"Two people?" I asked.

She nodded. "Yes. A man and a woman. It sounded like they were speaking Russian and they were very angry."

"Both of them?" Did that mean Luka and his thugs had returned? Did Peppin also speak Russian? What were they arguing over? Was Katya in danger?

There was a knock at the office door. It was Earlene, fresh from the focus group meeting and clutching today's edition in her manicured hands.

Chapter 27 Graham

"*What?* You were going to take a job at another paper and never even tell me I had a kid?"

"Maybe I was, maybe I wasn't." Elizabeth lifted her chin defensively.

"How the hell did that happen? I thought you were on birth control!"

"So something went wrong! Shit happens! Either way, how could I say yes to marriage with a man who puts himself in these situations, Kinnon? Somebody who's off chasing the next big headline or the next big story because he gets some kind of adrenaline thrill out of it? What happens when something blows up in your face and you don't come home for good? How could I do that to a baby — our baby?"

"A couple days ago, you were telling me how bored you were with your job! Then you tell me I can't be involved in mine?" I ran both hands through my hair in frustration. "What do you want?"

"I want my kid to have the kind of childhood I had," she said.

I threw my hands up in frustration.

"I want my parents close by so they can visit their grandchildren. I don't want to be bouncing around the country because we move from newspaper to newspaper," she continued. "I want to sit with my husband and kids at the supper table every night, not holding dinner because he's off on some breaking news story somewhere. I want summers up on Lake Erie."

"I can't promise you that—nobody can!"

"Why not, Kinnon? Why not?"

"Because stuff happens to everybody and you can't assure anyone their life is going to be smooth sailing. For God's sake, look at me!"

Elizabeth sighed, resting her hands on her ample hips. An awkward silence hung in the air between us. Why was this relationship suddenly so complicated? When did the woman I thought I could bare my soul to, talk to about anything and everything suddenly turn into someone I didn't know?

"When were you going to tell me you were pregnant?" I demanded.

"I don't know."

"You weren't going to… to end it, were you?"

She looked down and sighed again then looked me in the eye. "I don't know."

"Did it cross your mind that I might want to be a part of that decision?"

"It's my body, Kinnon. I'm the one who has to carry the baby. I figured I'd decide once I got to Akron."

The coffee maker beeped and I turned around to pour each of us a cup. I handed Elizabeth her mug and slid into the dinette chair, awash in anger and pain.

"I can't change who I am, Beth, any more than you can," I began. "I'm going to chase stories — that's what I do. As a human being, I have an obligation to do something to make this world a better place."

"Oh, please — get off your journalistic high horse. You don't have an obligation to come home every night to your kid?"

"When I know about him, yes. How can I provide for a kid I don't know about?" I stopped as realization swept through me. "You're running because you feel trapped. It's why you started looking for a new job."

"That's not true, Graham."

"Yes it is. You think you live in a predictable little town, work at a predictable, boring little job and suddenly, you're pregnant. All you can see are walls going up all around you. You didn't see my proposal as a way to get out of a bad situation. You saw it as the last door to your future closing."

Beth was silent. Her hand gripped the coffee cup tightly, her knuckles white. The surface of the hot liquid quivered.

"That's the real truth, isn't it?" I asked.

She sat her coffee mug down on the dinette table and moved toward the door.

"I have to go now."

I grabbed her arm. "If you don't want to get married, that's fine. If you want to go to Akron, that's fine too. But if you decide to have this baby, I'm going to be a part of this kid's life, whether you like it or not. I'm going to be the dad that I never had. I'll pay child support. I'll make sure that this kid never wants anything. Just let me be a part of his life."

"Please, Graham, let go of me."

"It's my kid, too."

Bursting into tears, she pulled from my grasp and left. This time, I knew she wouldn't come back.

***

Two hours later, I sat in Sheriff Roarke's office.

My old Toyota was parked at the curb; I'd returned the Mustang to the airport rental office.

Benny would be looking for that car, so going back to my old junker made sense. I couldn't afford the daily charges much longer anyway. It didn't matter anymore if I needed to hide from Elizabeth—whether she liked it or not, we were connected for life, or at least the next 18 years.

"So how did it go?" Roarke looked like he could use some sleep. "What happened?"

"Basically, I introduced myself to him, told him who I was."

"You told him you are his son?"

"I had to. He took one look at me and recognized me. We really just talked about personal stuff."

"That makes sense. He isn't going to invite just anyone to the next Aryan Knights meeting. He's going to want to know who he's dealing with before he does that." Roarke shuffled some papers on his desk. "I do have a couple things I need to pass on. Last night there was an incident in Collitstown where a black volunteer's car was burned. He'd had a confrontation at a mall earlier in the week with a white man who fits Doyle McMaster's description."

"McMaster might not be the only one in on it. When I met with Benny Kinnon, he had injuries to his hands, like he'd been in a fight or something."

"That so?" Roarke pushed a copy of the Collitstown police report across the desk at me. "These guys who are so proud of being white and right are usually too scared to show their faces when they pull this crap."

I nodded.

"They don't even have the balls to come in and ask for something in person. I got this today requesting a permit for a rally. Chief Marvin McGinnis also got one and the city manager got one. They want to rally on the courthouse steps but didn't specify a date." Roarke pushed a letter across his desk. There was no signature on the letter, just the scrawled words "Grand Wizard of the Aryan Knights."

"Are you going to grant it?"

"More than likely — once we get a firm date and time and a verifiable name to contact. Their right to free speech is guaranteed by the Constitution, same as you or me. The police chief and I just have to get together to make certain that there's plenty of space between these guys and protesters. This could get ugly fast, not to mention the cost of security."

"Can't you bill them for the costs?"

"When we don't bill any other group that wants to rally on our courthouse steps? How fair is that when groups like Mothers Against Drunk Driving get to kick off their events for free? Or when that anti-abortion group from the college holds their rally every spring? I have to have all hands on deck for that thing. If I charged the Aryan Knights for security and no one else, the ACLU would be all over me like nobody's business."

I nodded. "True."

"When are you going to see him again?"

"Hopefully tonight."

"What time?"

"He doesn't know I'm coming. He said he didn't want to see me again, so this won't be a pleasant visit."

"You need to be careful."

We were silent for a moment. I decided to take the conversation in another direction.

"I saw on front page of the *J-G* this morning that Jerome Johnson got shot," I said. "Addison included the part about the goats being slaughtered. Do you think Doyle McMaster had anything to do with that? I can't believe that the owner was hiding from the Russian mafia."

"I couldn't either when Addison called me this morning. Like I told you, when Johnson came by the other day, he wouldn't file a report. He told me that he went ahead and buried the animals on the farm, and he just wanted extra patrols in the area. I don't know if he'd talked to anyone else or not. If I'd known the owner of the place was in witness protection, we might have been able to keep him safe."

"Maybe when I meet with Benny Kinnon tonight, we'll get some answers."

"We will need you to wear a wire when you think you've gained his trust and he's going to give you some good information."

"That may take a while. He told me he doesn't want to see me again."

"Then why are you going back? Let me get one of our undercover guys—you don't have to do this, Graham."

"Yes, Sheriff, yes I do. This is personal."

Chapter 28 Addison

"Addison, do you have a minute?" Earlene stepped into the office. "Oh, I'm sorry."

"No, don't worry," said Dr. Reed. "We're finished."

The two professors stood and each shook my hand politely. I walked with them to the door of the newsroom at the top of the steps.

"Please tell your readers what Terrell was really about. Don't let him end up as a footnote in this whole mess," Dr. Reed said.

"I will." I nodded and watched them as they walked down the front stairs to the lobby. At the bottom of the stairs, Dr. Reed took Dr. Simms's hand, each taking comfort from the other in their horrible loss.

I returned to my office and closed the door. Earlene had taken one of my battered wingbacks, scooting it close to my desk and spreading today's edition across my desk.

Here we go, I thought.

"Everything OK?" I asked as I sat down behind my desk. I hoped I sounded nonchalant.

"I really do need to allocate some resources for you to update this office." Earlene looked around. "A little paint and some new furniture would do wonders for this place."

"Is that what you came to tell me?" I asked, tentatively.

"No, what I came up here to do was talk to you about a couple things," she began.

I swallowed hard.

"When I set up that group," she continued. "I didn't realize who I was dealing with. Mr. Spotts is, well… a handful."

"I'm glad you saw that firsthand," I said simply. "He can make my day a living hell, but it's people like Spotts who can sometimes come up with the best stories. So, I try to listen whenever I think he's got something — and even when he doesn't."

"I saw that. I also had a chance to look over your murder story on today's front page."

I winced, waiting for the ax to fall. What would she do? Compliment my diplomacy with Spotts — that was a stretch — then curse my story?

"I have to admit that when I first saw the story, I wasn't real happy," she said, touching her over-sprayed pageant hair. "I don't like surprises, Penny, not when I find my husband in flagrante delicto with other women, as several of my lawyers referred to it, and not when I find a story of this magnitude on the front page of the paper I've been entrusted to run!"

"You weren't here. I didn't know how to get in touch with you and we had a deadline," I said.

"You always knew how to get hold of Daddy when you had a big story!" she snapped.

"Your daddy knew what the hell he was doing!" I snapped back. Exhaustion was getting the better of me; I could feel holes in the filter between my mouth and brain getting larger. I didn't care. I'd been up for fourteen hours on too little food and even less sleep, all in pursuit of one murder story. No pseudo-Texas bimbo was going to tell me how to do my job. "I knew I could trust his judgment! I don't know that about you. All I see is you looking to everyone but my newsroom staff and me when it comes to news. Suddenly, I've got a focus group filled with egos and wackos led by a woman who's never been in a newsroom in her life, telling me how they want me to do my job!"

Earlene pulled back, regaining her composure. "Excuse me?"

The words didn't stop.

"Earlene, since you've been here, you've tried to learn a lot about the newspaper business, and I respect that," I said. "But you still don't know the what news is."

"Do go on." Earlene sat up straight, her words dripping in sharp Texas sweetness.

"I know that newspapering is a dying business, and I know that small town papers probably won't be around fifty years from now. We need somebody who can lead this newspaper, somebody who can take it into the future. The perception here is that you came back with a pile of cash from your last divorce with no place to put it and a lot of time on your hands."

Earlene was silent and I saw I'd just poked the bear — a tall over-dressed blonde bear.

"I'm sorry, Earlene. You can fire me or whatever you want to do. I'll be gone by five o'clock if that's what you want," I opened my side desk drawer and began to sweep the pictures of Duncan and Isabella, as well as Suzanne's family Christmas picture from my desktop into my purse.

"Let's quit the dramatics, shall we? I don't know what you've heard about me over the years, but let me tell you one thing—I am the owner of this newspaper and as such, I will run it the way I see best," she began. "And as such, you will look into Mr. Spotts' complaints about his neighbors."

"You're kidding me. What's next, barking dog complaints?"

"If that's what I want covered, then yes, you'll do stories on barking dog complaints!" Earlene said sharply. She sighed. "After you left, the meeting got really out of control—Mr. Spotts just wouldn't quit jawing about his neighbors and their loud parties, but it is clearly something that he feels is an issue and if he sees it as a problem, we need to do what we can do to fix it. I'm also angry that you didn't called me to tell me about the murder I see splashed all over my front page."

"I don't have your cell phone number!" I shot back. "Nobody in this building does!"

She held up her hands. "You will have it by the end of the day. And another thing, I want you to know that my father is the only reason I won't let you go through with quitting."

"What's that supposed to mean?" I stopped cleaning out my desk.

"He's put a lot of stock in you over the years, for whatever reason. As far as I'm concerned, what I've seen here today is someone who'd rather go her own way rather than take any kind of new direction."

This from somebody who has a four-foot tall equestrian self-portrait behind her desk? Someone whose editorial sense is limited to how soon she can spend her dividend check and who lives on alimony? The words almost slipped from my mouth, but I bit my tongue.

"Earlene, I'm the one who made the first call to the sheriff about that homicide," I said instead.

"You were?" Earlene's eyes, framed in Bambi-grade false eyelashes, widened.

"Yes. Katya Bolodenka came to my door at two this morning, scared out of her wits. We took her back to her farm and called Sheriff Roarke."

"I wasn't aware of that."

"That homicide call went out over the radio," I continued. "Everyone with a scanner in three counties heard it. The television remote trucks were practically blocking the road out there at the scene. If we hadn't covered something that big, in our own backyard, we would have looked like…"

"Fools," she finished for me. "I had a long talk with Daddy before I came up here and while he said our first obligation is to our readers and you're the best at doing that, I have not been impressed with your attitude."

I set my family photographs back up on the corner of my desk, but didn't speak.

"That said, my father doesn't want you fired," she repeated. "He's still the majority shareholder in the newspaper, so until such time as that changes, I have to listen to him. But what I want is somebody to get out there to Mr. Spolts' house as soon as possible and find out what the hell—" In Earlene's fake Texas accent, the word sounded like 'hail' —"is going on out there. And if I think the story is worth doing, the story is worth doing. You hear me?"

This time, it was my turn to sigh. What the hell else was I going to do? Go home to the farm and make Duncan and Isabella crazy?

"OK," I said. "I'll stay."

"Oh, and I've had two messages from some guy who says his name is Agent Peppin," she said.

I swallowed hard. "What did he want?"

"I don't know. I haven't called him back yet, but when I do, I'm going to tell him that I stand behind the story and you, despite the kind of crap I've had to deal with here today."

She left, slamming the door behind her. I caught a glimpse of Marcus, Elizabeth and Dennis, all wide-eyed at what they'd overheard.

I laid my head on the stack of papers on my desk and tried to get my bearings. No matter what she said, the barking dog thing was going to wait until tomorrow. I needed sleep and food, but more important, I still needed to know what happened at the Lunatic Fringe Farm.

I needed to get back out there and soon.

Knowing Terrell — or Jerome, as I wanted to keep calling him — had a fondness for getting involved with the wrong woman couldn't have been easy for Dr. Reed or Dr. Simms. I didn't believe it was the sole reason he was killed. Katya Bolodenka's refusal to follow WITSEC's rules got him killed.

By entering her tapestry in the state fair, and by consenting to a story for the *Journal-Gazette*, she'd broken the rules to keeping her safe — and those around her alive.

We had just done what we would normally do, what any other small town paper would have done: celebrated the accomplishments of our residents. Did putting the story up on our website—as part of that newsgathering process—lead to her husband and his thugs locating her? Probably. But what was I supposed to do? Am I supposed to start asking story subjects whether or not they've got some deep dark secret that puts their lives at risk before I run every story? *Pardon me, you don't happen to be in any kind of protective federal custody, do you? I need to know before I do this story.* That's just plain nuts. She had the chance to say no to the story when Elizabeth first called her.

I sat up and reached over to the window behind my desk, pushing it open. Between the focus group, Earlene's rant and my conversation with Terrell's/Jerome's parents, I needed a cigarette.

Finding a pack in my center desk drawer, I lit one and drew the smoke into my lungs, exhaling out the open window. My thoughts continued to churn.

Katya hadn't committed a crime—she'd only witnessed one, the murder of the homeless man in the basement of her Brighton Beach home. How fair was it that she be forced, for her own safety, into a situation where she couldn't contact those most dear to her? How would I react in that situation?

It might be easier for the gangsters themselves to step away from the life they've lived and assume another identity. I'd read books on Italian Mafioso who turned states' evidence and disappeared into witness protection. They had to know their new identities and lives were the true reason they were still alive and one word, one hint at who they'd been could get them killed.

But what about their family members, the wives and families, who, like Katya, never committed a crime? Whose only sin was to fall in love with a crook? It had to be harder for them to have their lives upended, their identities wiped away and any connection to home severed.

Clearly, Katya was trying to maintain ties with those she loved as often as she possibly could, with disastrous results. She repeatedly contacted her sister Svetlana against her handlers' orders—and then Svetlana, her husband and her baby daughter, all ended up dead at the hands of Kolya Dyakanov's thugs.

Then she'd relocated again, this time from Virginia and with animals acquired from another protected witness, here to Jubilant Falls.

How long had she been here, anyway? I didn't know. Duncan and I rarely drove down that road—we would have seen the animals if we had.

Regardless of how long Katya Bolodenka had been there, she'd had to find something to fill her time. Figuring she was safe, figuring no one would look for her in rural southwestern Ohio, she wants to get comfortable, settle in. She couldn't do any of those things that most folks would do—take a cooking class, learn to sew, join a book club—without having to repeat her intricate new life story, a life story she'd been given to keep her safe from harm, the result of a crime she did not commit.

So, she turned to her art. Where she learned weaving and dyeing was anyone's guess. But, she'd literally worked with what she's got—the fleece from the animals in her barn, and the life story she'd been forced to tell.

So she'd woven a tapestry, one she wanted to be recognized for. And, like anyone else, she wanted to reach out into the new community she found herself living in. So what could hurt if the state fair likes what she does? Who was going to come looking for her in Jubilant Falls?

She didn't count on me.

I wondered if she'd even told Jerome she'd entered the tapestry. Did she have to drive up to Columbus to enter it or could she have mailed it in? She knew how to drive — she'd come down to the newsroom to see me about the slain animals while I was in a meeting with Earlene. Graham and Elizabeth spoke to her and Graham took her over to the police department to see Gary. Somehow, though, I couldn't see her driving the hour to Columbus without protection — and Jerome would have likely put the kibosh on her entering anything. If she mailed it in, that marshal at her side would never have known about it. So, when the tapestry won, it was no surprise that the photo didn't have her in it. Our story had seriously blown her cover.

Over the years, I'd seen the damage that secrets could do — every one of the big stories I'd covered had hinged on someone unearthing a truth that someone else never wanted uncovered. I'd even seen the damage secrets that do within my own family. But those secrets were different, based in shame or whatever the current definition of sin was.

Katya's secrets weren't based on her shame or her sin. Her secrets were truth, the life she'd lived and the connections she'd treasured. So when she did the right thing by reporting a murder, she'd been thrown into a world not of her own making, a fiction she was forced to uphold for her own life expectancy — at least until she testified against her husband.

She was given a new name, a new history, taken from all she had known and all she had loved, and then stuck in what anyone else in her Brooklyn neighborhood would undoubtedly have thought was deep in the sticks.

Lonely and alone, she'd turned to the man who was sworn to protect her. How did that happen? I'm not sure I really wanted to know, but the things people did for love, or sometimes, just sex, boggled the mind. Did she even know Jerome's true identity? I doubted it. His identity needed to be protected as much as hers.

I drew the precious nicotine into my lungs again and exhaled out the back window, tossing the cigarette into the alley below.

I still couldn't figure out the argument Dr. Simms and Dr. Reed overheard. Who was Katya arguing with? Was it one of Kolya's thugs? Someone else? I needed to get over to the farm to find out.

***

The Lunatic Fringe farm was bathed in summer's late afternoon sun as I steered my Taurus up the gravel drive. It was hard to believe that fifteen hours ago, this driveway had been clogged with law enforcement officers and the road with television remote trucks.

The sound of the wind rippling through the corn was all I heard as I pulled up to the old farmhouse and parked my Taurus.

It was one of those perfect summer afternoons that made me glad I lived in Plummer County. Down the road, cows grazed in the fields and birds, balancing on the electrical wires, sang out boldly. A bee flew past my head, buzzing loudly as I swatted at it.

I stepped up onto the porch and knocked, then turned around to survey the land around it. I was close enough to smell the fresh paint on the porch and front wall near the door, where the man I knew as Jerome Johnson had laid in a pool of his own blood, just a few hours ago.

No answer. Maybe she's in the barn, I thought to myself.

Back down the front steps, I stepped backward into the driveway to get a look at the upstairs windows. The front windows were open, the curtains fluttering in the summer breeze.

"Hey! Katya! It's me, Addison!" I cupped my hands around my mouth and yelled. "You here?"

Silence.

I followed the gravel drive as it curled behind the house, walking toward the little cottage and the barn.

Thwack! I spun around as the old screen door slapped against the back door frame.

"Katya?" I called.

Still no one. The wind caught the old wooden screen door again and again, and it flapped like a broken wooden wing.

Why would that door be open? I wondered. Could something have happened? Had Luka or any of Kolya Dyakanov's other creeps returned? What if they'd killed her? I pulled the door open and stepped into the house.

In the kitchen, breakfast dishes sat in the sink—a coffee mug, half full, and the remnants of a bowl of cereal, a spoon.

"Katya? Katya? Are you here?" I called.

From the kitchen, I walked through the dining room and into the living room where we'd first met.

Katya's tapestry hung in two slashed pieces on the wall and the pictures of the murdered Svetlana and her daughter in front of St. Basil's Cathedral lay on the floor next to the cheap, particleboard coffee table. The chairs were overturned and someone had ripped the cushions open on the cheap, brown couch, as if searching for something.

I knelt and picked up one of the photos. The glass was broken and a shard had pierced Svetlana's face. If Katya was gone, if she'd disappeared back into witness protection, she wouldn't have left these behind.

I ran upstairs. I remembered the master bedroom was at the front of the house, when the Larsens lived there. I threw open the door to see two enormous looms and the spinning wheel Katya had used for the story we'd done. One loom had a thick and heavy project on it, maybe a rug. The other was serving as a catch all for finished tapestries, weaving tools and partially wound skeins of yarn. Fleeces sat in black plastic trash bags, yarn overflowed from baskets and books littered the room, but it looked more like creativity flowing than a raid.

"Katya?" I called again. "Katya, are you here?"

In the next bedroom, the mattress had been pulled from the frame and bedclothes covered the floor. The dresser drawers were open and clothing hung over the sides. The closet door was open and more clothing lay strewn across the floor.

The other bedroom and the upstairs bathroom looked the same—someone had come through and tossed it, in search of whatever they thought Katya was hiding. Another quick look didn't reveal any blood or evidence of any possible clean up. If Luka and his hoods harmed her, they hadn't done it here.

But what if she were safe? Where had she gone? Had she disappeared back into the witness protection program? If she had, why wouldn't she take those most precious items — the photos of her dead sister and her niece?

There had clearly been a struggle here. Something awful happened. Who had Jerome's/Terrell's parents heard arguing with her?

I pulled my phone from its belt holder and dialed Duncan's cell.

"It's me, Penny. I'm over here at the Lunatic Fringe and Katya's gone."

Chapter 29 Graham

It was dusk when I pulled into the lot at the Travel Inn. The door to Benny's room was slightly ajar and yellow light shone around the edges of the dirty window curtains.

There were several pick-up trucks parked around the barely-open door, and, with my Toyota's window down, I could hear men's voices coming from inside. What was going on? Was it a meeting? Were they making plans for the rally the Aryan Knights wanted to have on the courthouse steps?

I didn't want Benny to see me yet. I parked the Toyota in front of the last motel room, furthest from his and walked around the back of the building. I knew from being here on previous stories that the baths for each room were at the back of the building, each with a small crank-out window of frosted glass. Every room had a window air conditioner in the front, but not all of them worked and the owner was never real concerned about getting them fixed. I could only hope Benny's was one of those rooms and, along with the open front door, that back window would be open to let a breeze come through — and bring conversation out.

A narrow sidewalk, cracked and uneven, ran along the back of the building, next to a gravel driveway where an industrial Dumpster sat. From the corner where I parked, I could see cheap pink cotton curtains fluttering out the back of a bathroom three rooms down—Benny's room.

I tiptoed down the sidewalk and, once I was beneath the open window, leaned my back against the wall to listen. I considered bringing a reporter's notebook with me, but changed my mind at the last minute. Recording everything on my smart phone was a better choice. That way, I could keep an eye out for anyone trying to sneak up on me rather than having my head buried in the effort it would take to take notes. I hit the 'on' button, set the phone on the edge of the windowsill and began to listen.

"Ben, you've got to do something with that little asshole," a male voice said. "He's way out of control."

I recognized Benny's slow sardonic laugh. "No he won't. He's a pup, just trying to show he can run with the big dogs. I can handle him."

"You better! He's going to bring the cops down on us with all his shenanigans and we're going to be the ones holding the bag."

"No, you won't," Benny said, calmly. "I keep telling you, I've got him under control."

"Is he going to be there tonight?" someone else asked.

So what was tonight? I wondered. A meeting? Where would it be? And whom are they talking about? Doyle McMaster?

Benny grunted. "I figure he is," he said.

Another truck, this one a diesel, pulled up and cut its engine.

"It's him," Benny said.

The truck's door squeaked open and slammed shut. The men inside Benny's room were silent as the sound of footsteps entered the room.

"Hey, ya'll," said a young man's voice, a voice just a little younger than mine. I wanted to stand and peek through the window. Was it Doyle? As often as I'd covered McMaster's lengthy, though petty, criminal career, I hadn't heard him speak very often — unless it was during an arraignment, when he told the judge "Not guilty, your honor."

Whoever this kid was, he wasn't welcome. Only Benny answered, "Hey."

"I got those letters delivered for you."

Letters? Like the one Sheriff Roarke got requesting the rally on the courthouse steps?

"You weren't fucking stupid enough to do it yourself, were you?" Someone else asked.

"Naww — I had my sister's kid do it. I gave him five bucks for each one he delivered — he's like ten years old. He thought he just got a big ole pile of cash. If I did it myself, my probation officer would have nailed me to the wall. So where's the meeting?"

"Same as usual," Benny answered. His words and his tone turned expansive and sarcastic. "However, gentlemen, before we get the opportunity to preach the virtues of a pure white race to those who would let the Jews and the niggers and the queers destroy God's great country, we need to discuss a little fund raising. This organization doesn't run on good will alone."

Someone closed the front door of Benny's hotel room. There was a thump, like something dumped on a wooden surface, like a table. Someone else whistled low and long.

"That's heroin, isn't it?" the young man's voice asked. "Jesus, I don't think I've ever seen a whole brick—"

"Would you shut up?" a man's voice said. "Can you for once just not run your goddamned mouth?"

"Kid," Benny said. "Just to be sure, go back there and shut the bathroom window."

I snatched the smart phone from the sill and flattened myself against the wall as someone entered the bathroom. There were the sounds of the door closing, a zipper coming down and a stream of urine into the toilet, then the flush of water. I held my breath as a hand reached out and pulled the window closed.

So, even though Benny Kinnon had kicked his own heroin habit long ago, he was serious when he told me he didn't think twice about selling it.

I sprinted around to the front of the building, to the door of Benny's room. I knocked and the conversation inside stopped sharply.

"Who is it?" Benny called out.

"It's me, Graham. I wanted to talk to you again. About this morning."

Benny's hands were around my throat before he was completely out the door. I winced in pain as he pushed me against the truck, the pickup's chrome grill slamming into the middle of my back. His face was close to mine; I could smell his sour breath and see his scraggly beard.

"Did I not tell you not to come looking for me again?" he hissed.

"I just wanted to ask one more thing." I raised my hands in self-defense.

I saw stars as he slammed my head against the truck's hood. "No more questions! You hear me?" he screamed, spittle forming at the corners of his toothless mouth. Veins stood out in the swastika tattooed on his neck. "No more questions!"

"OK! OK!" I said.

He loosened his grip and I fell to dirt. Behind him, the barrel of a gun poked through the window curtains. Benny's dirty hands reached out and pulled me up by my shirt.

"You shouldn't have come back here," he said. "I told you that for your own good."

"Who's in there with you?" I pointed at the gun barrel. Benny turned around and waved. The gun disappeared from the window.

"Listen kid. I'm going to give you one last bit of advice." His words were hard. "Those guys in there, they're not the Sunday school set your idiot mother obviously raised you with. They'll kill you just as soon as look at you. I'm telling you for your own goddamn good — these guys don't screw around. Get the hell out of here or you'll end up dead."

Out of the corner of my eye, I saw a decrepit four-door Impala with primer grey fenders pull up beside the truck.

"You OK, Benny?" I turned my head to see who spoke. It was Doyle McMaster. His John Deere baseball hat was smeared with grease and his jeans were torn. He held a knife blade in his hand. So who was the young man's voice I heard in the motel room? The one who delivered the rally letters? Some other stupid kid who was getting sucked into Benny's world?

"Yeah, I'm fine." Benny turned to me and brushed the dirt from my shoulders, smiling sardonically. "Now get the hell out of here. I mean it."

He shoved me toward the road.

"Don't come back. I told you why."

As I walked away, McMaster spoke.

"You know that guy?"

"Nope," Benny answered.

"I think I've seen him before. He looks like that prick from the paper."

"A reporter?" Benny asked. "Nah—he's not smart enough to be a reporter."

I hung my head, walking briskly across the rocky motel parking lot to the busy road, hoping McMaster or Benny wouldn't follow. The words stung, worse than I thought they would. I fought the urge to go back and punch them both. There was a diner at the corner. I could sit there for a few minutes, recover my composure and have a cup of coffee, while waiting until it was safe for me to go back to get my car.

I waited until I hit the sidewalk to pull out my cell phone and called Judson Roarke on his cell phone as I walked toward the diner.

He picked up on the second ring.

"What's up? You OK?" he asked.

I explained what I'd heard about the meeting and the heroin and that I had the whole thing recorded on my phone.

"That changes the whole situation," Judson said, thoughtfully. "You're sure they said heroin? Did you see anything?"

"All I saw was the barrel of a gun in the window."

"Hmmmm."

"So what happens now?"

"I think it's time we bring in some of our undercover guys. This could get really dangerous really fast and I can't put a civilian like you at risk."

"But—"

"Listen, we appreciate all you've done for us."

"There's a meeting tonight—"

"No." Roarke's tone was sharp and commanding. "You don't go there—that's an order. It's too dangerous. I want you to bring in that recording and let us take it from there."

"Yes, sir," I sighed.

Roarke disconnected the call, just as I reached the diner and stepped inside. I took a seat in a booth where I had the best view of the front of the Travel Inn. I ordered a cup of coffee. It would be a little bit before I could walk back over there to get my car. In the meantime, I'd have to figure out what my next step would be.

Chapter 30 Addison

I don't know what to tell you." Duncan shook his head as we made one more pass through the ransacked house. "It looks like someone was searching for something, but it doesn't look like any body was hurt or killed here."

"Let's look in the cottage. Maybe there's something there."

Like the farmhouse, the cottage door was unlocked, so we walked in. Here, too, the furniture was cheap, upended and slashed, as if the search that began in the farmhouse continued. In the bedroom, sheets were torn from the double bed and a single vicious slash exposed the stuffing and springs within. Men's clothing hung from the sides of the open dresser drawers; dirty boot prints marked the clothing on the floor.

Again, it looked more like a burglary than a murder.

Duncan scratched his head. "Have you checked the barn?" he asked.

"No, I haven't. Come to think of it, I didn't see any animals in the pasture," I answered.

"Jerome, or whatever his name really was, told me they don't do well with the heat, so he had cooling units and fans installed," Duncan said. "The llamas and alpacas might be in the barn. Let's go see."

"But if she's not here and the animals are, that might mean those mobsters came after her," I said. "We need to call the sheriff."

"And if they're not there, she's been relocated in witness protection and she's just plain gone. You can't do anything about it."

"But it doesn't explain why the place has been tossed like this. Katya never would have left those pictures of her sister."

"In her situation, it might be best not to ask."

I sighed. He might be right.

"Well, let's go look in the barn at least," I said.

A few steps from the cottage and we were in the barn. Huge livestock fans hummed in a wide aisle between the two rows of box stalls, pushing the heat from the late August sun back outside. Walking up and down the aisle, Duncan and I saw the stall's dirt floors dotted with small piles of manure. Flakes of fresh hay stood in feeders, but there were no animals to be found.

To our right, the door to an office stood open. Duncan stepped inside and flipped on the light. A metal desk sat in front of a window, which looked down the driveway, toward the road.

On the wall by the door, I recognized several racks of halters and leads. There was a stack of buckets and black rubber feed bowls beneath them.

Kitchen cabinets, possibly reused from someone's kitchen, hung on the walls above a small sink, and contained familiar medications for parasites and other home veterinary supplies.

That didn't surprise us — Duncan and I, like most farmers, did a lot of the routine vet work ourselves. Annual vaccinations or treatment for worms or scours were things we often handled at the farm. It looked like Jerome and Katya did the same thing for the llamas and alpacas.

Duncan pointed to the corner where a split-open bag of feed lay on the floor, grain strewn across the floor. A few other bags of feed lay haphazardly on wooden pallets against the wall.

"Who ever dropped this was in a hurry, Penny."

Sighing, I knelt and scooped up a handful of sweet-smelling grain.

"We need to call the sheriff. Something has happened here."

"I don't think so. She's gone, Penny, and she's taken the animals with her. Witness protection relocated her again."

"But we don't know that for sure!" I cried. "This place has been trashed. She could be in danger."

"And she could just be gone. If the Russian mafia knows she's here, she'd have to leave real damn fast."

"I suppose." I let the grain fall from my hand back onto the floor. "Still, I'm going to call Jud Roarke and Gary McGinnis to see if they know anything. God knows I won't get anything out of Agent Peppin."

Duncan extended his hand to help me stand. "You just need to let her go, Penny. It's over."

***

After dinner, Duncan, Isabella and I were settling down in front of the television to watch a movie when Gary McGinnis called me back. I quickly explained what I'd seen at the Lunatic Fringe.

"I can't tell you anything, either," he said. "I know the sheriff's office turned the murder case over to the feds for investigation. Jud Roarke and his folks are completely off of it."

"But why would the place be trashed like that?" I asked.

"I don't know. Maybe they did it themselves, to send folks like you or those mobsters down the wrong trail."

"But she would have taken her sister's pictures with her," I argued. "Those were her most precious possessions. They were laying on the floor, with the glass broken."

"Then go ahead and call Jud Roarke or Bob Peppin, but I doubt if you'll get anything out of them."

Phone calls to the sheriff just repeated what Gary told me.

"I'm off the case," Sheriff Roarke said. "I can't tell you anything, even if I knew it."

Peppin didn't even answer his cell phone. I groaned in frustration as I disconnected, not bothering to leave a voice mail.

"Let it go, honey," Duncan said, patting my knee. "Why don't you just call it a night? You've been up an awful long time — you're exhausted. And turn that stupid police scanner off. Odds are, nothing is going to happen tonight that you can't pick up first thing tomorrow morning."

"I guess so."

Kissing him and Isabella on the cheek, I went upstairs to bed, unsure about what happened to Ekaterina Bolodenka, whether she was safe — or whether she was still alive.

Chapter 31 Graham

Two cups of coffee and one greasy burger later, the sun was still taking its time going down and yet no one had ventured from Benny's motel room. If there was a meeting, it wasn't going to be until after dark.

The lull was giving me too much time to think — and not just about Benny.

I pulled out my phone and with my thumb, flipped through the photos there. Most of the pictures were of Elizabeth and me, with our destination in the background, stupid cell phone selfies of us together, taken at arm's length. We were grinning then: there were pictures of a Saturday at the Cincinnati zoo, Elizabeth holding a pair of concert tickets outside a theater, another selfie of a kiss as a rainbow arched above us in a field of green grass.

My thumb hovered above the delete button, but I couldn't take the next step.

Why did she want to keep her pregnancy secret from me? Did she feel that trapped here in Jubilant Falls? Did she think I'd be a bad father? Just because of my job?

As painful as it was, it didn't matter now. She was going to move on with her life and I was going to move on with mine. I just had to ensure that I was a part of that kid's life, no matter what.

I felt a twinge as I rubbed the goose egg at the back of my head, my gift from Benny. At least I wasn't going to be that kind of father.

"Sir, we're closing." Smacking her gum, the waitress laid my bill on the table. She pointed at the clock above the door with her pencil. "It's eight o'clock."
I pulled a couple bucks out of my wallet and walked from the diner as she locked the door behind me and the diner's fluorescent lights went dark.

I walked across the Travel Inn's broken parking lot, looking at the curtains in Benny's room, hoping he, or the gun barrel I'd seen wouldn't appear until I got in my car.

I slid into my front seat and slipped the key into the ignition. After a few attempts, the engine turned over. I looked over to my left as engines from two pick up trucks in front of Benny's room also came to life. Dusk was falling, obscuring the driver's faces as the men pulled away from the front door, leaving Benny's junker truck and Doyle McMaster's Impala behind.

What was going on inside? Was Doyle McMaster convincing Benny of my identity? Was Benny still blowing him off, convinced I wasn't smart enough to be a reporter? Or was he enraged that now that I had other motivations for contacting him?

I had to smirk at my earlier reaction to his words. Why did I let that hurt me? Why did the opinion of the man who sold my mother drugs, then used her for sex and beat her up, matter to me? Why had it been so important to me to track him down and ask him stupid questions about my past?

As crude as he was, he got one thing right: We never get the parents that we want. They all have faults, say or do things someone in their right mind wouldn't do. Sometimes, they're driven by fear or the belief that they're just plain right. Some of them make incredible mistakes that change the lives of everyone around them — and sometimes they even learn from those mistakes.

Benny was not one of those who would learn from his mistakes. He would bounce from crime to court to prison and back, convinced the world around him wasn't nearly as intelligent as he was, but still not smart enough to realize that it took true guts to keep a job, raise a child and be a man.

My mother was one of those who learned from her mistakes and who tried to show she loved me, however imperfectly it may have played out. Sometimes her love showed itself through Bill's checkbook parenting, but as a result, I can't say I was neglected in any way. She worked hard to change her life.

My mother made sure that I had everything, as she herself worked hard to bury her own sordid past by having her past court records sealed and building a new persona as the wife of an Indianapolis manufacturing mogul. Maybe she hoped that I was young enough to forget those early bad years and remember only the good times after we were reunited.

It wasn't like she'd kept a secret from me; I knew where I came from. We just didn't talk about it. She'd even said she was surprised I waited this long to ask her the particulars. I had food, clothing, a good education and a roof over my head, thanks to Mother and Bill—and a moral grounding from the Jesuit brothers who educated me. Why bring up the past? I saw that clearly now.

And this child of mine, the one Beth was carrying, would wonder about his situation some day, in the same way I wondered about mine. He—somehow, I'd begun to personify this baby as a son—he'd come to me with all his questions, just the way I'd gone to Benny.

I could hear the question already. *Why don't you and Mommy live together?*

What Elizabeth decided to do was her choice. I'd asked her to marry me—and likely would again if I even saw her— but she was the one to make the decisions at this point. I'd have to live with her ambivalence and react accordingly. She would be a good mom, in her way, and yes, she would be living close to her parents, so there would be family there when she needed them. All I could do was tell the truth, and be a part of the kid's life to the best of my ability. My kid, my son, wouldn't be a twenty-seven-year-old man, wondering why I'd disappeared or why I'd never called.

Four motel doors down, Benny and Doyle stepped outside and into their vehicles. I slid down in my seat, hoping they wouldn't see me. Neither did. They waved at each other as the vehicles backed away from the door.

There was no redemption in Benny, not as a father and not as a man.

Maybe that was what I was looking for when I first agreed to help hunt him down. Maybe I was looking for someone who, like my mother, had done his time, cleaned up his life and made a contribution to society. I saw clearly that now that this wasn't the case — and never would be.

Tonight he would preach hate and, somewhere, sometime, sell death to fund his gospel.

Tonight, that would come to an end.

My car's transmission clunked ominously as I threw it into reverse and, at a distance, followed the truck and the sedan down the street.

***

The county roads were lush and green, over-hung with trees. Stars were beginning to come out in what would be a clear summer night. We were deep in the bowels of Plummer County, on roads that were barely wide enough to accommodate any oncoming traffic, had there been any, surrounded on all sides by fields of corn, soybeans and alfalfa.

On the right was a yellow bungalow, its paint peeling, the yard seemingly cut from the surrounding field of grass. It had been someone's American dream once: in the dark, I could just make out a chain link fence enclosing a back yard with a swing set and dog house, both considerably younger than the home itself. It wasn't any more. Foreclosure notices hung on the front door and window.

One driveway led directly to the house and a narrow one-car garage. Another shot off from the main drive through the grass field toward an old bank barn and back toward the road.

Sitting nearby was the stone foundation of another building, probably an older, original farmhouse, filled with weeds and saplings.

McMaster and Benny pulled into the drive and parked outside the barn. I kept going, about a quarter of a mile to the next driveway. I pulled in and parked beside another old farmhouse, shielded from the barn by a patch of old-growth trees.

"If you're looking for the damned party, it's next door." An elderly man, small and wiry, sat on the front porch in a worn bathrobe, his birdlike arms crossed across his chest. The front windows were open; I heard a parrot caw and cackle inside. "And you can tell all your buddies, this time, if it's still loud after ten o'clock, I'm calling the police."

I stepped up onto the porch, extending my hand. "I'm not here for any party. I'm Graham Kinnon, with the *Journal-Gazette*."

"Thank God! Somebody down at that stupid paper finally listened to me!"

"Listened to you?"

"I met today with that new lady publisher you've got. She seems real nice, a hell of a lot more sympathetic than that editor you've got. What's her name, Addison something? She's a cold one, she is. Anyway, your new publisher actually listens to what people have to say! I told her that somebody ought to be looking into these loud parties that go on over here." Spotts gestured with his sharp chin toward the neighboring barn. "She told me somebody would be out to talk to me about it. I just didn't think it was gonna be today."

This must have been the meeting Addison was attending that Elizabeth told me about when she came to my apartment. I tried not to smirk, realizing whose porch I was standing on.

It belonged to Melvin Spotts, whose voicemails into the newsroom were filled with absurd conspiracy theories and right-wing cant. After Addison went home at night, Dennis would play them on the speakerphone so we could all get a laugh.

A few of them were actually crazy enough to make sense.

When that happened, Addison had city reporter Marcus Henning chase it down, but Spotts' messages were never anything other than the paranoid ravings of someone convinced Watergate lurked behind every government office door.

"You know, I went to school with that new publisher's daddy. I swear that family always thought they was better than anyone else," Spotts continued. "Just because they owned that newspaper, they all held their noses in the air."

"So what kind of parties are going on there?" I asked.

"You gonna write this down? You ain't got no notebook."

"You're right." I walked back to my car and pulled a notebook from my glove box and a pen from the cup holder, rejoining Spotts on his porch. Even though I knew who he was, I had Spotts spell out his name for me before I began. "So tell me what's going on."

"Like I told your publisher, 'bout once a week, they come down here with their pick-up trucks and their loud music. There's a bunch of them and when I call the sheriff, I don't get any response."

"So how long has this been going on?"

"About a month—and I tell you, I'm getting darned sick and tired of the lack of response I get from that new sheriff. Raise my taxes to buy new dispatch equipment and then don't even come out to my house when I call 911? Have you looked into whether they spent that money like they said they did? I'll bet you that my tax dollars aren't going where the county said they would."

"I don't think that's the case, sir. I did a story on the new dispatch equipment about a month back." I tried to steer the conversation back to what was going on in the barn. "So what kind of things do you hear over at the barn?"

"Loud music, and talking. Somebody's always talking."

"Like on a microphone?"

He shrugged. "Maybe so. I take my hearing aids out before I go to bed, so I can't always understand what they're saying."

"Do you get the impression that it's a group meeting of any kind? Or just a loud party?"

"I get the impression that somebody's trying to keep me from getting a good night's sleep!" he snapped.

"If you don't mind, sir, I'd like to leave my car here and walk over there to see what's going on."

"Fine with me. Maybe you can get them to quiet it down a little before things get out of control."

I left Spotts sitting on his front porch and slipped into the woods.

Chapter 32 Addison

A phone call from Dr. Bovir woke me at just about one-thirty.

"What's up?" I asked, pulling a pair of jeans from the bedroom floor and stepping into them. I balanced the phone between my cheek and my shoulder as I dressed.

"I need you to come down to the morgue," said Dr. Bovir in his Pakistani accent.

"You can't tell me why?"

"Just come down, please." And he hung up.

Duncan barely grunted his acknowledgement as I left for yet another story in the middle of the night. It would be his responsibility — for the second day in a row — to get the Holsteins milked if I weren't back in time.

About twenty minutes later, I was leaning against the fender of my old blue Taurus, finishing a cigarette.

Wonder what this is about? I wish Graham Kinnon were here. This shit always happens when I'm short-staffed.

I ground my cigarette into the sidewalk in front of the emergency room before I stepped between the automatic double sliding doors. This early in the morning, the main doors had long been closed and all traffic had to come in through the ER.

I looked around the emergency waiting room, quiet at this time of the morning. A couple of patients were waiting to see the doctor. A man, his workingman's clothes dirty and his face bruised, probably from a late night bar fight, held an ice bag against his jaw. A drop of blood congealed in the beginnings of a day's growth of beard below his nose.

Across the room, a mother, dressed in jeans, sweatshirt and fuzzy slippers bounced a crying baby on her lap, a panicked look on her face. In the corner, an elderly man sat reading a year-old issue of *Golf* magazine. A worn woman's coat and scuffed purse lay in the chair next to him.

"I'm here to see Dr. Bovir," I said to the nurse behind the desk, showing my press pass.

Like a lot of small town coroner's offices, Bovir's was in the basement of Plummer County Community Hospital, just south of Jubilant Falls' downtown.

The nurse picked up the phone and punched in the morgue's extension on the keypad.

"He told me you'd be here," she said. She was silent for a moment. "Dr. Bovir? Yes, she's here. I'll send her down."

The nurse hung up the phone and pointed toward the hallway. "Just go down there, toward the elevator. The morgue is—"

"I know." I cut in. "I can find it. Thanks for your help."

My dirty white athletic shoes squeaked as I walked down the hallway, echoing off the empty walls. I stopped at the end of the hall and pushed the button to call the elevator. The soft ding of the approaching car echoed through the hall. I stepped inside and punched the glowing white 'B' button.

Dr. Bovir was waiting for me when the elevator doors opened in the basement. "Thanks for coming this late at night, Mrs. McIntyre," the coroner said, bowing slightly.

"No big deal. What's going on?" I pulled my reporter's notebook and a pen from my purse, uncapping the pen with my teeth.

"We need you to identify a body."

I arched an eyebrow. "The cops usually do this with a photo and the next of kin downtown. What's the deal that you need me, of all people, to come into the morgue to do the ID?"

Bovir didn't answer, but simply took my elbow and led me into the morgue.

Inside, Robert Peppin stood next to the steel autopsy table beside a wall of individually refrigerated drawers for corpses, his arms folded and his foot tapping.

His eyes hardened as I came into the room.

I didn't speak; I just nodded sharply in Peppin's direction.

Bovir lead me toward one of the steel examining tables in the center of the room, where a body lay covered in a sheet.

"Can you identify this person?" He folded the sheet down to the body's shoulders.

I gasped.

The woman lying on the slab had bullet wounds to her left eye and cheekbone. Her matted black hair fell around her naked shoulders and around her face. The back of her head, which rested on a metal headrest, was a mass of congealed blood, brains and hair where the bullets had exited.

I grasped the side of the steel slab for balance and closed my eyes to block out the horror as vomit rose in my throat. After a moment of silence, I let out a long sigh.

"Oh, Katya Bolodenka," I said softly. "I'm so, so sorry."

"You ought to be," Peppin said. "Ekaterina Bolodenka was the sole witness who was going to put Kolya Dyakonov away for a long time. Now, with no witness, we have no case, thanks to you."

"You listen to me, Peppin, and you listen to me good." I poked a finger into the agent's chest. "I'm not responsible for the death of Katya Bolodenka — or whatever goddamned name you've given her. Blame me all you want, but I didn't kill her. I just did my job. Your agency had a witness who couldn't play by the rules, protected by a man who couldn't keep his pecker in his pants. Don't you think the fact they were sleeping together compromised her situation a little bit? I'd say it was your agency and your marshal who failed Katya, not me."

"Please, Mrs. McIntyre, Agent Peppin—" Bucky Bovir stepped between us.

"I'm not done," I said, pushing him aside. "Somebody trashed that farmhouse—I was there this afternoon."

"What?" Peppin stepped back.

"That's what I said. Where did you find her body? Because there's no evidence she was killed in the house, unless you've already cleaned that mess up, too."

"I'm not at liberty to divulge that information," Peppin said, recovering his composure.

"Then you better be prepared to be skewered in tomorrow's paper because I'm telling the whole damned story. I've talked to Jerome Johnson's parents—I know his real name was Terrell Simms-Reed. I know what happened when he was a Marine. If you want to pin the responsibility for her death on anybody, you ought to look in the mirror because that's what my readers are going to see tomorrow."

I turned sharply and walked from the morgue.

***

Back in the hospital parking lot, I sagged against my car door, gazing at the moon, my left hand searching through my capacious purse for cigarettes.

I pulled one cigarette from the pack, placed it between my lips and lit it, taking my eyes off the moon only briefly.

I inhaled deeply; my shoulders sank as I exhaled sadly.

I'd have to go home and tell Duncan about it, of course. In all the years I'd been at the *Journal-Gazette*, there had been many murders and no doubt would be many more. Each of them had been tough in their own way, but why did this one seem so tough?

Maybe because I'd gotten to know the woman, I thought, scanning the sky for stars, trying to ignore the tears rising in my eyes. Maybe it's because I'm losing my edge. Maybe, after twenty years, I should confine myself to sitting in front of the computer, editing stories and filling pages. I could throw these kinds of stories at either Graham Kinnon or Marcus Henning. They would do just fine. I could avoid getting involved that way…

"When pigs fly," I said aloud.

Still, just a little bit ago, it all seemed so simple. I blinked back my tears and ground my cigarette into the pavement. No, I wouldn't go home and tell Duncan. I'd go into the newsroom. I'd write the story, post it to the website, then throw it on the front page. Earlene could tell me she didn't like my attitude and she could fire me for all I cared.

To hell with what happened next. Let somebody else go do a story on noisy neighbors. It was *real* news I was after.

Chapter 33 Graham

"I thought you were bringing that digital recording in.
It's been two hours and no one in my office has seen you
yet." Judson Roarke's voice was harsh on the other end of
the cell phone call.

The patch of woods between Spotts' house and the
abandoned barn was thick with underbrush, made darker by
nightfall. I had to stop and catch my breath before
answering.

"I still am. I just haven't gotten there yet."

"I told you not to go after Benjamin Kinnon and Doyle
McMaster. I told you it's too dangerous."

"I had to wait until it was safe for me to go get my car.
It was parked in the Travel Inn lot. I had to hole up in that
diner around the corner until they left."

"So where are you now?"

"I think I know where the meeting is being held." I
gave him Spotts' address. "Next door, there's a yellow
house—I think it's foreclosed on because there's some kind
of notice taped on the door—and back at the rear of the
property, there's an old barn. They're meeting there."

"How do you know that?"

"C'mon sheriff," I joked. "You know I don't have to reveal my sources."

"You screw with me and I'll charge you with obstructing official business."

I sighed. "OK, the truth? My editor met with Melvin Spotts today and he complained about the loud parties that have been going on there. Benny's and Doyle's trucks are parked there right now."

Roarke disconnected without another word.

I shoved my phone back in my shirt pocket and kept walking, moving the brush from my path with each step.

Roarke wasn't stupid. He knew where I was — he and every deputy in Plummer County were probably on their way, lights and sirens, busting ass down every narrow country road in Plummer County to converge on this place. I'd given him Spotts' address and he could further hone down my location by pinging my cell phone signal off the nearest tower.

So why didn't I turn back? Why didn't I just let Roarke finish the job like he was duly elected to do? I only had to walk back to my car and tell Spotts the sheriff and his posse were on their way. I only had to tell him he wouldn't be having any more problems, park my butt in my Toyota and wait for the fireworks to begin.

Why did I continue my trek to the barn?

Because Benny abandoned me as a child? Because he'd abused my mother? What good would that do now? It wouldn't change anything that happened back then. Were my actions, like Elizabeth said, self-righteousness and self-seeking? Was I just hell bent for a front-page story? Maybe she was right. Maybe I was the adrenaline and glory hound she said I was.

No, the truth was I just wanted to see an end to the calamity this man left in his wake. I wanted to see this end. Only then could I say I'd put the disaster that was my father behind me.

One final push through the undergrowth and I could see the back of the bank barn. Light shone through the slits in the thinning bare walls, black from age and weather. I could hear Benny and Doyle's voices inside.

Wire farm fencing along the edge of the property kept me from getting closer. I walked a little farther north, toward the back of Spotts' property, searching for a break in the fence line. Before too long, I found it: a place where it had rusted and an animal, probably a deer, pushed on the fence until the brittle tines gave way, leaving a hole big enough to crawl through. I got down on my hands and knees and crept through.

I looked down to brush the leaves and dirt off the knees of my pants and looked up — right into the barrel of Doyle McMaster's shotgun.

He grabbed my collar and yanked me to my feet.

"Boy, I don't know what you're after, or what you've told Bennie, but right now, you're trespassing." Spinning me around, Doyle pushed me toward the barn, the shotgun barrel between my shoulder blades.

"Bennie is my father," I said, my hands in the air. "I just wanted to talk to him back there at the hotel."

"From what I could see, he wasn't much interested, now was he?" He jabbed the gun barrel into my back. "Keep walking."

"Whose property is this?" I asked as we continued up the dirt bank to the barn's sliding doors.

"It was mine, until this country decided it didn't need honest white workers any more," Doyle said.

"How's that?"

"What do you mean? You are as stupid as Bennie says you are."

"No, I'm serious. Tell me what happened."

We stopped outside the door of the barn. I turned to face Doyle, but he didn't lower his gun.

"Get inside." McMaster pushed me through the open door and into the dark barn. I stumbled over something and fell on my face. I tried to get up, but a sharp kick in my side knocked the wind out of me. Groaning, I curled up in a fetal position.

"Lookee here, Benny," Doyle said. "Look what I found crawling around outside."

Benny rolled me over, his toothless face coming into focus as my eyes adjusted to the semi-darkness of the barn. I could smell his acrid breath as he bent over me.

"Didn't I tell you not to come looking for me boy? Didn't I?" he hissed. He gave me a sharp second kick. I felt a rib snap, and I sucked in my breath to keep from crying out.

"Get him up — tie him up over there," Bennie commanded.

Doyle grabbed me by the shoulders and dragged me toward the center of the barn floor where a rusted hay wagon and tools were laced together with generations of spider webs and brown dust. Doyle grabbed an old wooden chair from beside the wagon and pushed me into it. Benny pulled a handgun from the back of his pants and held it in my face as Doyle tied my hands and legs to the chair.

"I want to know what you're doing here," Benny demanded.

"I told you. I wanted to talk to you. You're my father."

"Bullshit." Benny swung the gun at my jaw. I cried out in pain as the butt struck the left side of my face and blood filled my mouth. I tried to answer as the gun butt came back, striking just beneath my right eye. "Talk to me, you whelp son of a bitch. Tell me the truth."

I hung my head, trying to wipe the blood from my mouth onto my shirt before I answered.

"I know why you came to Jubilant Falls," I said. I gasped between every couple words as I tried to control the pain of the broken rib. "I know about the Aryan Knights. I know what you're trying to do here."

"Who told you?"

"The police and sheriff had you under surveillance, but they didn't have anybody who could get close enough without you figuring out they were cops."

"So they send a fucking reporter?" Doyle came around to face me. "As soon as I saw you outside the Travel Inn, I knew who you were. "

"I volunteered," I gasped, as blood spilled from my mouth. "I wanted to see the asshole who got my mother sent to prison."

Doyle replied with the flat of his hand, striking my face. Benny stepped up and blocked him from striking me again.

"Let me handle this," he said. "I told you what happened between your mother and me, didn't I? I told you she was one dumb junkie bitch, didn't I?"

"I wanted you to know what happened to her, what happened to me."

My phone in my shirt pocket rang. Doyle reached over and pulled it out. Sheriff's Roarke's name and cell phone number showed on the phone's glass face. Doyle showed the phone to Benny.

"Answer it," Ben said, nodding at me. "Let him talk."

Doyle slid a dirty finger across the phone's glass surface to answer the call and held it to my ear.

"Where are you, Graham?"

"I'm here—in the barn," I gasped.

"You OK?"

Doyle pulled the phone from my ear before I could answer. Pushing the speaker button, he held the phone in front of me.

"Sheriff, this Doyle McMaster. We got your little snitch right here. You try to come get him and he's dead."

"Put Graham back on the phone," Roarke demanded.

"I'm here, Sheriff," I said.

"You hurt?"

"He's gonna be hurt worse if you try to come in here and get him," Doyle said.

"Who's in there with you?" Roarke asked. Doyle and I looked at Benny, who shook his head.

"Nobody here but family," I called into the phone.

"You—" Benny swung his pistol again. Stars exploded in my head and everything went black.

***

I don't know how long I was out, but when I came to, floodlights streamed through the two barn windows and thinning barn walls, flooding the dark interior with harsh white light.

Judson Roarke's voice boomed over a bullhorn:

"We need you to release the hostage, Mr. Kinnon. He needs medical attention. Let him go and we can end this peacefully."

I was still tied to the chair.

My shoulders and hips ached and, as I ran my tongue around the inside of my swollen mouth, I could feel a couple upper molars move. The light stung my eyes, which were nearly swollen shut, and it hurt to breathe.

Benny was at the wide sliding barn door, holding Doyle's shotgun with one hand and shading his eyes against the bright light with the other, peeking through the cracks in the wood. He didn't respond to Roarke's request.

Doyle sat in front of me on another old wooden chair, twirling Benny's handgun by the trigger guard. My cell phone sat on the dirt floor between us.

"Nice to have you back," Doyle said. "You've made us quite the center of attention now."

I groaned and spit blood from my mouth.

"Let us at least see him," Roarke continued through the bullhorn. "Let us know he's OK."

"You hear that? You got us into a bit of a situation," Doyle said. "The sheriff and all his buddies got this place surrounded. He's calling you a hostage."

"Isn't that what I am?" I slurred.

"Naw," Doyle smirked. "You're a martyr to the cause. Ain't none of us getting out of this one alive, least of all you."

I shook my head slowly. "No. That's not going to happen." Gasping for breath, my head fell to my chest.

Doyle stuck the gun barrel under my chin and lifted my head with it.

"Sure of that, are you?"

"You won't get away with this." I tasted blood in my mouth again and spit it on the dirt floor. Doyle pulled the gun away and began twirling it on his index finger as I silently watched.

Despite my pain, I knew there were a lot of guys just like Doyle McMaster in Jubilant Falls. I wrote about them every day.

In another age, they didn't need college. They graduated from high school — or didn't — and worked for thirty years at a factory job before retiring with their pension, or made a living from the farm that had been theirs for generations.

Their wives stayed at home and raised their children according to their well-thumbed King James Version of the Bible, which they read from each morning, as well as at Wednesday and Sunday services at little fundamentalist churches on back country roads.

In Doyle's world, there were no grey areas. Life was black or white, right or wrong. A man worked, a woman kept the home. Children were disciplined with the back of a hand to not talk back. Life's rules were strict and clear: men and women, blacks and whites had their roles to play in this world. You saluted the flag and thanked God for your blessings, as long as those same gifts weren't extended to those who really didn't deserve them.

But then their world changed: the factory jobs and the secure future they provided disappeared. Without educations or union jobs, guys like Doyle found they couldn't support themselves working at fast food joints or stocking shelves at a big box store. Brown-skinned immigrants with accents and religions they couldn't understand began to fill a world they were increasingly cut out of, working at jobs these angry young white men couldn't dream of getting.

Now it looked like I was going to die with one of them.

"What happened to make you like this, Doyle?" I asked, trying to get the question out in one breath.

The gun stopped spinning and Doyle looked up at me. "You really want to know?"

"Yeah," I gasped. "I really want to know."

Doyle smirked as he began his tale.

"This farm was in my family since as long as I can remember. My grandfather farmed it and before that, his grandfather farmed it before that. Then my dad got the farm after he comes back from Vietnam and he ends up selling everything off piece by piece, thanks to Jew bankers. You know the crazy old man who lives next door? That was my grandparents' house. My dad lived there after they died, but sold it to that crazy bastard just to pay the taxes. I grew up in that yellow house out there." Doyle gestured toward the barn door. "All I had was that house and the fifty acres I caught you trespassing on. I got the right to shoot your dumb ass for that right now, no questions asked."

Doyle jammed the gun barrel into my shoulder. I cried out in pain.

"But if it's in foreclosure—" I managed to wheeze.

"Shut up!"

Doyle jammed the barrel into my shoulder again.

"Doyle! Stop it!" Benny called from his post at the barn door.

"Tell me your story, then let me go," I said, feeling weak. "I'll tell your story. I'll put it in the paper."

"What's going on in there? We want to see the hostage." Roarke's voice boomed over the bullhorn.

"I'm not done yet!" Doyle called out, then turned back to me. "You wouldn't do that. You're just trying to con me."

I nodded. "Yeah, I would. Tell me the rest. What happened next?"

"My old man had to go to work at Traeburn Tractor, because he couldn't make a living farming anymore. Then when Traeburn closed, he lost his job. He started drinking, and then when things got really bad, he shot himself."

"I'm sorry."

Doyle didn't hear me. He was on a roll, now. "I'm tired of the white man getting screwed. I lost my job at the auto parts plant, then I got my hours cut at the hog farm—all because these damn Mexicans will work for nothin' and the niggers are getting the jobs that belong to real Americans."

No doubt he'd lost his job with each conviction and jail term, but Doyle's thought process defied any logic. I'd seen it before. It wasn't his fault—it was everyone else's.

And people like Benny Kinnon came along, claiming to be the fix for their problem, the outlet for their rage. But guys like Doyle were too dumb to see him for the con man that he was, looking only to gain from their pain over the loss of a world that existed only in John Wayne movies.

"So why did you punch Jerome Johnson?" I asked.

"A man's got a right to express an opinion doesn't he? I'm expressing mine and that nigger takes offense at me calling it the way it is? The man hit me first! Then I don't know who that other asshole was who jumped in, but Jesus." His words trailed off.

"What about the goats?"

"What goats?"

"Two cashmere goats were decapitated and gutted at Johnson's farm after you got in the fight with Johnson. You didn't do that?"

Doyle scoffed at me. "Hell no."

It must have been the Russians, then, trying to send a message to Katya Bolodenka. Does Addison know that, I wonder?

"I left a message for that white woman who lives there, though."

"What kind of a message?"

Grinning, Doyle stopped twirling the gun and pulled a knife from his boot, the same knife he had in his hand at the Travel Inn.

"What did you do?"

"Paper said she was sleeping with that Johnson guy."

"Did you hurt her?"

He smirked and with a sharp motion flung the knife between my feet. I gasped as it shot into the dirt, vibrating slightly.

"Like I said, I left a message for her. I cut up every piece of furniture in that place, just to let her know that kind of race mixing won't be tolerated here. She'll think twice before she leaves a door unlocked again."

On the floor, my phone rang. Doyle reached over and picked it up; it was Roarke's cell phone number. Doyle slid his finger across the screen and held the phone in front of my face. "Go ahead. Talk."

"Hello?"

"It's Sheriff Roarke. Are you OK, Graham?"

I looked at Doyle, who nodded. "I could be better."

"What do you need? Do you need food? Medical attention? We're trying to do everything we can to get you out."

Doyle pulled the phone away from me. "He's not coming out alive any more than Benny or me," he snapped.

"Don't let it end this way, McMaster," Roarke said. "Don't let anybody get hurt and it will go easier for you."

"If you let me go, I can tell your story," I said. "I can't tell your story if I'm dead."

"Bring him out, McMaster," Roarke said. "Let him come out. "

Benny stepped back from the door. "We open those doors and the cops will kill us all."

"Who is that?" Roarke asked on the other end of the call.

"Benny Kinnon, Sheriff," Benny said.

"Well, Mr. Kinnon, we have the barn surrounded. We've searched your truck. We found the heroin you hid in the wheel well. If you come out peacefully, with Graham, I'll personally guarantee your safety. I'll talk to the prosecutor about a reduction in charges."

"I open these doors and we all die in a hail of bullets. I'm not stupid."

"I promise you. Bring Graham to the barn door and let him go. You give yourself up peacefully and nobody dies."

Benny glared at him as Doyle ended the call.

"You got me into this," Benny said. "You better get me out."

"I'll bring him up to the front of the barn, but I ain't guaranteeing anything once those doors slide open," Doyle said. Roughly, Doyle pulled the knife from the ground and cut the rope from around my wrists and ankles. I cried out in pain as both men yanked me to my feet.

In front of the barn door, they let go of me. I sank to my knees, stars swirling in my head, and my breath coming in painful gasps. I couldn't have run if I wanted to. Doyle tied my hands behind my back again as Benny held the cold shotgun against my head. When he was done, both men stood with their hands on a sliding door, Benny on the left, Doyle on the right.

I swallowed hard and looked up toward the rusted track that held the two doors closed. Would they even open? Tears began to fill my swollen eyes and roll down my bruised cheeks.

This was it. I would never know my son. Elizabeth would tell him I died chasing a damned story, I thought. She was right. I'd do anything to get a byline. And for what? After a few years, they'll move on. She'll get married and her husband will adopt him and unless he asks about his real father, I'll just be a footnote in his life history.

Benny called out. "We're at the door."

"On the count of three, open the door," Roarke answered. "One... two..."

With a groan, the barn doors slid apart and the floodlights blinded me.

"Hold your fire! Everyone! Hold your fire!" I heard Roarke yell. On my right, Doyle cocked his pistol in slow motion.

"Look out!" I screamed. I tried to roll away as Doyle's gun flashed. I groaned as the bullet exploded in my right thigh. There was another shot, this one from my left, and Doyle fell to the ground, his chest an open cavity of fabric, blood and deer shot. Benny, my father, stepped forward into the glare of the floodlights, dropping the shotgun as he raised his hands in the air.

Chapter 34 Addison

The blue of a computer screen was the only light in the newsroom as I made my way upstairs, the horror of Katya's bloody face still fresh in my mind.

It was nearly two in the morning. I could have gone home, slept a few hours and then come back to do this story. No one else had it, not the big metro in Collitstown, not any of the TV stations. If I wrote it now and threw it up on the website, maybe even sent it to the Associated Press, everyone would have it by dawn.

I didn't care. Two people were dead and a federal agency was partially responsible for their murders. I was going to write this story and expose how serious errors in judgment led to both deaths. Everyone in Plummer County, if not the state of Ohio, should know why that happened. Once I slapped this story up on the website and across the front page, everybody would have a piece of it and I hoped they did.

Earlene could fire me for not going after the barking dog story first — or for whatever damned reason she wanted.

I flipped on the overhead lights, sat down at the nearest computer and logged onto the editorial system. The computer beeped, letting me know it was ready for me to start. It was time to hang one Agent Robert Peppin out to dry.

By ADDISON MCINTYRE
Managing Editor

A Youngstown Road woman linked to the murder of a federal agent Tuesday has herself been shot, the latest in a case reportedly linked to a string of questionable New Jersey pain clinics, allegedly run by Russian organized crime figures.

Although law enforcement officials would not release the details of the murder, the body of Ekaterina Bolodenka was identified early Thursday morning at the Plummer County Morgue. She was shot at least two times in the face.

On Tuesday night, sheriff's deputies found a U.S. Marshal known as Jerome Johnson dead on the porch of the farm that Bolodenka owned.

Bolodenka was the wife of Kolya Dyakonov, who reportedly ran a chain of fraudulent Medicaid pain clinics where doctors on his payroll dispensed painkillers such as Oxycontin and Oxycodone to members of the homeless community. New Jersey authorities have linked these clinics to an explosion of drug overdoses and deaths in the area.

Bolodenka was placed in witness protection by federal authorities after she reportedly witnessed her husband killing a homeless man in her Brooklyn neighborhood of Brighton Beach.

She was the only witness against her husband, according to Agent Robert Peppin.

"Without her, we have no case," he said.

Originally relocated to the Shenandoah Valley of Virginia, Bolodenka ignored orders from her keepers that she was no longer allowed to stay in touch with her sister Svetlana, Svetlana's husband Alexis and their infant daughter Nadezhda, called Nadya.

When members of the Dyakanov's gang reportedly heard Katya had been in contact, all three, including the baby, were reportedly killed when Svetlana and Alexis would not reveal Bolodenka's location.

Following their murders, Bolodenka was relocated here to Plummer County and the Youngstown Road farm, along with a number of llamas and alpacas from another witness, where an agent reportedly named Jerome Johnson was assigned to protect her.

Just as Bolodenka had secrets, so did the man protecting her.

Johnson, who's real name was Terrell Simms-Reed, was a former Marine, assigned to the American Embassy in Moscow. He spoke Russian and was trained as a military policeman, according to his parents, but his military career was cut short when his commanding officer found he was involved with Russian prostitutes.

Simms-Reed received an honorable discharge and following his return to the States, found a job with the U.S. Marshal Service, where he was assigned, often under assumed names, to provide protection for Russian-speaking witnesses, such as Bolodenka, until they could testify.

Bolodenka told members of the *Journal-Gazette* staff that she and the man she believed to be Johnson were romantically involved.

Agent Robert Peppin, who is heading up the investigation, would not comment on where or how Bolodenka was killed, but suggested that a *J-G* story last Saturday on Bolodenka was responsible for her death.

The *Journal-Gazette's* first story was about Bolodenka's background, and how she had won at the state fair. She later admitted that the Witness Protection program fabricated the information she provided for that story. She also identified Johnson as her farm manager.

A visit to the Youngstown Road farmhouse by J-G staff yesterday afternoon found Bolodenka was not at home, but the house had been ransacked and much of the furniture slashed.

Peppin, questioned at the morgue, would not comment.

The story needed one more line, one more paragraph to make it complete. I stepped away from the computer to think.

The police radio was quiet, not really surprising at this time of the morning, but out of force of habit, I decided to check it anyway. I walked across the room—it was off.

Shit, I thought to myself. I knew who did it—Earlene had the weekly cleaning service under orders to turn off anything they found still using electricity when they came through after midnight.

Who cares? It could stay off until I got back in here for deadline—not that I needed anything else on my plate. I made a mental note to call Graham Kinnon and see how his stepfather was doing after his heart attack. Maybe I could talk him into coming back from family leave a few days early.

Across the newsroom, I heard my cell phone ring deep in my purse.

Probably Duncan, I thought to myself as I walked back to the desk to answer it. I didn't recognize the number. Was it Peppin? Maybe Dr. Bovir?

"Hello?"

"Addison, it's me, Elizabeth Day." Her normally tough voice was quiet and scared.

"What's up kiddo? Why are you calling me at this time of the morning?"

"It's Graham. He's at the hospital. He's been shot."

Chapter 35 Graham

"Hey. You awake?" It was a woman's voice, soft and gentle.

My swollen eyes opened slowly as I felt the stupor of anesthesia temporarily recede. I was in a hospital bed. A nurse touched my shoulder, speaking softly. With the light glowing gently behind her, she seemed angelic. As my eyes focused more, I saw she had red curly hair trying valiantly to escape the bun pinned atop her head, and green eyes that danced in the halo of her smile. She wore a stethoscope around her neck and I wanted to see how far her freckles descended into the V-necked collar of her blue surgical scrubs.

I wanted to tell her, too, how beautiful she looked, but my words were garbled and slurred. I couldn't move my right leg, but why? The memory of Sheriff Roarke and his deputies rushing into McMaster's barn returned.

Once again, I heard the gunshots, felt the pain and I saw Ben standing in the glare of the floodlights as he was handcuffed. I remembered EMTs surrounding me, working frantically to stem the bleeding in my leg. I remembered Roarke standing above Doyle McMaster's dead body, shaking his head as I was placed on a gurney and rolled to the ambulance.

I groaned.

"I'm sorry—just nod," the nurse said.

I complied.

"You have two broken cheekbones. You also have a pretty good concussion and a broken rib. Do you remember being shot in the leg, Mr. Kinnon?" Now that she knew I was awake, her voice was loud and she over-enunciated her words.

I grunted in assent and tried to reach down to touch the bandages, but I was too loopy to find my leg. She took my hand and placed it on top the covers.

"You're OK now. Your leg is still there. The bullet went through the outside of your thigh, but doctors had to go in and get some shrapnel. They also checked for shrapnel damage to the artery in your leg, which was fine. That means you've had an angiogram, so I need you to lie very still. Are you in any pain?"

I groaned and nodded.

"Hang on here and I'll give you some medication."

My redheaded angel injected something into my IV line and patted my shoulder. I caught a glimpse of a gold band on her left hand. *Damn*, I thought drunkenly as I slid back into darkness.

Several hours later, I was back in this universe and allowed to sit up slightly.

Before her shift ended, Red came back to see me and brought me some chicken broth I could sip through a straw and a little bit of soda.

There was a knock at my hospital door.

It was Addison, with today's paper in her hand.

I waved her in, feebly, trying to give her a lopsided smile through my bruises.

"You look like shit," she said.

"Thanks," I mumbled.

"I ought to kick your ass for this latest stunt," she said, spreading today's paper across my lap. "But, damn, it's the best front page we've had in a while."

Two stories, both with Addison's byline, shared the top of the page. The headline **Farm owner shot** sat on top a story that went down along two columns, with a one-column picture of Katya Bolodenka, cropped from the picture Pat had taken last week.

Next to it, another headline **Reporter wounded in standoff**, filled the remaining four columns, including a photo of McMaster's barn, still surrounded by sheriff's cruisers and headshots of me, McMaster and Ben.

Across the bottom, Elizabeth had a preview story of this weekend's Canal Days festival with a photo of volunteers working on two garden club floats.

I pointed to Ben's mug shot.

"He saved my life," I said slowly.

Addison nodded. "Sounds like it, from what Judson Roarke told me. He filled me in on everything you were doing, by the way. Ben Kinnon will be charged with inducing panic, possession of heroin with intent to distribute, kidnapping, possession of a weapon under disability and a couple assault charges. He's going away for a long time. "

I nodded. We were both silent for a moment.

"I wish you'd told me what you were doing, Graham," she said.

I shrugged. "It was personal stuff. It didn't belong in the newsroom," I said.

My broken rib made it hard to breathe deeply, but maybe as a result of the pain medication, I was getting better about stringing a sentence together.

"Like you and Elizabeth? Did that belong in the newsroom?"

I felt myself blushing through my bruises to the roots of my hair.

"She's the one who called me and told me you were shot," Addison said. "Apparently you handed your phone to one of the EMTs and asked them to call her, before you blacked out."

"So, um, what all do you know?"

"I know you two were seeing each other for about a year and I know she's pregnant and I know you guys have broken up."

I sank back into my pillows. "Sorry."

She shook her head. "There's nothing to be sorry about. You work with people long enough and sometimes relationships happen. Ask me one day about John Porter, the man who sat at your desk before you did. Elizabeth also told me that going after this Benjamin Kinnon guy was kind of a personal quest for you."

"It was," I said. "He was never more than a name on my birth certificate, but after I thought Elizabeth was pregnant, my thoughts kind of changed."

"From what she told me, you knew he was scum to start with."

"Yeah, I did. When Chief McGinnis told me he was living here and suspected to be involved in some hate crimes, I wanted to see if I could meet him, figure out if he's anything like me—or if I'm anything like him. They didn't think one of their under cover cops could get close to him."

"So you volunteered. Why does that not surprise me?"

Again, I shrugged.

"Then you find out he's dealing heroin? And holding Aryan Knights meetings in that barn next to Melvin Spotts' place? I swear to God, I'm listening to every word that crazy old man says from now on out," she said.

I tried to smile, but my face hurt too much.

"So," Addison said slowly. "It's none of my business, but what are you going to do about the baby?"

I shrugged. "I love her, but she won't marry me, Addison. I've asked. I don't even know if she's going to go through with the pregnancy."

"After deadline today, she asked me if she could move up her last day to next Friday. Apparently, the *Beacon-Journal* needs her to start sooner."

"And I told you my stepdad had a heart attack," I said. "She's feeding you a line. She wants to leave town before I have a chance to beg her to stay."

"Maybe she is, maybe she isn't."

"I don't want to lose her or the baby, but don't have a whole lot of options at this point," I said.

"Just do everything you can to keep in touch with that baby after it's born. I have a feeling I don't need to tell you what it's like to grow up feeling abandoned," Addison said. "My mother left my father when I was six. I never saw her again and it wasn't until a couple years ago I knew she'd died."

"Really?"

Addison nodded. My face was probably too bruised and beat up to show much shock. Even though we all knew her dad, Walt, a retired state trooper, Addison never revealed a whole lot about her childhood.

"And I know I'm not the one to talk, but being a parent means you learn to live with a lot of different things, not just dirty diapers and a lack of sleep. You learn to live with uncertainty over the damnedest things, like whether or not a kid will remember something you said in anger, or if they've forgotten it in ten minutes. You'll stress over everything you do or say to that child, what toys they play with, what food they eat, or like my daughter, what genes you've passed on. And then, somewhere along the line, despite everything you've done or tried not to do, they end up OK and they still love you."

"I hope so."

"Life's messy Graham—you see that every day. In this business, there are those who like to think that we are above the nastiness and the pain we report, but we're not. We show up at all these public disasters—car crashes, murders, drug raids— and we think we would never do anything to put ourselves in that situation. We won't drive drunk, we won't get addicted, but you never know what happens in someone's life to put him or her there at that moment. We all have our own shortcomings that we have to live with, and those shortcomings don't usually get shown to the world. Some times they do, sometimes they hide behind an unbelievable mask of lies and denial. Some are buried so deep, folks don't even know where they are."

"Benny told me that we never get the parents we want."

"That's true. On the opposite side of that coin, sometimes people often don't get to be the parents they want to be, either because of something they've done or a situation they find themselves in. But they make the best of it, like I know you will with this baby."

"Benny told me that these guys he associated with would just as soon kill me as look at me. Doyle was going to kill me when those barn doors opened. I'll never forget the sound of that hammer being cocked." I sighed. "After Benny shot him, I remember this look on his face as he was getting handcuffed. It was like 'I did this for you,' almost. Maybe not. I don't know. It's all in such a haze."

"You never know. My mother was wearing a locket with a picture of me in it on the day she was killed by a drunk driver outside of Chicago. At that point, she hadn't seen me in four years, but I obviously meant something to her. You and Elizabeth will do fine, whatever happens. I know you will. You got a heart, Graham, underneath all your tough-guy exterior, and that will take you far."

I pointed at Katya Bolodenka's headshot. "So is she dead?"

Addison sighed. "Yes. Dr. Bovir had me come down and identify her body this morning. That whole situation just makes me sick. Jerome Johnson's parents stopped by the farm to talk to her and heard her arguing with someone in Russian—and his name wasn't really Jerome Johnson, I learned. By the time I got over to the farmhouse to check on her, she was gone. Somebody had gone through the house, though, and slashed every damned piece of furniture in the place. The place was trashed and she was gone. I guess they came back and took her someplace else to kill her."

"The Russians didn't trash the house," I said. "Doyle did that. He told me he did. He told me he didn't kill the goats though. I asked twice."

"What?"

"Yeah, he told me slashing the furniture was payback for her involvement with Johnson — he called it 'race mixing.' He showed me the knife he used to cut everything up. Said the house was empty and the door unlocked, so he just went in and started cutting stuff up."

"I'll call the federal agent on the case and let him know — if he'll take my call. He's too damned arrogant to speak to the press," Addison said. "I've got to get going. Earlene gave me the rest of the afternoon off — I've got to go home to get some sleep. I'll let you read the story, but I can't help but feel Katya Bolodenka got let down by a whole bunch of people along the line, even me."

"When I get back, I can call the folks in New Jersey and find out where the case stands, whether Katya Bolodenka's husband will be released or not."

"You need to worry about getting better. I'll keep on that story, OK? I'll see you later."

With a wave she was gone.

For the rest of the afternoon, I had a steady stream of visitors.

Sheriff Roarke stopped in to bring back my cell phone.

"We got the audio recording off your phone," Roarke said. "It's going to be used in Benjamin Kinnon's trial, so expect a call to testify."

"I figured."

"If it gets that far. I understand from the prosecutor that his lawyers have already suggested a deal."

"What about the hate crimes?"

"Ben Kinnon can't be connected to those directly — it looks like he managed to manipulate Doyle McMaster and a couple others into doing the leg work. Whether or not they can prove Kinnon incited McMaster or any of the others to commit them remains to be seen. That's up to the federal prosecutor. What charges get kicked upstairs to the feds and which ones stay here, they are still figuring that out."

I pointed at the newspaper lying on my bedside table. "Did you see that Russian woman on the Lunatic Fringe farm was shot and killed?"

"Yes I did. When I talked to the feds this morning, I gave them the information about Doyle's slaughtering her goats."

I shook my head. "Doyle told me he didn't do that."

"He can burn a man's car, get in a fistfight at the feed mill —"

"And slash the furniture at Lunatic Fringe —" I interjected.

"He did that, too? I hadn't heard about that one." Roarke shook his head in disgust. "Let's physically abuse your fellow man because you believe he's below you, but by God, livestock deserve better treatment. That's just plain sick."

After he left, Marcus Henning came by to visit, then Chief G and Dennis Herrick. There were flowers from my parents, Earlene, and the newsroom. Sportswriter Chris Royal dropped by on his way to an inter-league scrimmage he was covering, but by the time visiting hours were over, the one person I most wanted to see — Elizabeth — never came to the door.

I was hurt, but I wasn't surprised — just incredibly, incredibly alone. I turned out the light above my bed and went to sleep.

***

I had a cab bring me home the next afternoon. I tipped the driver extra for carrying my plastic bag of personal belongings as I negotiated the steps on my crutches and hobbled into my apartment. My broken rib made using crutches absolute agony, but I promised Red before I was discharged that I'd keep moving so I wouldn't get pneumonia.

As I sank onto the couch and lifted my leg onto the coffee table, there was a knock at the door.

"It's open!" I called out.

It was Elizabeth, carrying a big foil pan of lasagna and a plastic container of salad. She was wearing tight floral pants that ended just below her knees, a pair of orange flats and a loose white tee shirt with a large red rose printed across the front and shoulder. She set the food down on the kitchen table.

"I didn't want you to starve while you were off work, Kinnon, so I thought I'd bring you something," she said. She didn't move from beside the table.

"Thank you."

"Don't get any ideas. We're all taking turns in the newsroom to make sure you've got at least one hot meal a day. Today was just my turn."

Silence settled like an uncomfortable fog as impenetrable as the distance between us.

"Did you hear? Next Friday is going to be my last day," she said finally, drawing circles on the tabletop with her fingertip.

"I heard."

"We're meeting at the bar across from the courthouse for drinks after work. Do you think you can come?"

"You want something this ugly sending you off to Akron?" I pointed at my bruised face.

In a few steps, she was beside me on the couch. She reached up and touched my face, smiling sadly.

"You're a little beat up, but you're not ugly, Kinnon. You never were."

"Oh Elizabeth," I whispered, drawing her as close as my broken rib would allow. Tears rose in my swollen eyes. "Please, don't go, please. Stay here. Marry me. We'll be a family. We can make it work."

Gently, she kissed each purpled cheek.

"I can't Kinnon. I just can't."

Then she stood and, without a word, walked out the door.

Chapter 36 Addison

The sun was just beginning to peak over the horizon Friday morning as Duncan and I headed out to the barn for milking. Already the air held the promise of all the heat and humidity a late Ohio summer could bring.

"You look like you got caught up on your sleep," Duncan said, taking my hand. "I think you slept twelve hours, in between the nap you had yesterday afternoon and the sleep you got last night."

"I think I did, too," I answered, squeezing his hand in return. "I feel halfway decent this morning."

"You seem like you're coping a little better with Katya Bolodenka's murder this morning." Duncan caught me sitting on the front porch last night after dinner, surrounded by cigarette smoke, trying to shut out the horror of Katya's bullet-ridden face as tears streamed down my face.

"I'm OK, I guess, although I can't help feeling like I never got a good hold on that story, that I was on the periphery in a lot of ways." I shrugged.

"Like how? You reported on the information you received, then when you found out it was false, you reported on that, too."

"Yes, but the meat of the story didn't happen here—the organized crime, the illegal pain clinics, the murder in Katya's basement and of her sister's family. Those were big city stories. It feels really strange to have it all come to a head here in Jubilant Falls."

"Yeah, I suppose so. I never would have thought we had white supremacists moving into Plummer County, either," Duncan said. "But I guess Graham's whole deal showed that wasn't true."

"The Aryan Knights moving in makes more sense to me than the Russian Mafia," I said. "People like Benjamin Kinnon prey on guys like Doyle McMaster. The ignorant, the ill-informed and the down on their luck are easy pickings for folks like that. Plummer County isn't the isolated little backwater we grew up in, Duncan."

My husband sighed as he pondered. "So what's your day look like?" he asked, after a moment of silence.

"Not much. I've got the last preview story for Canal Days to do and then later this afternoon, I've got an interview with a candidate for Elizabeth's job. The newsroom staff was also going to have dinner and a couple beers next week before she goes, by the way."

We reached the door of the barn and I stopped talking only to take a slurp of coffee from the mug in my hand before stepping inside to smell the warm, familiar odor of cattle, straw and manure.

"Graham's getting out of the hospital today and she's supposed to take him dinner. Tomorrow is my day to take him a meal. You want to just eat someplace Saturday and then I can take him some carryout food?"

Duncan didn't answer. Standing in the barn doorway, he stared down our drive.

"You expecting someone?" he asked.

Coming up the drive were two large Ford pick up trucks, both pulling a gooseneck livestock trailer, their dual rear wheels kicking up gravel in the early morning light. The headlights were bright, obscuring the faces of the drivers.

"No-o-o…" I said slowly. "No."

The first truck stopped. The driver's side door opened and a tall, thin woman stepped from the cab.

I gasped. The last time I'd seen that face it was covered in blood. Her left eye had been pulpy red hole, matching the identical bullet wound in her cheek. The curly black hair, now peeking from the back of her baseball cap, had been bloody and filled with brain matter as her body lay on Dr. Bovir's exam table.

"Katya! Katya Bolodenka! You're, you're not dead!"

Opening her arms, she ran to hug Duncan and me. As we embraced, I saw Agent Peppin step out of the other truck, slapping a work glove against the fender of his truck as he ambled casually toward us. His semi-automatic pistol hung from his belt and I could see the bulge of his Kevlar vest beneath the gray tee shirt he wore.

"Yes! I am alive! I am so sorry for what we had to do at hospital," she said.

"What the hell is this all about?" I demanded as Peppin, shoving his work gloves into his back pocket, stepped closer. "Now I've run a story about a murder that didn't really happen!"

"Pretty awesome make-up job, though, don't you think?" Peppin smiled. "That nurse at the ER desk? She was one of ours, too."

"I could just slap your arrogant face," I said.

"Before you do, hear me out. After your story about Agent Johnson ran in the paper, we had to do something to keep Miss Bolodenka safe. We knew you weren't the usual small town journalist who'd take our word if we told you she was dead. We also felt if she went missing, you'd come looking for her. We had to come up with some other solution."

"So you haul me down in the middle of the goddamned night to identify someone who's not really dead? And let me make a fool of myself screaming at you? And induce me to run a story that's obviously not true?"

"Pretty much. Technically, we didn't 'haul' you down. You came when Dr. Bovir called," Peppin smirked. "But you also told me a few things we didn't know. We had contacted Agent Johnson's parents and knew they were coming to claim the body. What I didn't realize was you'd spoken to his parents and knew his real name and record. I also didn't know someone had come through the farmhouse after we left and slashed the furniture.

"But when it all came out in your story the next day, it was perfect for us. It didn't make us look good on the surface, but that gave the whole scenario more credibility. While WITSEC has a largely successful record at keeping relocated folks safe, when we've failed, it gets a lot of press—bad press."

"So why did you call my boss, Earlene? You weren't going to ask we not run the story, were you?"

"Believe it or not, I respect the role the press plays in this country. You can be an incredible tool to solve crimes and a major pain in my ass. I wanted to sit down with her and you about the possibility of planting some information in your story, something to help us locate the men who killed the man you knew as Jerome Johnson. By the time she called back, your newspaper was already printed, but either way, she wouldn't budge."

Duncan looked at me and raised an eyebrow.

"Luka and Maks were stopped in Pennsylvania, on their way back to Brighton Beach," Katya said. "They tell agents two more of Kolya's thugs are sent to kill me—and then them, since they didn't get job done first time. So agents show them your story on the Internet and they think job is complete."

"When they think they're next, they turned on Kolya Dyakonov and spilled their guts," Peppin grinned, rocking on his heels.

"And I get to look the fool—again," I said.

"On the contrary, Mrs. McIntyre, your story cemented the case for us. Luka and Maks corroborated Miss Bolodenka's story of the murder she witnessed, as well as the murder of her sister Svetlana, her husband and baby. More charges are going to be filed today in New York."

"I can't believe this," I spluttered. "You come busting ass up my driveway, tell me I've been conned again and expect me not to report on that?"

Peppin pulled a photo from his back pocket and handed it to me. It was a group of somber people, dressed in black, standing around a casket in a big city cemetery.

"You do what you want. I'm in no position to stop you. Our official statement is that following her murder, Miss Bolodenka was buried in her family plot in Brooklyn. Here is proof. We're going to give it to a couple television stations later today."

"You got Dr. Bovir to go along with this whole scenario, too!"

"Your coroner took some convincing, but in the end he realized that if we were to fake her death, we would need to have everything documented. He saw the value of presenting a good solid case and keeping a witness safe. There are full autopsy notes, both audio and computer files, now on file at the coroner's office, should anyone decide to check."

"What about the farm? That was in her name, too?" I asked.

"It's already been sold," Peppin said.

"Please, keep secret for me," Katya said. "I am to be relocated yet again. I have learned my lesson and they are giving me one more chance with another new name and story. I had to talk Agent Peppin into letting me come here to tell you truth and say goodbye."

"It can be harder for relocated family members to understand they need to live within WITSEC's rules," Peppin said. "The made guys, the gangsters — they generally know that if they break their cover, they die. The wives, the daughters, the sons, they don't understand it as well. Sometimes, they don't have any clue what their husband or father really did for a living. The program is often much harder on them. Letting her tell you the truth and letting her say goodbye is the one thing we could do before we relocate her again."

"But what about the picture of your sister?" I asked. "I went back to check on you and found it on the floor. I knew you wouldn't have left it behind willingly."

"Even if I don't have their pictures, I will always have her and Nadya in my heart," Katya said, tapping her chest. "And when the trial starts, it will be big news that I am dead witness, back from grave to testify. Maybe you come to Big Apple and report on it then?"

I took the photo from Peppin and shook my head. If I reported that I'd been taken again, there wouldn't be anything left to my credibility — or that of the *Journal-Gazette*. And the reason behind the story would be what? To once again put Katya in danger? What choice did I have but to go along with all this?

I sighed.

"You got names to go along with this photo?" I asked.

"No. Just say 'unidentified members of the family' in the caption. You can even quote me," Peppin said. He turned to Katya. "The sun is almost up. We've got to get rolling if we want to make it to our next destination before its too hot for these animals."

"So, you taking the llamas and the alpacas with you?" Duncan asked.

"Yes. I am too attached to them — they are like babies to me," Katya smiled. "Where I am going has room for them."

"I really didn't want to take them again, but we had no place else to send them," Peppin said. "The sheep and goats were pretty easy to find homes for. I couldn't leave the llamas and alpacas behind without care and most of the rescue operations asked too many questions."

"I was angry he want to leave them — we argued long and hard about it," Katya said. "I did not know this man spoke Russian!"

"So it was you she was arguing with when Dr. Reed and Dr. Simms stopped by the Lunatic Fringe?" I asked Peppin.

He nodded. "She made a pretty good argument for taking them. Knowing you, I thought you'd be back around to check on things, and I couldn't risk another story showing up in your newspaper."

Katya hugged us both again, and then she and Peppin headed back toward the trucks. With a wave, she jumped confidently into the cab and started the engine. Expertly turning their trucks and trailers around, Katya and Peppin headed back down the driveway. At the end of the drive, they turned right and headed into the sunrise.

I looked at the photo in my hand. Sitting at the side of the casket was a woman in a black dress and sunglasses, holding a tissue over her mouth, surrounded by serious looking family members, all in black and standing among the many tombstones. Tall, leggy and thin, curly black hair cascaded down her shoulders from beneath a wide black hat. A short muscular man, wearing a black suit and a thick gold necklace stood behind her with his hand on her shoulder, apparently comforting her. The goatee gave everything away.

It was Katya, sitting at what was supposed to be her own funeral with Peppin pretending to comfort her.

"I'll be damned," I said. "I'll just be damned."

In the barn, one of the Holsteins lowed softly.

"C'mon, Penny," Duncan said. "The girls are waiting for us."

I stuffed the photo into the back pocket of my Carhartt's and followed him into the barn.

Chapter 37 Graham

Six months later

"Breathe, baby, breathe!" I wrapped my hand around Elizabeth's and looked her in the eye, trying to get her to focus as the contraction swept through her body. Sweat covered her face, shining in the harsh light of the delivery room at Akron General Hospital. Face to face, we breathed in tandem, short, heavy, chuffing sounds: *hee, hee, hee, hoo, hoo, hoo,* like we'd learned in Lamaze classes. The contraction stopped momentarily and she fell back against the pillow. Someone had put a surgical cap over her naked head.

'You did this to me, Kinnon," she gasped, trying to catch her breath. "This is your fault."

"I seem to remember you were a willing participant, Mrs. Kinnon," I whispered.

She smiled and I released her hand, catching a glimpse of her wedding ring, a plain gold band framed by the little solitaire.

Before she could respond, another contraction rolled over her and we began our synchronized breathing again.

This morning, I'd rushed up to Akron as soon as she called to tell me her water broke, speeding up the highway before the sun came up.

It was now early evening.

"Just a few more minutes and you can begin pushing." The doctor looked up from between her legs, which were swathed in sheets.

Another contraction came in another wave. We locked eyes and began breathing together again.

"C'mon, baby, c'mon," I whispered. "You can do this."

"Kinnon, I—" she began and froze. Her eyes rolled up in her head; her lips turned blue. The heart monitor at her side began to shriek and her hand fell away from mine.

"Elizabeth? Elizabeth?" I cried. I turned to the nurse at her side. "What's going on? What's happening?"

Control gave way to chaos as the sound filled the room.

"Quick! Get him out of here!" The doctor barked. "Get him out of here! I need the crash cart!"

"No! No! What's happening?" I cried as a nurse shuffled me out into the hallway.

"Sir, you need to stay here," she said firmly. "We have an emergency and it's best that you stay out here and let us handle it."

I could see the panic in her eyes. I grabbed her by the arms as she tried to reenter the delivery room.

"What's wrong with my wife? What's happening?" I demanded.

"Sir, I don't know. You just need to wait here." She peeled my hands from her arms and dashed back inside. I caught a glimpse of someone standing above Elizabeth with defibrillator paddles as a baby cried.

I sank against the wall as more staff rushed past. Someone came out and led me to a private room, furnished with a chair, a coffee table and couch, where I sat alone, sobbing and rocking.

We married four months ago, on a Friday morning in the judge's chambers at the Summit County Courthouse. It hadn't been a conventional marriage, but then, I never expected anything else. Her parents and her brother attended. Mother and Bill were in Boca Raton and couldn't make it, although Bill sent a big check.

She wore a vintage peach maternity top with a wide white collar, black skirt and Kelly green flats with her purple wig. The bouquet of white roses rested in her hands on her wide belly. Still limping from my wounds, I wore a navy blue suit, with a matching boutonniere. I'm not sure what the judge thought as he pronounced us man and wife.

On Monday, I returned to Jubilant Falls.

For the next sixteen weeks, that was how we lived: Each Friday after work, I would get in the car and drive to her apartment, handing off the police scanner to the new reporter in the newsroom. If Elizabeth had the weekend off, that was great. If she didn't, she came back to Jubilant Falls and stayed at my place on her days off. With some of Bill's check, I bought a minivan and a car seat, trading in the Toyota. A crib now sat in the corner of my living room, matching the one in the baby's room at Elizabeth's apartment.

The drive was tedious, but the reunions bliss. I teased her about how convinced she was that we could never make it work.

She thrived in Akron. Her coworkers and editors loved her and the future looked bright. Until there was a job there for me, it was best I keep the job that I had at the *Journal-Gazette*.

The remainder of Bill's check sat in a joint account, waiting to be used as a down payment on a house when that job came through. She wanted a Cape Cod-style home and we spent the weekends poring over the real estate listings on line, the laptop resting on her expanding belly.

That was the plan.

That was how we were going to live our lives, our whole lives.

She understood dinner wouldn't always be at the same time and she probably couldn't stop me from going hell-bent for stories.

I promised her summers at Lake Erie. I'd promised.

"I can't lose her, not now!" I cried to the institutional tan walls.

The sound of the ticking wall clock was my only answer as I sank back against the couch, feeling hollow.

It was half an hour before someone knocked and I jumped up as the door opened. It was the doctor.

"Where is she? How is Elizabeth? What about the baby?" I asked.

He pulled the surgical mask down from his face. Pain filled his eyes.

"I'm sorry. We lost her. It could have been an aneurysm or a stroke, but we won't know for sure—"

"*Noooo!*" The sound of my grief bounced off the walls.

The door opened again as the nurse, the same one who'd pushed me into the hallway, walked in, holding a small squalling bundle. Her eyes were red from crying.

"I'm so, so sorry about your wife. It's a girl, Mr. Kinnon," she whispered, handing me the baby. "It's a girl."

I took the bundle from her and sat back down on the couch, cupping my daughter's head with my hand, filled with equal measures of awe and loss and love.

A pink knitted hat covered a mass of brown hair. I laid her on the couch and opened the blankets, examining ten perfect fingers and ten perfect toes. Her skin was red and blotchy, with white cheesy spots in places. I couldn't tell if her deep blue eyes could focus on anything or not. Above her diaper, there was a clip over her umbilical cord; around it, her skin was stained with iodine. She turned her head to the side and opened her mouth, making a sucking sound.

"Oh God," I whispered. "What do I do now?"

"She's hungry," the nurse said softly. "Let me get you a bottle."

"What are you going to name her?" The doctor ran his finger tenderly across her forehead.

"We were sure it was going to be a boy," I said, taking the baby into my arms. The nurse came back with a bottle and handed it to me. "She didn't want to know ahead of time. We hadn't even chosen a girl's name until last week. This is Gwendolyn Elizabeth Kinnon."

I leaned over and kissed her forehead as she hungrily sucked from the bottle. "Your mommy would have loved you very much, Gwennie."

***

Three days later, on a cold, wet February day, we laid Elizabeth to rest, next to her grandparents in a Shaker Heights cemetery.

I barely remember the ceremony or the people who attended.

I just remember bouncing little Gwennie on my shoulder as she howled through the service, giving voice to all our sorrow. Elizabeth's death made the front page of the local section of the *Beacon-Journal*: Reporter dies giving birth.

I stayed at Elizabeth's parents' house as we worked our way through her personal belongings and her mother helped me through the basics of baby care. After a week, I tucked everything in the van, fastened Gwennie into her car seat and, wearing Elizabeth's wedding rings on a chain around my neck, headed back to Jubilant Falls, loaded down with diapers, baby clothes and grief.

Addison, Marcus and Dennis met me at my apartment and helped me unpack the van. I sat on the couch, giving Gwennie a bottle as my spare and Spartan living room turned into a frilly, pink nursery.

After they left, she fell asleep easily in the crib. I sat cross-legged on the floor, watching through the slats of her crib as her breath came rhythmically. I leaned my head against the side of the crib and tears rolled down my cheeks.

"It wasn't supposed to end like this, Elizabeth," I whispered. "What am I supposed to do now? How am I going to raise our baby? How am I going to do my job?"

Gwennie's deep blue eyes opened, fixing on me. I scooted over to the crib and slipped my hand through the slats, laying my hand on her belly. Her mouth curved into a gassy smile. A tiny hand, still pink and splotchy, worked its way from beneath the swaddling pink blankets, and locked on my index finger.

In that second, in that motion, I saw her mother. Every joy, every pain, every time we found each other in the dark of night, in tenderness and need, they all resulted in this little pink-wrapped miracle in my living room. In this little girl, I realized I would have Elizabeth forever.

My shattered universe would come together again, not immediately, but day by day and piece by piece, as we built our little family around those memories.

"We're going to do this, baby girl," I whispered. "We're going to be OK."

About the author

Debra Gaskill is an award-winning journalist with more than 20 years of experience in newspapers in Ohio. She has an associate's degree in liberal arts from Thomas Nelson Community College in Hampton, Va., a bachelor's degree in English and journalism from Wittenberg University and a master of fine arts degree in creative writing from Antioch University.

She and her husband Greg, a retired Air Force lieutenant colonel, reside in Enon, where they raise llamas and alpacas on their farm. They have two adult children and one grandson.

She is the author of three other Jubilant Falls novels, *The Major's Wife, Barn Burner,* and *Lethal Little Lies.*

Connect with Debra on her website at www.debragaskillnovels.com or on her blog, http://debragaskill.wordpress.com. You can also connect with her on Twitter at @Debra Gaskill.

If you liked *Murder on the Lunatic Fringe*, please leave a review on the website where you purchased the book. Your support is greatly appreciated!

MYSTERY

Gaskill, Debra

Murder on the Lunatic Fringe.

20318168R00173

Made in the USA
Middletown, DE
23 May 2015